The Writing on the Wall

JENNA RAE

Bella
BOOKS

Acknowledgments

Thank you seems like a small phrase for the love, support, and encouragement I have been offered by my family and friends. I especially want to thank Ben, Josh, Lee, Morgan, Dan, Gracie, and Pumpkin.

I have been the fortunate recipient of help, guidance, and insight offered by the brilliant Kathalina Chandler, Morgan Curtis, Karin Kallmaker, and Katherine V. Forrest. Many thanks, also, to the dedicated staff at Bella Books for all that you do.

About the Author

Jenna Rae is a California native who grew up in and around San Francisco and lives in northern California. She teaches English, mostly as an excuse to talk about books and writing and reading. When she's not writing, teaching, or reading, Jenna likes to garden, crochet, and try out new vegetarian recipes. She is the devoted servant of two occasionally affectionate and frequently sleepy cats.

CHAPTER ONE

"Your front porch makes you look like trailer trash."

Toxic words presented with a wink and a kiss—classic Janet.

They hurt, more maybe than they should have. More than police Inspector Del Mason cared to show, anyway. So she'd ignored the comment and pretended not to believe it.

But neither Janet nor any other woman had crossed Del's threshold in months, and it was time to make it more inviting, if she wanted one crossing it again. So, nearly six months after Janet's caustic comment, Del tore out the whole thing—an easy task, given the state of the wood—and started over from scratch.

Now she was almost finished and feeling pretty good about the new porch and its sturdiness. It was plain, functional and solid. She was stomping back and forth across it to make sure it was sound when a flash of glare off a windshield caught her eye. That was the first time Del saw her new neighbor, a little brunette who was chugging along in a battered old Buick. She slowed in the driveway of the empty house only long enough to reach down and fumble for something, the remote to the garage door opener, maybe. Then she trundled right in without a single glance around. It was surreptitious. To Del's mind, surreptitious was a fancy word for sneaky. She didn't like the woman's behavior.

Del had decided long before to turn a blind eye to any activities of her neighbors that were not heinous and was pretty good about sticking to that. So if she'd seen a moving van or the new homeowner looking around to get a feel for the neighborhood, she'd have gone back to work without a moment's thought. But in this case Del watched the wheezy old car and its driver disappear into the mouth of the garage three doors down and across the street. And then, nothing. That was what got her speculating.

Del had toured the pretty yellow Edwardian a few weeks before, knowing that it wouldn't be on the market for more than a month or two—homes in the heart of the Castro never sat empty for long. Del had been lucky enough to buy many years earlier, during a period of flat home values, and she'd still only barely been able to afford the smallest and most rundown house, one that had been through a plumbing disaster and a kitchen fire.

Sneaky Buick chick must be loaded. Software guru? Venture capitalist? Tort lawyer? But if she could afford that house, why was she driving a rusted beater? Hipster affectation? That seemed unlikely. The woman wasn't young enough to think the battered brown beater was ironic. So, what was the deal?

Not knowing made Del irritable. She tried to dismiss her unfounded pique and went back to work, keeping an eye out for the inevitable truckload of furniture. But as the afternoon wore on and no truck appeared, Del found excuses to stay out front. She tried to talk herself out of loitering in wait. But it was odd for an owner to sneak in like that without even looking around. And who moves in with nothing at all? And who in San Francisco drives a ratty, old car, unless it's by necessity? There hadn't even been a pile of stuff in the backseat.

She finally gave up and went inside her own house. She'd restored her creaking Victorian to a livable state, but it still needed more lighting and new windows and doors. She definitely needed to finish the walls in the garage and get her junk organized down there. Unlike most of the neighbors' homes, hers boasted no granite counters or stainless steel appliances or fancy woodwork. She'd done one project at a time, always on a tight budget, and the house looked like it. But she had learned how to do wiring and plumbing and how to refinish the floors and how to put up drywall, and every time something worked right, a little part of her thought, I did that. The neighbors might live in fancier digs, but most of them probably didn't know how to wire a house to code.

She snuck a peek out her front window. What was the story? Had she moved from overseas? Was she an eccentric millionaire? A flipper? A spoiled, erratic heiress? She for sure wasn't a poor cousin who'd inherited the house. Jerry Tartan had sold it to finance his retirement on Maui.

Washing up and building a salad to go with the steak she'd left marinating all afternoon, Del shook her head at her own idle curiosity.

The shrilling cell phone broke into her thoughts, and she wiped her hands on her jeans, reaching for the call that meant some family was about to get bad news.

***

Through most of the next forty hours, Del focused on the latest domestic dispute turned deadly. It was dismayingly familiar: wife tries to leave controlling, violent husband or boyfriend or whatever and gets killed for her trouble.

The killer was always a likable guy, handsome and charming and successful. The victim had always seemed happy and in love, and no one could believe that this had happened. Except for a sister or cousin or best friend who'd been sure that something was wrong. "I tried to help her. But she kept going back to him!"

She'd heard the same thing hundreds of times.

"I know," Del would murmur, and she did know. She felt compassion for the victims, but she also felt—and fought—disdain for them, especially the ones with kids. How could they put their kids through that? How could they want to be with someone who was usually abusing the kids, too?

Looking at one of the crime scene photos, Del shook her head... Ana Moreno's face was gone, replaced by a mash of bone and dried blood and flesh.

"Fuckin' hamburger," muttered Inspector Mark Milner, the lead detective on the case. He pulled the photo out of her hand and stared at it in apparent fascination, then dropped the photo on Del's desk.

"Yeah." Del didn't know what else to say. Milner had said it like he was impressed by the damage. He'd already commented twice that the murder was "a waste of a perfectly good piece of ass" and stared at Del as if daring her to object.

Del ignored his baiting. He was a caricature, a bitter, burned-out, alcoholic cop. Arrogant, more than a little sexist and homophobic. He wasn't her partner, never would be, and she let his comments slide. She focused on solving the murder.

Not that there was much question who'd done it. Restraining orders, safe houses and social workers notwithstanding, it was very hard to protect a person once someone had decided to kill her. And the victims always knew that. This one had. Ana Moreno had done all the things she should have, once she'd decided to leave. She'd gotten a temporary restraining order, she'd filed for divorce, and she'd documented the abuse and the stalking and the threats. There was a nice thick file on Del's desk, bulging with pictures and emergency room receipts and transcripts of threatening phone calls. After all of that, the victim was something of a legal expert. She probably could have gotten a job at a law office if she'd survived.

But she hadn't stood a chance. Five feet tall, a hundred pounds, against a guy twice her size—Del shook her head, wishing she could really talk to the killer. *Did it make you feel like a big man, beating on a woman who barely came up to your chest?*

That wasn't something she'd ask, of course. She'd never had a real conversation, an honest conversation, with a killer.

Despite all of Ana Moreno's efforts, the ex had barely had to break a sweat to get to her: he just followed her home when she picked up the kids from school. She'd moved out of the shelter into an apartment near her new fast-food job and the kids' school.

"She didn't want to put the kids through a change of schools," a neighbor said, blowing smoke sideways, away from Del's face. Middle-aged, bleach blonde, she had that wide-eyed look of shock people always seemed to have around death. And maybe a little hopped-up, guilty glee at not being on the slab. "She was a good mom, you know?"

"Yes, ma'am. Thank you for your help."

Were you home? Del wanted to ask but didn't. When she was screaming for her life and her bones were breaking and she was gushing blood, were you home? Did you hear it? Did you turn up the TV to drown out the sounds? The apartment complex housed over thirty units, and the walls were almost thin enough to see through, but nobody had heard a thing. There was no point in asking.

Two days after the phone call that had meant her steak would go uneaten, Del finally returned home, having watched Milner take credit for the arrest of the husband. After last year's fiasco in the press, she'd be trailing along after one arrogant ass or another and letting him take credit for her work until her reputation recovered. And guys like Milner were more than happy to do so.

She reviewed the case as she parked her beloved Honda Rebel and tried to ignore the piles of scrap wood and tools and pipes in the garage. She'd been the one to notify the victim's parents, a baffled, vaguely embarrassed older couple, both tax accountants in Oakland. She'd seen the two kids, both still silent and watchful, sent into the grandparents' care. The team had collected the evidence that proved that the husband beat his wife with a chair, and then pieces of the chair, until she was dead. It was Del who'd gotten his confession, a gift she hadn't expected. He'd gotten aroused telling her about it. He'd gone into great detail about the sounds and the feeling of it, gotten flushed and short of breath rhapsodizing about the smell.

She'd smiled at him, encouraging him, nodding and leaning forward breathlessly, as though he were telling her an exciting, sexy story. He'd kept his hands below the table, and she'd pretended not to know or care that he was getting off on telling her about it. The heavy table had rocked into her chest over and over, and she'd pretended not to notice that or the squealing protests of the chair as the killer raced toward climax and the end of the story.

She tried to clean off the memory of his excitement by scrubbing her hands. Her face was hot, her stomach sour, and she had to let it go. The woman was dead. There'd be another one tomorrow or the next day or the next, killed for the crime of falling in love with the wrong person. She rolled her eyes. Okay, enough.

She sniffed Sunday's steak after freeing it from the tinfoil she'd stuck it in two days before and decided to grill it. In the cool of the backyard, she sipped an icy beer and waited for the grill to heat up. *I'm drinking alone again. That can't be good.*

She sighed, settling with care into her one rickety lawn chair. She'd wrestled it out of a pile in the garage after Janet had taken her good patio furniture, the table and chairs set she'd saved up for over a year to buy. God only knew why Janet had even taken it all. She certainly hadn't needed it. Of course, Janet wasn't the type to go without whatever her whims demanded.

Del's body ached with weariness. She let out a slow breath, trying to let go of the hurt and disappointment that had been her closest companions for months. Janet had loved eating outside, had insisted on it whenever the weather allowed. That was how Del had gotten in the habit of grilling. Janet liked to eat outside, but she hated to cook.

Well, that's one thing, anyway. Janet might have destroyed her career, ruined her peace of mind, broken her heart, stolen her good patio furniture, and made her miserable—damned if she didn't sound like the world's worst country song—but she did get Del grilling her steaks instead of frying them.

"What kind of hillbilly fries a steak?" Janet had demanded

the first time she saw Del throw a slab of beef in a frying pan. Del scowled in what she pretended was mock outrage and shook a spatula at her. Janet tried to grab it, but Del held it up over her head, laughing at Janet's expression. They made love then and there, Del reaching out to snap off the gas before smoke could fill the whole house.

Trailer trash. Hillbilly. Janet had known exactly the buttons to push, hadn't she?

Musing about the cost of new patio furniture reminded Del of her new neighbor. Did she have any stuff in that big house yet? Was she sleeping on the floor? That hardly seemed likely. What kind of furniture was she likely to have, this woman in the big, fancy house, driving an ancient boat on wheels? Maybe she was the chintz and lace type. Or the black leather and chrome type. Maybe floor cushions, clay pots, and hand-woven rugs?

Funny, she thought, how someone can move in right down the street and still be a total stranger. Of course, the whole Welcome Wagon could have come and gone a dozen times. Once a case started, Del tended to get pretty wrapped up in it. The neighbors seemed to accept her as a sometimes presence. She set her steak on the grill, resolving for the umpteenth time to find more balance in her life: less work, more fun.

***

The next few weeks made her forget that resolution. She was stumped on a headache of a cold case, last year's murder of a young prostitute whom no one seemed to miss or even to know. Her days and nights were tied up with chasing down leads when she connected the girl to a group of street kids who stuck together and subsisted in the Tenderloin and did not cooperate with cops.

Then she was pulled into a missing persons case. The department scoured the city for a minor who'd disappeared from his exclusive prep school in Sea Cliff. After the city paid dozens of cops overtime for a week, it turned out he'd run away because his daddy wouldn't buy him a new ride after he totaled his second sports car. By the time Del could get back to the murdered girl, the street kids had moved on. She forgot about patio furniture and the new neighbor and nearly everything. Sometimes even Janet slipped her mind.

She came home one evening to find a SAFE flier on her door and made a face in response. She didn't want to go. She was tired, for one thing. For another, she didn't want the whole neighborhood to know she was a cop. They'd get squirrelly over their illicit drug use, or, worse, call her every time someone drove by playing loud music. SAFE, the community outreach branch of the department, had a lot of potential upsides. She just didn't want to be a part of it.

Phil and Marco, her next-door neighbors, were the organizers of the meeting. Marco had been harassing Del for months about it, knowing she'd eventually cave. He didn't remind her that she owed him. He didn't need to. His scrawled "M" on the flier was enough to compel her. A few hours later, Del slipped through the crowd and headed straight toward the food arranged on the dining room table. Marco shadowed her and raised his eyebrows when she dug right in.

"Really? Not even a hello?" Marco hissed, and Del mumbled an apology.

"I'm glad you came," he whispered, his expression softening.

Del shrugged. "If I'd known there was gonna be food."

"Hmmmn."

Marco was the only person she'd confided in after the end with Janet. He'd listened to her, commiserated with her, brought her food and liquor. Now, every time she saw him, she thought of that time. She was grateful for his kindness but had to fight the temptation to avoid him. He had seen her at her worst. It was in his eyes, that knowing, and she couldn't stand to see it.

She swallowed hard, trying to clear her mouth, wanting to say something like thank you and unable to do so. He patted her arm and murmured something she didn't quite hear but read as commiseration and encouragement.

Marco moved away to join Phil in front of the fireplace. Ignoring the introductions of the various neighbors, Del scanned the room. Maybe a dozen people were seated. Another dozen or so hovered around the edges of the room, and Del was glad to see that most of them were familiar. She zeroed in on the new neighbor. It had to be her. She was the only person Del didn't recognize. It was hard to see much of her, because her head was down.

Phil asked the stranger to introduce herself. Startled, she blushed and stood with thinly disguised reluctance. She looked like a recent escapee from some crazy Christian cult. Too pale, no makeup, crazily long hair, dowdy clothes.

"Hi." The woman's soft voice barely reached around the room. "My name's Lola, Lola Bannon. I just bought the yellow house, the one with the white door?" Several people nodded and smiled, but Lola Bannon was looking down and probably didn't see them.

She sat, cheeks still flushed, and Del examined her discreetly as the meeting progressed. Pretty eyes in a baby face. Thirties? Average everything, height, weight. Maybe. Her figure was hidden by bulky clothes, boxy gray sweater, jeans, cheap sneakers. No purse, no jacket. Bulge of keys in the left front pocket of very loose jeans. Sick? Drugs? Maybe not, the fair skin and brown eyes were clear. But the eyes were ringed with deep, dark circles. Someone wasn't getting much sleep. The woman was vanilla wafer, all the way. No, not even that—soda cracker without the salt.

Del almost missed it. She had lost interest by then and let her gaze drift over to Marco. It was his smile and the surprise in his eyes that made her look back.

Lola Bannon was smiling at Marco, and she was—Del couldn't think of a word that sufficed. Beautiful. Stunning. Breathtaking, that was it. She was breathtaking. Wow. Del sucked in air, fighting the urge to laugh. She looked like a completely different woman! Suddenly, she had sparkling eyes, pink cheeks, and a sweet, sensual mouth. How could a smile change someone's face that much?

Del could usually sum people up in short order. It was part of her job, and she had developed the habit long before her training at the academy. But Lola Bannon was hard to read. Del narrowed her eyes, intrigued. Lola's smile faded, but her eyes were still bright. She nodded at something Phil said, and then smothered a laugh when he told a joke. Del smiled at that and was surprised to realize that she was attracted to the little mouse. When was the last time she'd been attracted to anyone? Not since Janet. Not that it mattered. She was done with love forever. Allergic to it. Sick of it. Closed for business forever. She fixed her gaze on Phil, willing herself not to sneak glances at Lola and only cheating three or four times.

She tried to look attentive to the topic of "Noticing Suspicious Behavior or Persons" per the annoyingly reflective laminated sign propped on the fireplace behind Phil and Marco. The SAFE rep was wrapping things up quickly, and Del turned back to the food as soon as she decently could. Tomorrow was Friday, and she might actually get to have a real weekend. Maybe. If nobody cheated or lied or stole anything or burned the toast or forgot to water the plants or whatever it was people did to make somebody want to kill them.

CHAPTER TWO

Lola sat at her computer, watching the cursor blink. She was starting a new chapter and was stuck. Her fingers twitched. Stop thinking, she told herself. Just stop thinking about it and do it. But she couldn't.

"What's wrong with you?" Orrin's voice was low, not yet angry, almost conversational. She shook it away. Not real, she reminded herself.

Orrin had asked that question a lot. So had more than one social worker and nearly every foster parent. Even Mrs. Polachek, a good-humored mountain of a woman with seemingly endless patience for just about every other kind of personal failing, had been baffled and irritated by Lola's inability to speak up, to answer even the simplest question. She'd never mistreated Lola, but she hadn't exactly warmed to her, either.

One day, she asked Lola what her favorite book was and received only a worried frown in response. Lola wasn't sure how to answer. Was Mrs. Polachek familiar with *The Faerie Queene*? It wasn't really a book, not the way Mrs. Polachek meant, but it was Lola's favorite story. What if Mrs. Polachek didn't recognize Spenser's epic poem and thought it was a kid's picture book and told Lola to read something more appropriate? What if she thought Lola was showing off? Or that she was lying? She might get really mad. There were too many bad possibilities, and Lola panicked and couldn't answer. She had tried very hard to please Mrs. Polachek by cleaning up after the other kids, getting up with the little ones at night, staying awake to avoid having loud nightmares that would wake up the whole house. But obviously it hadn't worked. Mrs. Polachek waited a long time for an answer, resting her thick arms on her massive chest and eying Lola's downcast face.

Finally, she said, "I can't put my finger on it, Lola, but there's definitely something wrong with you. What do you think it is?"

Lola, ten or so at the time, shrugged and apologized and waited to be released. Then she went to the bathroom and looked in the mirror, trying to figure it out. *What is wrong with me?* There were obvious answers. She was neither charming nor beautiful. She was bright enough, but not really anything special. She was not charismatic or personable or friendly. Too quiet. Too plain. Too timid. She had always been disappointing. Maybe, she thought, that was why my parents didn't want me.

But there were a lot of people who were not charming or beautiful or charismatic or anything special, and they had parents and even friends. Lola didn't find it hard to believe that she was unlovable. But, like Mrs. Polachek, she couldn't quite put her finger on the reason why.

She thought about imitating the popular girls at school and in that way become more lovable. Popular girls seemed to know by some instinct who was powerful and who was weak. They teased and tossed their hair and flirted with the powerful, and they flayed the weak mercilessly. And they could accurately assess the constant, and to Lola, unreadable, changes in an invisible power structure, seemingly without effort. How did they do that? Could she learn to do what they did? No, she decided after much thought. She could not. She was doomed to flounder alone in the uncharted sea of humanity.

At the neighborhood safety meeting, Lola noticed Marco's concern for the blonde woman when she darted over to the food. He'd mentioned her to Lola the day before, Del something? He seemed very fond of her, though he also seemed wary of saying much about her. She was certainly attractive. Lola watched her with interest. Aside from being famished, she also seemed very guarded. She stood with her arms crossed, her feet planted wide. Like a Roman guard or something. A cop, no doubt about it. She scanned the room, her face inscrutable. A Roman guard crossed with an Amazon warrior. The Faerie Queene, Lola thought with surprise, she's like the Faerie Queene of the modern age. The fanciful thought made her smile, but she ducked her head to hide this. Del, though she looked like a proud, beautiful Faerie Queene, might think Lola was laughing at her.

She's strong, Lola decided, fiercely independent, and maybe standoffish. A throwaway kid? She was beautiful and obviously unaware of it, but she looked hard, too. Tough, prickly, maybe disdainful. A little mean, perhaps? A good person to avoid, probably. Lola also noticed Del's scrutiny after the embarrassing introduction of herself she was forced to make. She saw Del dismiss her as nothing special, a boring nobody. This irked her for some reason she couldn't name. Generally she liked to let people's gazes glide over her. Maybe, though, it was time for that to change.

She thought about this the next day while showering. She was still using a cache of shampoo and soap cadged from a housekeeper's cart and drying with a threadbare motel towel. I'm a thief, she'd realized only after driving away from the shabby fleabag she'd lived in for a year. I have now become a person who steals. This didn't feel as bad as she'd have once thought.

She was still sleeping on the floor, using her coat as a blanket and sweater as a pillow. Ever since she'd left Folsom, she'd spent all her waking hours writing, unable to focus on anything else. She loved having the freedom to focus on that. But it wasn't good, living like that for too long, first in the motel and then in the new house, and it was time to make this place a home for herself.

A home, wasn't that what she'd always wanted? Of course, she'd wanted a family, too, but it was well past time to accept that she would never have that. She shook that aside to focus on the fact that she finally had a real home of her own. It had been terrifying, signing all of those papers, committing to this place. And she hadn't originally planned to buy at all. She'd looked online after her lawyer warned her about the tax implications of her new money.

"Buy a house," he said, "or you'll lose all your money to Uncle Sam."

She liked the way he said that, Uncle Sam, as though there were some greedy old man waiting to snatch cash from her wallet. She made a wish list and sent it to the top fifty realtors in the state, unable to choose a city or a neighborhood. Among the dozens of listings she received, this was the only one she felt a connection with. It was almost tangible, her desire for this house, and she defied logic and practicality and a lot of fears to get it.

Her new home was a symbol of everything she wanted to become. It was bright and open and uncluttered. It was filled with light, and she'd only reluctantly and with some difficulty installed curtains and drapes. And it was clean and fresh smelling and untainted by any old memories. It was a complete break from everything she'd ever known. Her mind skirted away from the subject of everything she'd ever known, and she repeated her new mantra aloud: "The past has passed."

The house belonged where she did, in the here and now. Best of all, it was hers, bought and insured in her name alone and belonging only to her. As proud of the house as she was, it was hard to believe they'd let her buy it. Surely she didn't deserve such a beautiful house. What if someone came and took it away from her? This thought crept into her mind often, though she knew there was no real reason to be afraid. Was there?

She snapped her fingers and pushed away the question. It's okay to be happy, she reminded herself. It was time to start over, to make a new and better life, and all she'd done was skulk around and bury herself in writing. Enough of that. It was time to start living. She peered into the bathroom mirror and wondered what her new life would be like, and who she would be in it. Her reflection looked pale and scared and not at all brave, and she turned away from it.

"The past has passed," she repeated, and her voice echoed in the empty hallway. Time for a new life and a new Lola.

Lola's resolve to take action carried her through the next several weeks. She made a beeline to the nearest consignment store, grim with determination to make the house her own. She bought beds and chairs and tables and paintings, not with any plan in mind but because things appealed to her. She even broke down and bought towels and sheets and blankets, picking over the discount and thrift store bins with care. She didn't want to waste a single penny, but she wanted to only buy things she really liked. Orrin would have disapproved of everything, she knew, and that made her like them all even more.

Even now, she was frugal in her choices. She tried to talk herself out of her worry, but she agonized nearly as much over a fifty-cent towel as she did over an eighty-dollar couch. Whether a thing was stylish or valuable wasn't a consideration. She bought a battered ottoman upholstered in rich, gorgeous red, knowing that it was old and worn and should be reupholstered. She didn't care. She loved it. It felt warm and real to her. Orrin would have pronounced it junk. Her hand rubbed its velvet side as though to soothe it, and she was glad she'd rescued it from the thrift store.

"Don't worry," she whispered to the thing, "I'm old and worn out, too."

When the house was finally furnished, she decided to work on her appearance, again feeling that she was somehow defying Orrin. It was both exciting and scary. On the morning of her appointment at the chic salon down the street, she counted out the cash she'd allotted for the day and realized that it was more than she'd spent on furnishing the entire house. She was horrified by the wastefulness of it.

"Well," she asked the mirror, "is it a waste, really?"

She'd cut her own hair with kitchen shears since she was twelve. She wanted just once to go to a real hair salon and see what she could look like if she were someone else, some better and luckier version of herself.

She forced herself to walk into the upscale storefront, immediately intimidated by the lavish décor and fashionable clientele. Her feet wanted to carry her back out again, but she smiled with false courage and let a smooth young woman lead her to a chair. She'd chosen the salon carefully, figuring the outrageous prices would make them be nice to her. It was strange and a little scary, letting all those strangers stare at her and touch her and discuss her like she was a problem to be solved.

"Those eyebrows," one young woman lamented, tilting her elaborately pierced face and frowning at Lola.

"Don't worry," a voice murmured from somewhere out of Lola's sight, "Pasha'll fix them. She's a genius."

"Good God, look at that hair," one young boy said, frowning. "What is he doing with that hair?"

"He's cutting off about two feet of it," said an authoritative voice from somewhere she couldn't see, and Lola twisted around to see a tall man wearing all black. He was the most beautiful human being Lola had ever seen. She gaped at him, unable to greet such a magnificent creature. He was blinding, with white-blond hair and deep blue eyes and tanned skin and white, white teeth. He was hard to look at, like a searchlight with eyes. She turned back around and gripped the arms of the chair.

"Hello, Lola," he said, his voice softer.

Lola smiled in his general direction, but she was muted by terror. What on earth could someone so beautiful think of an ugly, horrible, frumpy nobody like her? This had been a huge mistake. She was definitely in the wrong place. She tried to think of a way to leave.

"Hi." She forced out the word but couldn't tell if he heard her.

"Don't you hate that?"

She looked up into the mirror at his reflection's eyes, nonplussed out of her shame and fear.

"You know, people talking about you like you're furniture?"

She grimaced, trying not to agree too enthusiastically. "I guess it's a professional hazard."

He shook his head. "Not at all. Just unprofessional. And rude."

"Sorry, Adonis," murmured one beautiful young woman. She actually batted her eyelashes, tinged a bright purple, and he laughed. Lola exhaled with relief. He wasn't angry? No, he really wasn't. It was okay.

"Behave, children," he said, shaking a finger, and the cool, glamorous youngsters actually giggled! Lola suppressed a smile.

So, this was Adonis. The receptionist had said that he would try to stop by but wouldn't have time to do her whole makeover.

"He's overbooked for months," the receptionist had chirped. "It's a privilege to be seen by one of his protégés."

"Thank you for stopping by," Lola said in his direction, assuming that he would turn her over to a junior stylist.

"Trying to get rid of me?"

Lola opened her mouth but couldn't speak, afraid he was offended, but he laughed again.

"I'm not going anywhere," he said, and she raised an eyebrow.

Maybe he'd had a cancellation. Maybe he enjoyed a challenge. Maybe no one else was skilled enough to fix such a huge mess. That was probably it. That was certainly it. He couldn't let her walk out of his salon looking like an ogre. It would be bad for business. That made sense. She nodded grimly.

"Smile! Today is going to be the best day of your life," he promised, and Lola tried to comply.

"O—kay," she said, and he laughed.

"I'm serious." His dark eyes widened. "Listen, I know this is scary. But by the time I'm done with you, you'll be able to hold your head up high." He leaned over and peered into her eyes. "Lola, I see you. You've hidden yourself behind all of this," he waved his hands, "and now it's time to unveil the real you. Little Lola, Lolita mia, no more hiding."

He was so beautiful. Even without his gorgeous hair and stylish clothes and perfect teeth, he would have been beautiful. How could he understand what it was like to be unattractive? Of course, weren't his kind words part of what she was paying for? She was plain, at best. She knew enough to know that. But arguing would only force the poor man to pile on more empty flattery, so she just smiled and murmured something that sounded like agreement.

"Are you donating the hair?"

"If you think they'll want it."

He didn't respond. He just ran his fingers through the lengths of her hair, pulling it away from her head and letting it drop against the side of the chair. It was so heavy! She hadn't noticed that it hung past her hips. How long had it been since she'd cut it? Several years, at least.

"Of course, I'll donate it. And, Adonis," she leaned back to look him in the eyes, "thank you."

"I haven't done anything yet, Lolita. Don't thank me until I'm done waving my magic wand." He flashed a brilliant smile and started plaiting her hair. She saw that he was done talking to her. He seemed completely focused on something inside his own head. Was that what she looked like when she was writing? None of his assistants or protégés or whatever they were seemed inclined to interrupt him. They stood back as if watching a great artist at work. Even other clients turned to watch him.

Were they laughing at her? She forced the thought away. They're being nice to you, she reminded herself. Isn't that enough? Adonis ordered her to close her eyes. She drifted into her favorite daydream, in which she had made all the right choices instead of all the wrong ones.

Some unknown time later, she was still sitting there with her eyes closed. A soft something danced lightly over her eyelids, and it tickled. Her head was cool. Her hair felt gone, just gone. She snaked a hand out to see if Adonis had shaved her head, and he lightly slapped her hand away.

"No cheating, Miss Doolittle. You turned yourself over to Professor Higgins, and I'm not done yet."

She giggled, and she and Adonis both chuckled when someone asked who Professor Higgins was. Maybe Adonis is right, she thought. I haven't even seen myself yet, but I feel different. I feel like maybe I could actually turn out to be a real person. She pressed her eyes shut tight, but a few tears leaked out, and she felt a hand press a tissue to them.

"I know," he said. "It's not easy, being beautiful."

That cracked up both of them again, and Lola relaxed and gave in. If Adonis had shaved her head, so be it. She sank back into her daydream.

Someone was putting more makeup on her. She'd worn lipstick before, and cover-up, but that was it. She worried that Adonis would be disappointed and she didn't want to let him down. He seemed so hopeful about all of this, but at the end she'd still be herself. She would open her eyes, and he would be disappointed but too polite to show it.

Pretend you love it, she told herself. Let him pretend you're pretty and that he worked miracles, and then you'll be able to leave, and it will all be over. You never have to do this ever again, and it's almost over.

Finally, the stylist pronounced her finished. She kept her eyes closed an extra second to prolong the suspense and heard Adonis groan in impatience. She felt herself smiling, and she finally looked in the mirror.

She could hardly process the image for a moment. Then she gasped out loud. The woman who stared back at her in the mirror was a stranger. She looked like some television version of Lola. Younger, prettier, and somehow more expressive, she had big eyes and shiny hair and a wide smile. It was weird. Kind of scary, even. She would not have recognized herself but for the crookedness of her teeth. It was like looking at a stranger. Like the old Lola had disappeared and been replaced by some better version of her. Lola saw her smile falter. Was that her reflection? Was it a trick mirror? Was she dreaming?

"You— "She couldn't continue.

"I know," Adonis said, tilting his head to the side. "You're right. I am an amazing, remarkable and talented genius, thank you very much."

"How—"

"I told you," he said, taking her hand. "You had yourself all wrong, Lola Lolita Doolittle. You thought you were supposed to be somebody's ugly stepsister, didn't you?"

"But?" At some point, she was going to have to be able to make an actual sentence, but it was still beyond her. She reached up and lightly touched her hair. It felt soft, like a baby's hair. Adonis pulled her hand away and held it. She shook her head slowly, and her hair flew around her face as though it were weightless.

"I don't understand." She frowned. "This isn't me. This isn't what I look like. I never looked like this. What did you do?"

"I knew, the minute I saw you, that you weren't my usual client. You weren't trying to be more than you were. You'd made yourself invisible, hadn't you? And now you're ready to stop being invisible. It's not magic, honey. It's just a little makeup and a haircut from this century."

Lola's eyes overflowed again, and Adonis smiled as she dabbed at them.

"Tommy," he called over his shoulder, "change Lolita's mascara to waterproof!"

"One more thing, and I don't want you to be insulted," Adonis said. "But you need to stop dressing like a fugitive from a chain gang." He pulled out a stack of magazines and showed her clothes she should buy. He asked her to pick a few things and then told her what was wrong with those choices. After a while, she was able to pick a half dozen items that Adonis approved of.

"Go shopping," he ordered, "and bring everything back to me so I can check it. I don't quite trust you, and I don't want you ruining my work with mom jeans and a baggy sweatshirt. Dress like someone with an ounce of self-worth, okay?"

She promised to do so and reached out to shake his hand. He shook his head and pulled her close for a hug. He'd spent more time with her than she'd ever imagined. And never once had he made her feel like an outsider or a freak. It was unnerving, having someone so dazzling treat her with such sweetness.

"Thank you so much," she whispered. "You've been so kind and so brilliant. Thank you, thank you, thank you!"

Change, she told herself while walking home, is good. This was a new habit of hers, coaching herself. Go team! She laughed at herself and saw a cute, tomboyish girl smile at her. Was she flirting? She couldn't be. Someone so beautiful would never look twice at someone like her, but the very possibility was exhilarating. She finally looked and felt like she belonged in this lovely, lovely place. As the sunlight dimmed around her, Lola wandered around her pretty new house and wondered what kind of person she would turn out to be, now that she could choose.

CHAPTER THREE

With Halloween a week away, Del realized that her porch was the only one with no pumpkin on it. She couldn't believe she'd let things go like that. The neighborhood kids had no patience for excuses come candy night, and she didn't blame them. But tonight was not the time to worry about that. She was on her way to her book club and didn't want to miss it again. She'd read the book three weeks before and barely remembered it, something about an alien or something? Whatever. She used to have friends, but now she spent much of her time alone, and it was wearing on her. Tess and the other members of the book club were all she had left, and she hadn't seen them since summer. Taking in the decorations and breathing in the cool fall air made her wish she were actually excited about the rapidly approaching holiday season.

Last Halloween Janet had talked her into wearing a costume, something Del hadn't done since she was a small child. They went as prisoner and guard, Janet in a sexy little uniform and Del in the stripes. Del left a huge bowl of candy on the porch and they joined the crowd on the streets. Del had felt lighter and freer that night than maybe ever before, even as she kept a watchful eye on the more ebullient gatherers. While the neighborhood had once been known for its wild Halloween debauchery, new ordinances and pressure from a variety of sources within the community had changed things to a more subdued hubbub. It was the perfect setting for Del's mood that night. She was in love with a beautiful woman who seemed to love her back, and she was happy.

Janet was more than just beautiful. She was both larger than life and unimaginably tiny. Everything about her seemed delicate. Her wrists, her shoulders, even her hips were bony. But her voice was loud, teasing and provocative and sexy and sharp, either purring or screeching and on the verge of hysteria. She demanded constant attention, and Del was surprised to find how much she enjoyed being in demand like that. Sometimes it was more exciting than exhausting. Sometimes it was not.

Janet was obsessed with her weight, always insisting that she needed to go on a diet. She dressed in the sexiest clothes and wore the highest heels, and she never went anywhere without full makeup. Del loved walking into a bar or restaurant with Janet on her arm. Every head in the place would turn to Janet, and she would strut along, head high, hips swaying, well aware of her sexual prowess. Her dark, heavily lined eyes and long, shining hair made her an exotic beauty in a city full of exotic beauties, but it was something else that made her special. What that was, Del never could figure out. Confidence, charisma, mystique, maybe? She certainly had all of them to spare. Janet was what Del's daddy would have called "a right good one."

They'd met in a bar. When Janet sauntered up and just stared up at Del, unsmiling, her chest stuck out like she wanted to fight, Del almost laughed. She thought that if the girl weren't such a knockout she'd seem ridiculous. But she was a knockout.

"You gonna buy me a drink, Stretch, or what?"

Del smiled and wished she had a hat to doff. Of course she bought the girl a drink. She had always been very confident with women. She was used to being the one to approach them, to seeing them blush as she charmed and flattered and teased them. It was disconcerting to have this tiny gorgeous girl walk up and seduce her. She'd been off balance ever since that night. She spent months growing to trust Janet and wanted something she hadn't wanted since she was a kid—real love, real trust, a family of two. And Janet seemed to want it too.

Late at night, after dinner and wine and Janet's detailed and apparently fictional stories about whatever school she'd worked at that day, they had long talks about their future together. Del told Janet things she never shared with anyone. She talked about conflicts within the department, about inept administrators, about the difficulties of being a woman and gay and a detective. She opened her heart, and for the first time in her life, shared everything she felt and thought. She never imagined that Janet, who listened to her every word with wide eyes and an attentive air, who ran to Del at the end of the day as if burning with passion for her, would turn around and stab her in the back. Del was still reeling.

It was six months after that first night in the bar that Del found out Janet wasn't a substitute teacher but a freelance reporter writing an expose on the SFPD. All Janet's stories about teaching were fictional. All those months, all those questions—in retrospect, it was obvious. She was never in love with Del. She was working her, using her to dig up dirt on the department.

When the article came out, first online, then in every local paper, and finally in a national magazine, everyone seemed to know Del was the source. Del wasn't sure how. She wasn't the only lesbian in the department, or even the station, but everyone knew that Inspector Del Mason was the one who'd blown it. She was never formally disciplined, but she was still paying for her stupidity in the contempt from her police colleagues and supervisors, their ostracism.

Whatever headway Del had made in the last several months in rebuilding her life on the job, she'd failed to make in her personal life. One minute, she and Janet were going to be together forever.

The next, Janet was a traitor who'd only been with her to use her. Del still felt raw, exposed and hurt and angry. Though she'd never been in the closet, she had always kept her personal life separate from her professional life. She'd certainly never made a public spectacle of herself. She also hadn't been anyone's fool since she was seven years old, and now, at forty, she felt like a hapless child all over again. Losing her head over a woman was a mistake she'd never planned to make, and one she did not intend to make again.

The thrumming of her bike brought Del back to the present. She headed toward the coffee shop, eager to touch base with the women from the book club. She only made it to the meeting about half the time because of the job but she enjoyed it when she did go.

As she carefully backed the Rebel up against the edge of the sidewalk, Del noticed a woman walking toward her in the gathering dusk. The new neighbor, what was her name? Linda? Laura? Lola. That was it, Lola Bannon.

"Lola?" she called, and the woman froze. She stood peering at the helmet that hid Del's face, poised on the balls of her feet like she might flee into the night.

"Hey, hi. Didn't mean to startle you. I'm Del, your neighbor. We met at Marco and Phil's. Remember?" Del pulled off the helmet and smiled in what she hoped was an "I'm a nice person and not a serial killer" way. Actually, she realized belatedly, they hadn't met. She scarcely recognized this woman.

"No. Yes. Did we? Hi, Del. Uh, I'm sorry," Lola protested, "I wasn't paying attention." She came closer and flashed a brief, reflexive smile. Even in the waning light of evening, she looked like a completely different woman from the one Del had seen in Marco's living room. Now Del was surprised she'd recognized her at all. She looked like that other woman's sexy twin.

She wore a lavender sweater and stylish jeans. A fitted leather jacket completed the look, and the new clothes showed off a shapelier body than Del had realized before. Her hair was tinted a warmer brown, no grays, and cut at least twenty inches shorter, in a style that framed her face and drew attention to her eyes. Those eyes, Del noticed, were even prettier than she'd thought, golden and sparkling. Her cheeks were a soft pink, and her lips looked full and glossy and rose colored. Soft. Full. Kissable.

"What are you doing here?" Del heard the brusqueness in her voice and saw Lola's shoulders hunch. Most people would bristle, not retreat. *She's more skittish than I thought.* She grimaced and saw Lola's face freeze.

What is wrong with me? Be nice. She gestured at the paperback Lola clutched. "Book club?"

She climbed off the bike and saw Lola take an unconscious step backward. This could get old, fast. Del felt like she was standing over a feral cat. She eased her body backward. Lola took another unconscious step, this time forward. *That* was interesting.

"Oh, uh, I saw the ad for a book club here, I mean, I saw it online, and I thought I'd check it out. Maybe. I've never joined a book club. How about you?"

Del nodded. "I've been coming for a while. I don't always make it, but nobody seems to mind. They're a nice group. What'd you think of the SAFE neighborhood thing?"

"Oh." Lola tilted her head, "Great. I'd never been to anything like that before. I thought it would be nice to meet my new neighbors."

But you didn't talk to a soul. You slipped out just as fast as I did. Faster. She held out her book, and Lola smiled, holding out her own copy of *Stranger in a Strange Land.*

"D'you like it?" Del asked.

"Like it?" Lola seemed to take the question seriously. Her eyes widened, and a small smile lit up her face, even in the dim light on the sidewalk.

Oh, but it was a beautiful smile. A real one, this time. Del liked the way that smile, brief though it was, warmed her in a way that was disconcerting. She reminded herself, *I don't even know this woman.*

"I did. You know, the 'grok' thing. That's a lovely concept, isn't it? And I think we all feel a little—alien, sometimes."

"What makes you feel like an alien?"

The question was too direct. Lola shook her head and shrugged at the same time. She gave an apologetic smile and looked away, turning toward the door. "We should probably go in, I think."

Del nodded at Lola's back and held the door. She leaned forward to hear Lola's barely audible thanks.

Del knew she could be intimidating with her height and build and cop's demeanor, and she tried to be as nonthreatening as possible, especially with this kind of woman. She generally treated people like they were witnesses—drawing them out, making them feel comfortable and safe, letting their personalities show themselves naturally.

Timid women she tended to handle with kid gloves, allowing them their space. Proving that she was nice and not scary. She felt like she'd bullied Lola, somehow. *I feel like a bad guy around her, and I don't like it. I'm not too sure I like her.* Pretty or not, sweet or not, she was all rabbit and no fight. But there was something intriguing about her. Del suspected, though she had no reason to do so, that there was more to Lola Bannon than met the eye.

The tables had been pushed around so the group could form a rough oval on one side of the brightly lit neighborhood hangout. It was a popular place and often hosted poetry readings, live music and book clubs. Because of this, regulars had become accustomed to clustering on the smaller side of the oversized coffee shop and bakery, leaving the larger side open for whatever was going on that night. Del thought of it as a kind of home away from home, one of the few places she could go and not feel like she was on duty.

Several members of the book club were already seated, sipping coffee and chatting. Tess, the book club organizer, had made arrangements with the owner, and now they always had a few carafes of coffee and some cups set on a table so that members could serve themselves. Their annual dues somehow supposedly covered the cost of this, although Del suspected that Tess ended up paying more than her share. She vowed, not for the first time, to address this privately with Tess. She didn't like the idea of letting the kid pay for all of them.

Del waited by the door to see what Lola would do. She saw her look around for Tess, who always wore a nametag when someone new was joining them—she was a natural organizer and facilitator and one of the reasons Del had joined the group. Del spotted Tess at the edge of the circle and smiled; her dark curls bounced every time she gestured or nodded or laughed. She was a lively, charismatic Cuban woman who managed to balance strength and softness with seemingly effortless grace, and she was one of Del's favorite people.

She remembered meeting Tess nearly a decade earlier, when a burglar had stabbed an elderly neighbor and Tess had managed to bring the guy down with a baseball bat, call for help, and save the neighbor's life without breaking a sweat. Del had given her a high five, which had earned her a sour look from her then-captain. She'd also asked Tess if she'd ever considered a career in law enforcement, something she still thought would be a good idea. But Tess was a nurse, and she had no interest in law enforcement. Del had expressed her sincere regret over this, and she'd seen that Tess was flattered. A few weeks after that, Tess came into the station to find her—she was recruiting for a local basketball league and had thought of Del. This wasn't much of a surprise. People always asked Del if she played basketball.

Del wasn't a great player, but she was pretty athletic, and her height and quick reflexes made her an asset. She played for six seasons and enjoyed hanging out with Tess and the other players, then quit when Janet complained that it took too much time away from each other. Tess approached her every few months to ask her back, but Del wasn't sure she wanted to play anymore—the younger players tended to throw elbows pretty freely, and she was no longer young enough to recover from bruised ribs in an hour or two. Janet's whining had just made for a good excuse. Tess, still in her early thirties, didn't seem to get that in ten years she herself would probably be more wary of contact sports.

Del watched as Lola approached Tess and introduced herself. Tess was her usual ebullient self and waved Lola at the coffee setup with some quiet joke that made Lola smile. Del smiled, too. She'd thought Lola would be too shy to walk up to Tess, but clearly she'd underestimated her.

Lola seemed to waver before choosing a seat that was as far away from everyone as possible, on the edge of the group. Del decided to sit opposite her. She would show Lola that she wasn't the big meanie she appeared to be. She exchanged greetings with Tess, her girlfriend Lin, and Rachel, a Barbie wannabe who'd tried on numerous occasions to develop a relationship with Del. Rachel was buxom, blond, and overtly sexy in a way that made most people fawn over her.

A badge bunny, Del decided early on, and was turned off, despite Rachel's obvious charms. Cops were like magnets to some people. The guns, the power, the danger—something about cops got certain women all lathered. Del had studiously avoided that particular pitfall, having watched too many of her colleagues run from badge bunny to badge bunny. It always ended in tears and betrayal and drama. Of course, Janet was all drama, yet another reason Del should have known better.

Rachel was holding hands with a tall, muscular butch in a Pendleton shirt and jeans. She even wore the requisite black boots. Cop? Firefighter? Military? Something like that. Tough, smart-looking, built like a prizefighter. Perfect. That should keep Rachel busy for a while. Andrea, an abrasive, aggressive woman with a habit of interrupting people, wasn't there, and Del was relieved. She and Andrea had butted heads more than once, and it only ever ended when Tess played referee. Del hated to put Tess in that position, and she tried to avoid conflict, but Andrea loved to wrangle and could never agree to disagree. Andrea would have intimidated Lola. Maybe, with such a small group, she would actually talk. Maybe. Two other women came in, arms around each other. They were both typically quiet, and Del nodded to them and to Rachel's seatmate. She saw Lola surreptitiously take in each woman and size her up. She seemed to be doing threat assessments, even on the least threatening people. Del narrowed her eyes.

She saw Lola catch her watching. She held Del's gaze for a moment, and Del realized that Lola had been aware of her scrutiny and was letting her know it. It was a ballsy move. Maybe she needed to stop underestimating Lola. In the light of the coffee shop, the changes she'd undergone were even more striking. She could have been a whole different person. She was more than pretty. She was a knockout. Breathtaking, that was the word that Del had thought of at Marco's, and it was a lot more evident now.

As the evening began, Del stayed a passive observer, an unusual role for her, as Tess led the spirited discussion. Del noticed that Lola, who merely listened for the first several minutes, eventually became an active participant. She wasn't assertive, but she did make a few insightful comments, which the rest of the group seemed to respond to. Challenged by Rachel on one point, Lola immediately backed down, and Del was unsurprised but disappointed. Tess took Lola's position then, but Lola didn't rejoin the dialogue. Too easily intimidated, too easily put aside. A shame. She seemed smart and kind of funny. And her hair smelled good. Del had noticed this when holding the door for her.

Still, Lola asserted herself again later and made a joke to prevent any argument, and Del was glad. This was going to be fun. Maybe Lola had a little fire, after all. Del caught Rachel's annoyed glance and suppressed a smile when Lee grabbed Rachel's knee to get her attention. *Good for you, Lee.* She saw Lola smiling faintly at the silent exchange. So, she's more observant than most. Janet was also very observant. Del shied away from the comparison and focused on the discussion again.

Soon after, the meeting broke up. Del waved goodbye to Tess and walked out right behind Lola. Her hair did smell good. Not too sweet, not too flowery, clean and light and fresh. Maybe they could be friends. Del missed having friends. And Lola seemed like someone who was very alone.

"Hey, Lola?"

She turned, and the top of her head came up to just under Del's chin. Del smiled more easily than she had in months. Why was it that everything Lola did was so damned cute?

"Yes, Del?" They stepped through the door together, and Del felt braced by the night air. Lola seemed to be slowly edging away.

"Uh." Why was this so hard? Del never had trouble talking to people.

She spat her words out more sharply than she'd intended. "I don't see your car." She gestured at her bike.

Lola made a walking motion with her fingers and smiled. "You walked here?" It sounded like an accusation. She had meant it to sound nice. Friendly. She saw Lola shiver. "Uhh. I should get going. Good night." Lola zipped up her jacket. "Nice to see you again, neighbor."

"Wait," Del called. "Listen. It's kinda far to your house and pretty cold. You know, and it's pretty late."

"Oh." Lola started to back away. "It's okay. I like walking."

"Well," Del tried to appear not scary and not crazy and not pushy. "It's just that it's kind of far and not really that safe this late." She shrugged and smiled. "Listen, Lola, we're neighbors, and if anything happened to you, I'd feel like crap. I have an extra helmet. Besides, I bet you've never been on a bike before, and it's kinda fun."

Del knew Lola could certainly walk home seven blocks just fine. But this would give Del an excuse to get closer to her and start building trust with her and developing the friendship she had decided to cultivate. She grabbed the extra helmet that Janet had worn and held it out in what she hoped was a friendly and not aggressive gesture.

Lola hesitated but then smiled, "Well, you're right. I haven't ever been on a motorcycle. Don't take this the wrong way, but it seems kind of dangerous."

Del nodded. "It can be, if you're not careful. But I am careful, and I promise, I'll get you home safe. What do you say?" She offered a scout's salute and smiled. She wasn't sure why she was pushing this. This felt like more than just being neighborly.

Lola appeared to be thinking it over. "Okay, but if I die, I'm coming back to haunt you."

Del's laughter gurgled out. She was definitely funny. And cute and smart and sweet. Not to mention, damned sexy in a leather jacket. "Deal."

She stuck out her hand, and Lola shook it. Her skin was soft, but her hand was cold. *Gloves. Next time, I'll bring gloves for her. Not that there will be a next time. But there might.* She sat and braced the bike, hoping Lola wouldn't chicken out.

Lola murmured her thanks and pulled on the helmet. She

eased carefully onto the bike as though it were a bucking bronco. Del swallowed a laugh.

"You all set?"

"Um, what should I do?"

"Well, pretty much just sit there and hold on."

"I think even I can do that."

Lola's arms hugged Del's sides, and her leather jacket rubbed against Del's, and her jeans rubbed against Del's. It was nice. Janet loved the bike, but she also loved bouncing on the seat and leaning to see around Del, and it was more dangerous than fun to ride with her. Janet also talked nonstop into the intercom, which was even more annoying. Lola was still and quiet and warm. She leaned with Del, instead of trying to anticipate the turns and guide the bike herself. She would be a good dance partner, the way she followed instead of fighting to lead. Lola's body was softer against Del's than Janet's, too.

Lola's arms didn't loosen at all, and her fingers grasped Del's pockets. She was scared of the bike, as she'd said. But the ride was smooth and uneventful. And over much too quickly. Lola climbed off as carefully as she'd climbed on. Del wanted to tease her but wasn't sure how she'd take it.

"See? That wasn't so bad, was it?"

Lola pulled off her helmet, and Del did the same. She grinned to see that Lola was beaming. "That was awesome! I didn't realize how, I don't know, how fun it would be."

Del laughed. "And we were only going twenty miles an hour. Imagine it at eighty."

Lola shook her head. "No, thanks. That sounds terrifying. I think twenty miles an hour is perfect."

Del laughed again. "Maybe I'll be able to change your mind."

"Sorry, but I doubt it."

There was a moment of silence.

"Thanks for the ride."

Del shrugged. "Thanks for trusting me."

"Take care, and thanks again."

"'Night."

Lola held out the helmet and flashed that knockout smile

again, and Del felt her whole body respond. It would be easy to lose herself in that smile.

Okay, she reminded herself, Lola is not your girlfriend. She never will be. She's not even your friend. Barely an acquaintance. But she parked the bike and went inside still thinking about Lola and her shy, sweet smile. And her warm, soft body. And the smell of her hair.

The next month went by quickly, so quickly that Del barely saw Lola or anyone else outside of work. She ran into her once in the grocery store, but Lola was heading out with a distracted look when Del was going in, and she didn't want to be a pest. She also saw her from the bike once. Lola was walking along, head high, hair blowing out behind her. She looked like a shampoo commercial. Then she saw Del and waved, and Del waved back, wishing she wasn't rushing to work and had time to stop. Every time she thought about going by Lola's to say hello, something came up.

Halloween came and went, with no more notice on Del's part than the requisite bowl of candy and uncarved pumpkin on the porch. She was occupied with several stalled cases, more scutwork, and was determined to clear at least one of them before the month was out. She was at a loss on the unidentified prostitute and put the frustrating puzzle aside for the time being. Now she was chasing her tail on three other unsolved murders and feeling useless. She wanted to get back to new cases and work a homicide she could actually solve. The cold cases were almost impossible to clear. They went cold in the first place because there wasn't enough evidence, and new, meaningful evidence was even harder to find long after the fact. She put in extra hours, covered all of her bases, approached each problem from a variety of angles, and still had no luck.

Frustrated, she rode home late one Friday night, vowing to take a day off soon. The next week was Thanksgiving. She glanced at Lola's living room window as she passed, noting two cats perched on the windowsill, eying the world outside as though they were tiny royal sentries. It made her chuckle out loud as she roared by, and she realized that she hadn't laughed since she'd last spoken with Lola. A month ago?

Oh, well. Book club is tonight. Bet I'll see her there. Maybe I'll see if she wants a ride. She remembered how it had felt when Lola had put her arms around her. And how it had felt to see her smile and hear her laugh. She was being ridiculous. The woman was practically a stranger. A pretty, smart, shy, funny stranger who liked to read. Del shook her head. Quiet little Lola Bannon was going to be trouble.

CHAPTER FOUR

Lola stood frozen at her front door, trying to decide whether she should walk to the coffee shop or just drive. She would have enjoyed the walk, but she was worried that Del would be upset with her or feel obligated to give her a ride. She didn't want to offend Del by ignoring her concerns, but she didn't want to feel cornered into accepting a ride, either. She knew that Del was just being nice, but taking a ride to someplace she could get to on her own felt like unnecessary dependence.

Was she overthinking things? She couldn't be sure. She sometimes wished she could see Lauren, who had been her therapist for a little while. But Lauren was well over a hundred miles away, and Lola hadn't spoken to her in over a year. Del, and the way Lola felt drawn to her, seemed like matters Lauren could have helped her sort through.

Lola was attracted to Del, and she didn't really want to be. She was far too raw, still, and it was too nice, leaning into Del's broad back and smelling the leather of her jacket. Lola had been truthful. She'd never been on a motorcycle before. It was such a surprise, the pure pleasure and freedom and power of it. It was a little scary, but they went only a few blocks, and Del seemed like a capable driver.

She seemed capable in a lot of ways. And nicer than she'd seemed at first. She was a less active participant in the book club than Lola had expected. And a careful listener, though you had to look closely to see her reactions to what people said. She kept her face pretty blank, but her eyes were expressive when she thought no one was looking. She was intimidating, in some ways—tough, independent and a little brusque. But tender and sensitive and sweet, underneath the bluster.

Okay, Lola, she chided herself. You don't even know this woman. You've met her, like, twice. And you've barely exchanged a dozen words. And maybe a few giggles. Del had a cute laugh. She always seemed surprised to find herself laughing.

Yes, Lola found Del attractive but intimidating. Lola also remembered the interplay between Del and Rachel and Lee, and she didn't want to get involved in a lot of craziness. Besides, if Rachel was Del's type, then she herself definitely was not. Orrin's snide chuckle sounded in Lola's head, and she had to second his derision. *Someone as beautiful as Del would never even look at someone like me. And she probably thinks I'm about as exciting as oatmeal. Not that I care what she thinks.* She smiled to herself. Well, she acknowledged, maybe I care a little.

Loath though she was to draw the comparison, Lola had to admit that some things about Del reminded her of Orrin. She was confident, smart and independent. She could be sharp. She didn't appear to tolerate foolishness. And she seemed to have the ability to read people very well—it was disconcerting, the way she seemed to be sizing Lola up all the time.

She also seemed very different from Orrin. She was both tougher than he and softer, somehow. She didn't seem to need to prove herself the way he always did. He had to be the boss all the time, but Del seemed like she didn't need to do that. When

Lola seemed nervous, Del backed off. Orrin would have enjoyed her discomfort, while Del seemed unsettled by it. She was a keen listener, but, unlike Orrin, she didn't seem to just listen long enough to find something to pick apart. Lola shook her head and scolded herself. You barely know this woman. Stop making a lot of assumptions about who she is based on nothing. She's just a neighbor. That's all.

Lola had been attracted to other women, but not like this. She wasn't sure how to handle the scary intensity of her attraction to Del. She was worried about making the right choices in women. She'd certainly failed to make the right choice in men. And, she reminded herself, Dr. Orrin Beckett had seemed nice at first. All people generally start off being nice. You don't know who they really are until they decide to show you. And they don't do that until it's too late for you to get away.

Not that Del was beating a path to her door. Lola heard her bike, early in the morning and late at night. Del seemed to work a lot, so maybe she was too busy to come to this month's book club. Maybe she didn't want to be around because she felt like Lola was right there, in her way. That seemed pretty paranoid, though—maybe she was just busy and hadn't given Lola a second thought for the last month. Really, that was the most likely scenario.

Suddenly resolute, she stepped out into the evening chill and trotted down the stairs. Just as she reached the bottom step, she heard a roar and saw Del's bike. Panicked, as though Del could read her thoughts, Lola froze again. Then she had to laugh at herself. *Really*, she thought, *you're freaking out because your neighbor is offering you a ride? Get over yourself.*

"Hey," Del called as she pulled up, "wanna ride?"

"I don't want you to feel like you have to," Lola started, but Del just handed her the helmet and waited. Lola was irritated by Del's assumption, but she was also warmed by the current of desire that ran through her when Del's fingers brushed against hers. She hesitated, holding the helmet, and Del pulled off hers and looked at her in a measuring way.

"Listen," Del said, over the grumbling of the bike, "if you'd rather walk, I'm not planning to kidnap you and whisk you off to book club against your will. Whatever you want to do is cool. I just thought you might want a chance to reconsider your speed limit of twenty."

Lola smiled. "I do like the bike."

"See?"

"But twenty is the absolute limit, okay?"

Del held up two fingers, as she had the month before. "Scout's honor, ma'am."

"You're silly." Climbing on and wrapping her arms around Del's waist, Lola found herself smiling into Del's jacket like a teenager. She giggled with sudden embarrassment—was it obvious to Del how attractive Lola found her? How could it not be? She was flushed and giddy with excitement and nerves.

When they pulled up in front of the coffee shop, Tess was on the sidewalk. It was clear she was waiting to talk to Del, so Lola murmured her thanks to Del and a greeting to Tess before heading inside so they could talk privately. As she opened the door, she heard Tess teasing Del about something, goading her, maybe.

She took a cup of coffee this time, lured by the aroma, and sweetened it liberally.

"You're like me," Lin said.

Lola jumped. She hadn't noticed the slight girl beside her. "I'm sorry, what?"

Lin smiled. "You like some coffee with your sugar."

Lola grinned. "If it were socially acceptable to drink giant cups of milk and sugar without coffee, I would do it."

"Me, too. Is Del gonna play?" Lin was dumping sugar into her coffee like it had to hold her over for the next month.

"Play?"

"Basketball."

She said it like most people would say "cockroaches," and Lola made a questioning face.

"Well, come on, they're all twelve feet tall and built like Amazons. I basically either have to stay home or play cheerleader."

They both looked over as Tess and Del came in. It was obvious that Del had turned Tess down, and Lin made a face.

"Too bad. If Del would play, then at least I'd have someone to talk to."

"Wouldn't Del be busy playing?"

Lin rolled her eyes. "Not Del. You."

Lola shook her head. "Oh, no. I think you have the wrong impression. Del and I aren't together. We're just neighbors. We barely even know each other."

"Really?" Lin regarded her with open scrutiny, and Lola blushed. "That's funny. I got the impression—"

"Sweetie?" Tess wanted to start the meeting.

Lin waggled her fingers at Lola and sat down.

Lola hurried to the same seat she'd chosen the month before, thinking about what Lin had said. She noticed that Del sat across from her again, and she felt self-conscious, smoothing her hair. She also noticed Rachel's open scrutiny and subsequent pique. Although Rachel had no reason to be jealous, Lola flushed with pleasure. Silly, she chided herself. Rachel could be a model, and Del's definitely attractive enough to get Rachel's attention.

She could hear Orrin's voice. "Come on, Lolly, she looks like a whore, but at least she's sexy enough to pull it off. You're not even in her league."

This was true. Lola glanced at Del and then Rachel, whose hand was firmly grasped by the very intimidating Lee. Lee caught her looking and smiled, and her smile was shy and sweet. Lola realized that she didn't know what Lee's voice sounded like. Had she spoken at the last meeting? No, Lola didn't think so. She watched as Lee kissed the back of Rachel's hand, and Rachel snuggled up against her, almost purring.

Lee looked like a kid at the world's best birthday party. No wonder Rachel liked her. She was physically more imposing than Del but seemed sweeter, more approachable. Like a teddy bear. Del was more like a tiger or lion—there was something catlike in her avid awareness of everything around her. Lola could almost imagine Del stretched out in the tall grass of some far-off savannah, supine and regal as a lioness dozing in the sun, eyes half-closed but taking in everything around her. She'd spring into action if needed, faster than the blink of an eye. This image danced in Lola's mind like a movie she'd seen in another lifetime, and she had to struggle to tune in to Tess's voice.

"Okay, ladies," she was saying, "who wants to start us off? Anyone want to lead the way?"

A chorus of voices answered her, and she smiled. Lola was a bit overwhelmed by the enthusiasm of the group and sat back to listen. They'd chosen *Reading Lolita in Tehran,* an autobiography by a university professor who created a secret literature class for women. Lola had devoured the book with greedy pleasure, often feeling like she was there with the class in that living room in Tehran, pulling off her headscarf and drinking tea and talking about everything.

Lola eventually worked up her courage to speak during a rare lull. "This story is so compelling, it transcends time, race, nationality, gender, religion, sexual orientation, political stance—"

She became self-conscious when she saw Del's close attention and faltered, but Tess, who'd rescued Lola the month before, picked up the thread and made Lola's point. Silently thanking Tess, Lola resolved that she would not need rescuing again. It was ridiculous. She was a grown woman, and she should be able to string together a sentence by herself. After all, she was supposed to be a writer! Orrin's phantom snorted in her ear, and Lola flushed.

It was some time later that Lin asserted that leaving one's homeland when it is troubled was an act of cowardice. "It's selfish," she concluded. "Self-centered. Really, it's a kind of societal treason."

Del argued that an oppressed person had the right to find a better life wherever she could, that suffering for the sake of suffering didn't help anything. She continued, "Don't you think it might be better to go somewhere safer and gain power there and then return home to make things better? What's the point of suffering alongside your neighbors, when you can leave to get help and then come back and help them? Doesn't that seem just as valid?"

Lola heard nothing but compassion in Del's assertion, so she was surprised and distressed by Lin's response.

"What do you know about it? Where are you from? Here, right? Where do you get off, Del, even having an opinion about it? You've never had to figure out how to live in a new country. You've never had to choose between two cultures. You're out of line." Lin's voice was loud, and Lola caught her breath and eyed Del.

"You'd want to stay and make things better. I get that." Del seemed so calm! Lola frowned and chewed her lip. Was this outburst a usual thing for Lin? Maybe it was all that sugar.

Lin's face was red. "No, you don't get it. If you did, you wouldn't say that it's okay to cut and run, just because it's easier. It's cowardly. What about the people you leave behind? What happens to them after you abandon them? They could get hurt, jailed, killed—and you would be okay with that? There's no excuse for that kind of selfishness. Would you just take off, when the going got rough? Come off it, Del, don't tell me you're a damn coward!"

Lin's increasingly loud voice and snapping eyes were hypnotic. Lola gaped at her in horror, and she edged forward on her chair, fighting the urge to flee. Her gaze darted to Del's face, certain that it would be red and angry, that her eyes would be flashing. It didn't seem to be happening, but Lola could hardly breathe. Any second now, she would fly into a rage. How could she not? Lola's cup was shaking in her hand, and she eased it down into the chair beside her, trying not to drop it.

Lola was afraid for Lin and afraid of Lin at the same time. She looked from Del to Lin and back again, waiting to see who would fly at the other. Surely Lin saw that Del could overpower her. Didn't she? Or was she counting on Tess to protect her? She looked at Tess, who was watching the interplay with apparent calm. Lola was confused. She looked at Del again, unsure what to expect.

"But doing what you have to in order to survive—" Del's eyes met Lola's suddenly. Her eyes widened a fraction, and she halted midsentence.

"Lin," she said, "I'm sorry. It's obvious you feel strongly about this. I don't. I didn't mean to upset you."

Lin immediately sat back in her chair. She shook her head.

Tess grabbed her hand, and they exchanged looks. Lola's gaze still darted between Lin and Del, and she stayed poised on the edge of her seat, uncertain what was happening.

"No," Lin's voice was soft, her cheeks bright red. "God, Del, I'm so sorry. I didn't mean to pick a fight, especially with you, of all people. It's just, you know, I wonder what my life would have been like if my mom hadn't run away from her problems. You know how she is. Would I have had a real family, and a real home, instead of one ghetto apartment after another? I don't even speak Korean. People look at me, and all they see is 'Asian,' and I can only speak English. Do you know how weird that is?" She shrugged and looked away.

"Well, *mija*," Tess crooned, "I can't teach you Korean, but I can teach you the language of love." She made a silly face, and Lin rolled her eyes.

"Okay," Tess stood, "I think that's *buenas noches*, ladies."

Everyone rose, and Lola saw Tess and Del exchange a small, conspiratorial glance. What was that about? Why wasn't Del mad? Would she be mad when they left? Lola took a deep breath, overcome with mixed relief and uncertainty.

Not everyone flies into a rage when they get mad, she reminded herself. Most people control themselves. She knew that was what she was supposed to think. Lauren had told her that. Lauren also told her that she needed to learn to trust people. Lola knew she was right, but it was a lot harder than Lauren made it sound. In retrospect, it had been ridiculous, thinking that the two perfectly nice women would get into a brawl at a book club meeting. People don't do things like that, at least not in public.

She watched as Del went over to Lin and said something that made her smile. So, things looked okay between them. But, how? Why? What was going to happen now? Was this the calm before the storm? Lola wished she'd never come to this book club, that she'd never met any of these people. There were too many things she didn't know. She was hopelessly unprepared for real life, and this realization hurt more than she could have anticipated. After everything she'd done and learned, she was still too raw, too uncertain, and too unsophisticated.

Her legs were shaky, and she waited as long as she could before rising. Del was waiting, chatting with Tess by the door. Hesitating, Lola noticed the way Del saw her coming and reached to get the door and stood back to let her through. She reminded herself that Del was probably polite to everyone. That she was just naturally a chivalrous person. That it didn't mean anything. That she wouldn't take out Lin's behavior on Lola. Why would she? There was no reason, was there? Still it was hard to walk past her. Del seemed totally relaxed. Everything was fine. It would be weird to not take a ride home from her now. It might hurt her feelings. Or make her mad. Still, Lola rushed by and jumped when Del's arm brushed hers. Then she stood frozen on the sidewalk. She was afraid to get on the bike and didn't know how to get out of it. It was irrational, and she knew it, but that knowledge didn't make her less afraid. She listened to Tess and Del say their goodbyes and couldn't make her breathing slow down.

Del eyed her, approached her as though worried she'd bolt. Was it that obvious?

"Everything okay?"

Lola nodded and swallowed hard. "Del?"

"What's up?"

She wasn't sure how to say what she was thinking. "I just—I wasn't—it was nice of you to let Lin be right. After she yelled at you and everything. Most people would have been pretty mad. I mean, I think so."

There was a long silence. Del's eyes searched hers, and Lola looked away. Had Del taken her comment the wrong way? She was cold and hugged herself. Why did I say anything? What if she's mad? Tears clouded her vision, and she blinked them away. Maybe, hopefully, Del couldn't see them in the gloom of the sidewalk.

"She was upset." Del said in a quiet voice. "I didn't mean to upset her like that, and I should have realized she'd be touchy about the subject."

"Why?"

Del laughed. She seemed to hesitate. "I'll tell you in a minute." She glanced over at Lee and Rachel, strolling by hand in hand and clearly oblivious to anyone but each other. Del smiled easily at that, and Lola took the moment to swipe at her eyes. Del seemed pretty relaxed. Not just pretending to be, but actually fine. Maybe everything would be okay. Del pulled on her helmet and waved at the bike. "Ready?"

Lola nodded and climbed on. Del wasn't mad. She was fine. Everything was going to be fine. Right? She took a deep breath and hugged Del's waist, closed her eyes, and inhaled Del's warm, clean scent. Del was fine. She wasn't going to do anything but drive her home and maybe tell her why Lin would be touchy about the subject, and that was it. She wasn't waiting until no one was around to get mad at Lola, right? She barely knew Lola. She had no reason to be mad at her. Right?

Too soon, they were in front of Lola's house. She climbed off with still-shaky legs, accepting Del's offered hand to keep her balance. Del took off her helmet and held it in her lap, then shut down the bike.

"Thanks for the ride." Lola wanted to escape, but she was almost as curious about how Del would act now that no one was around as she was nervous about it. Curiosity killed the cat, she thought, and dismissed that. Del wasn't mean. She wasn't dangerous. Del didn't want to hurt her.

"Let me know if you want to go for a real ride sometime. Out in the hills, I can really open it up."

"If that means go faster, I think I'll pass. You're a lot braver than me. But thanks." She stood awkwardly for a moment, unsure about whether to leave or not.

"You wanted to know about Lin?" Del's eyes were searching hers again, and Lola felt a flash of foreboding.

"I don't want to pry."

Del smiled. "No, it's okay. I've known Lin and her mom, Vivian, for years, so I should have known anything around her mom would piss her off."

"I don't understand."

"It's complicated."

Lola frowned, not sure what that meant or if she should ask. "Because her mom moved here from Korea?"

"Well, for a long time she was pissed because Viv wouldn't speak Korean to her."

"Why not?"

"Well, she wanted Lin to be American, you know? To speak English and be like the other kids. She figured that was the best way to help her succeed. And it worked—Lin got into Berkeley, got her master's, has a great job. She's smart and successful and totally Americanized. Viv wanted to give her kid the best possible life, and she did. That was why she came here and gave up everything like that. She didn't do it for herself. She worked every crap job she had to, sometimes two, for Lin. Everything was for her kid back then."

"Back then?"

"You caught that, huh?" Del tilted her head.

Lola wasn't sure whether she should ask more questions or not. She'd forgotten, if she'd ever known, how to read the subtle signals needed for conversation. She waited dumbly for Del to either continue or to dismiss her.

"Viv didn't date at all until Lin went off to college. Then she married the first guy who bought her dinner, and he happened to be the Holy Roller-type. All of a sudden, he's running the show. Says Lin is going to hell. Says Viv'll go to hell if she condones her daughter's 'lifestyle.' Tess is a demon leading Lin to her doom, and I'm a bad influence on both of them, blah, blah, blah."

Lola shook her head. "That's awful. Poor Lin!"

"Sucks." She shrugged. "What can she do?"

"Do you think they'll ever make up?"

"Not while Viv's married to the asshole."

"She picked him over her own daughter, after sacrificing so much for her." Lola wasn't surprised, but it still hurt to hear of one more woman choosing the man in her life over her child. Her real child, at that. Didn't that make a difference? She'd always assumed that it did.

"That's how it goes." Del shrugged, and Lola tried to read her expression. It was drawn and tight, and Lola blurted out a question before she thought about it.

"Did you and Lin used to date? Wait, don't answer that. It's none of my business. I'm sorry."

But Del was shaking her head. "Don't worry about it. And no. She's still growing up, as far as I'm concerned. She's a nice kid, though, and I'm glad to see her with someone like Tess. Plus, she makes Tess happy."

"Lin and Tess want you to play basketball."

"Yeah, that's not happening. I do miss hanging out with Tess, though." Del said, "I met her maybe seven or eight years back when she invited me to join her team, and we got to be friends. She's a lot like me, you know?"

"Tall?"

Del laughed, then she looked at Lola for a long moment. "You really don't know what I mean?"

Lola shook her head, but then she shrugged. "Kind of. You and Tess are both, I guess, not that girly?"

Del shrugged too. "That's as good a way to put it as any." She hesitated, giving a tired smile. "You don't look any different from a million other women out there." She waved her arm vaguely around. "I don't blend in like that. People look at me like I'm some kind of freak. Always have. I'm used to it, I guess, most of the time. Sometimes it bothers me. Makes me feel—"

Del stopped, frowning, and she looked suddenly vulnerable. Lola stifled an impulse to reach out to her. Then she thought, why not? But the moment had passed, and Del wore that tired smile again, and Lola's heart ached to see the weary resignation on her face.

"Anyway, Tess needed somebody to show her how to survive. Her family pretty much threw her away when she wouldn't pretend to be what they wanted."

Del's voice was steady, but Lola heard a world of pain in it.

Del smiled. "She doesn't need my help, not anymore. It's easy to be around her, especially now that she's happy with Lin. We understand each other, you know?"

Lola nodded. No wonder they were close. "It was kind of you, being there for her like that. Was someone there to help you, the way you helped Tess?"

Del shook her head.

"I'm sorry."

"No biggie."

But the shadow of pain in her eyes said otherwise. Lola again had the impulse to reach out to her and again let the moment pass.

"Maybe someday Tess's family will accept her for who she is. I hope so. What about your family?"

Del made a face, and Lola saw that she'd hit on a sore subject. She pictured Del, a lonely, confused, courageous young woman who defied every expectation of what a woman was supposed to be. It must have been so scary and so painful. How had she done it? Even now, how did Del have the courage to walk around in her own skin? What had it cost her, what did it still cost her, to be herself? Lola felt like an intruder suddenly. She had no right to ask personal questions.

"I'm sorry. You don't have to answer that."

Del shrugged, swiped at her lips with the back of her hand. She let go a shaky laugh. "Well, you know, families."

Lola was going to say, no, actually, I don't. But then they would be done talking about Del, and she was pretty sure that Del didn't open up like this very often. She cast about for a safer question.

"Did you introduce Tess and Lin?"

"Actually, I did. I'd just bought the house," she waved down the street, "but it wasn't really livable yet. No plumbing, no kitchen. The place was a disaster. So I was still living in the apartment and spending all my free time over here, working on the place. I needed help but I didn't have much money, between the rent on the apartment, my mortgage, the fortune I was spending at the hardware store. You get the idea."

Lola nodded. She tried to imagine buying a house and fixing it up herself and couldn't do it. Again, she was struck by Del's courage.

"Lin was home for the summer, about to start grad school. Viv hadn't married the asshole yet, so they were still close. Lin was such a good kid! She had a job at a shoe store, but she wanted to make some extra cash. I hired her as a helper, just to sweep and run errands, stuff like that." Del smiled. "She's the least handy person I've ever met, but she tried real hard. Cleaned up, sorted all my tools, ran to the store for supplies. She even managed to lay some tile. One day, Tess came by. Her dad was a plumber, and she was helping me with some stuff, making sure it was to code. They met, and it was like kismet. They've been together ever since." Del grinned, an open, easy grin that softened her hard features and brightened her eyes.

"I'm glad they found each other. They seem happy."

"Yeah." Del seemed tired suddenly, and Lola realized that she had been detaining her for several minutes and felt guilty.

"Thanks for the ride. And for not minding all my questions."

"No problem. G'night."

Standing at her door and waving goodnight, Lola wondered what it would feel like if Del grabbed her hand the way Tess had grabbed Lin's. She pushed away the thought. Del had never been anything but polite to her. She certainly wasn't making an effort to romance her. Besides, Lola knew she needed to learn to stand on her own two feet. She hung up her coat, glad that she'd chosen something warm. Her hands and legs were freezing after the short ride on the bike. Didn't Del get cold, riding around exposed to the air like that?

Hounded by the mewling kitties, she checked their food and water bowls. They followed her around as she checked the doors and windows and then went upstairs. She tried to imagine fixing the plumbing or putting on a roof. If anything went wrong in the house, she'd have to call someone to fix it. She looked over at the bathroom window where the curtain hung at a slight angle. She'd struggled just to put up curtains, and she hadn't even been able to do that right! She looked back at her reflection and tried to assure herself that it didn't matter.

"Useless, stupid, silly cow," Orrin said. She saw movement in the mirror and thought for a second he was behind her. She whirled around, choking on fear, but there was no one there. She went back through the house, checking all of the doors and windows again, opening the closets and peering under the beds. There was no one. She was imagining things. Oh, great, she thought. Now I'm crazy, too. Super. But it was normal to get spooked sometimes, wasn't it? People got spooked in movies all the time.

"Yes, Lolly," Orrin said. "Right before the monster kills them."

She sniffed, refusing to acknowledge his comment. But she did rush through her ablutions, wishing she were already safely under the covers. One of the kitties jumped up on the sink and got a paw wet, yowling in dismay at this indignity. As usual, the kitties' silly antics distracted her from the megrims and made her smile. She scolded Buttons and squeezed her. Queenie would never put up with being hugged like that, but Buttons just waited passively for her to let go.

"Oh, you're a silly girl." She buried her face in the cat's soft fur, surprised by how attached she'd become to the two little Dumpster refugees. They were strays, just like her. She looked in the mirror. Adonis had done what he could, and he'd definitely improved her appearance, but she was still an overweight, middle-aged, plain nobody with nothing to offer. And no amount of mooning would change the fact that Del was completely out of her league.

She decided it was time to try to meet someone, someone who wasn't Del. Someone she found attractive, but not so much that she'd lose her head. Someone not out of her league. She tried to imagine who that woman would be, but her mind kept picturing tall blonde women with short hair and strong-looking arms and long, muscular-looking legs and shy smiles and noisy, exciting, scary motorcycles.

"Stop it!"

Enough. No more daydreaming about Del. It was time to meet someone new and at least make a friend. She'd never really had one, and she needed to do that before she even considered finding a girlfriend.

She'd been thinking about looking online but had dithered. Well, she told herself, just do it. No neighbors, no police (she'd guessed at Del's profession the first day), and no one from the book club. Also, no one so physically imposing. She felt helpless next to Del, and she didn't like it. But she found herself remembering the feel of Del's broad back and didn't even realize she was smiling as she stooped to pet the clamoring kitties and climb into bed.

The fun of the evening and her daydreams about the future occupied her mind as she lay trying to fall asleep. But the memory of Lin's anger, and her own panic, intruded and kept her awake for a long time. Then her bad dreams came back for the first time in a long time, and they broke her sleep over and over. She woke with a scream a few hours before dawn, covered in sweat and tangled in blankets. She looked around the room, unsure if the nightmare had awakened her or if someone was in the room.

She couldn't shake the feeling that she was not alone. She was suddenly certain that someone was watching her. She turned on the light and looked. She checked the closet and bathroom and under the bed, feeling childish but doing it anyway. She couldn't let it go until she'd checked the whole house and even the garage. The feeling of being watched intensified as she searched, but there was no one. She forced herself to lie down and not to go check every room again. You're being paranoid, she scolded herself. It was over an hour before she dropped back into sleep.

By the time she woke up in the morning, she'd forgotten why the light was on and was busy assuring the kitties that yes, they would get breakfast, and yes, she would give them fresh water, and yes, they were the best kitties ever.

CHAPTER FIVE

Del spent Thanksgiving and the next day alone, wallowing in memories of last year. Janet had insisted they barbecue a turkey, and she threw a screaming tantrum when it was almost raw after five hours on the grill. It turned out, they realized belatedly, that the turkey should be thawed first. Del slapped her forehead and made a face. Janet's pique evaporated, and she burst into a big belly laugh that made Del smile even now, remembering. They put the turkey in the oven, and it wasn't done until nearly midnight. They waited up and ate turkey with their hands and drank beer and watched sappy old movies. Del couldn't believe it had all been a lie. That it was all gone now.

Del watched the Macy's parade and the Cowboys play football and old movies. She wore a Dallas sweatshirt in tribute to her daddy and bought a bag of booze in tribute to both him and Momma. She nursed a bottle of tequila on Thursday and another on Friday.

Two solid days of drinking hollowed out her skull and replaced her brain with a shattered drum line by Saturday morning.

"Oh, Lord, help me," she moaned, lying on the bathroom floor, her hot face pressed into the cool tile floor. "Sweet baby Jesus, I wanna die." She blinked, and she could hear the clicks.

"Never again! Make this stop, and I'll never drink again in my life."

And then the doorbell rang.

"Go away!" Del tried to yell, but her throat was too scratchy. Groaning, she struggled to her feet as the doorbell sang out again. She wall crawled her way down the hall, pulled her favorite old .38 from the drawer in the entry table, and looked through the peephole. She relaxed and eased the door open to find Marco peering at her with wide eyes.

"What?" Her voice was a raspy whisper. She had the urge to finger comb her hair but couldn't make her hand go that far north. She put the .38 back in the drawer, blocking his view of this with her body—Marco looked upset but not scared.

"Oh, honey!" Marco took in her disheveled clothes and bloodshot eyes. "Sorry, Del, I didn't know you were, uh, sick," he finished delicately. He appeared to be trying not to inhale. She must reek of alcohol and sweat and self-pity.

She shook her head, trying to think of a way to deny feeling like crap and unable to do so.

"Do you need anything, Del? Anything at all? Aspirin?"

Del softened. Marco wasn't the only person who reached out to her after the Janet fiasco. But he was the only one who ignored her curses and pouting silences and stubbornness. He brought her food and wine and offered compassion and friendship and wouldn't take no for an answer. Why he bothered, she couldn't imagine. She wasn't easy to get along with, from what she'd been told, but Marco seemed to just accept her as she was. He sympathized with Del, drank with her, and pronounced Janet a "lying, worthless, bitch of a whore," which made Del laugh. She smiled, remembering, and knew she couldn't turn him away.

She gestured at him to come in, wondering at the dizziness

this motion caused. If it were anyone else, she thought, and let it go. He was watching her now, and she realized she'd drifted off for a moment. She caught his eye and made a face that should have made him smile but didn't. Her internal antennae perked up. Something was wrong.

"I'm fine. What's up? How was Thanksgiving?" She knew he'd spent the day with his in-laws, who still had trouble accepting that he and Phil were married.

Marco shook his head. "You know how it was, Del."

"Yeah," she said. "But tell me anyway."

"No, it doesn't matter." He waved the subject away. "I need to talk to you." He eased past her and led the way to the kitchen.

This was going to be bad. Anything that trumped his nasty in-laws had to be serious.

While Marco made coffee and found some bread to toast, Del landed roughly on a chair. She watched him, trying not to get dizzy as he made his way around the kitchen.

"What's going on?" She was growing more worried than hung over by the second. Marco was focused on the toast, the butter and jam, the coffee and napkins. Whatever he wanted to talk about, it was serious enough to make him fuss over the foodstuffs and choose his words carefully.

"So," he began after several moments of silence, setting coffee and toast in front of her and settling down opposite her with his own cup. "You know Lola?"

Del nodded. She took a delicate sip of the hot coffee, hoping her stomach wouldn't send it right back. It would burn like hell all the way up if it did. It was better to focus on that than on the careful way Marco was bringing up Lola. Something bad had happened.

I knew it. I knew there was something wrong there. Adrenaline hummed through her, lighting up her whole body, and she struggled to maintain a cool demeanor. A memory danced around that cool and tried to ignite her: Lola perched on the balls of her feet, ready to flee. She breathed slowly and tried to stay calm. Another memory: Lola, worried that she might fly across the coffee shop and throttle Lin. Her face had been gray, ragged with fear. Del's stomach did a slow, painful flip.

"Del, you look terrible, and I'm sorry to bug you, but I don't know what to do. I think she needs help."

Del watched him. His hand shook when he raised the cup to his mouth. His hair was uncombed. He wore a T-shirt and sweatpants. Phil might walk around like that on a Saturday, but not Marco. She had maybe still been a little drunk when she woke up, but she was sober now. A crazy ex, maybe? This was something she'd wondered about the first time she'd spoken with Lola. One of her daddy's favorite sayings came to her—"Baby, sometimes it well and truly sucks to be right."

Her stomach hurt, but not from the coffee. She set down her cup with a quiet snick and nodded at Marco to continue.

"I know you don't like to advertise the fact that you're a cop, I mean, a police officer," he said, pushing his hair back. He hesitated, shrugged.

"Okay. It's okay." She waited. He would talk when he was ready. He picked up his coffee, watching her over the rim of his cup. He was clearly asking her to put on the badge.

Del inhaled slowly, clearing her head. *If I look tense, he won't be able to talk to me.* She nodded and pasted a calm, welcoming look on her face.

"Marco, I want you to tell me exactly what's going on." Even she caught the note of authority in her tone.

Marco took a deep breath. Good, his expression said, you can take charge and decide what to do. He wrapped his hands around his cup as though they were cold. His eyes were wide, remembering. "Okay. So last night we were walking home after dinner—Delfina's, of course." He paused and waited for Del's nod. He had complained more than once about Phil's attachment to the local eatery.

She gave the nod and waited. He'd get there faster if she stayed out of the way.

"I'm sorry. I don't know how to tell this. Uh, we were almost home, and Phil pointed at Lola's house, and I saw this guy. He was huge. Really scary looking. He was, like, grabbing at Lola, trying to pull her up the stairs, I think. We didn't know what to do! Phil ran over there and started yelling at the guy, and the guy let go and ran, and I called 911. She looked so scared! Oh, my God, Del, I've never seen anything like that. I didn't know what to do!"

His eyes searched Del's.

"You did the right thing," she murmured. People always seemed to need reassurance that calling for help had been the right thing, even when it was obvious. She surveyed and was glad of the calm in her voice, her face. She was doing a good job of keeping her feelings under wraps. But it wasn't without effort. She felt like she was on fire.

She didn't want to do this. She didn't want to picture Lola being hurt. She didn't want to think about what might have happened, what it meant. She didn't want to stay cool on the outside and pretend she had no feelings about this, but it was necessary. She crinkled her eyes at Marco.

"Which way did he run?"

"West." Marco pointed. "By the time we got there, she was standing up, and she had a black eye, and there was blood all over her face. Her shirt was soaked in blood, and it was so weird! She was trying to act like nothing happened. I told her I called the cops, and she was totally shocked. A cop finally came—at least twenty minutes later—and left in like five minutes. He acted like we were wasting his time, and she was trying to pretend it was no big deal. But she was shaking, Del, and her eyes were just—" Del watched him search for a word and then give up and shake his head. "I don't know. She looked really, really scared. Now she's not answering her phone or the door, and I'm worried. What if he came back and killed her? What if he's in there with her?"

Del's mind slowed down, picking apart the information. This is not your sweet new friend that this happened to, she tried to convince herself. This is just some woman, and you need to be cool.

"Did she know him?"

Marco shook his head. "She said no."

"You believe her?"

"Oh!" He chewed his lower lip. "Yes," he said, his voice firm, "I believe her."

"Okay." Though it was much more likely, Del knew, that Lola was lying. She fought a sudden, irrational anger at Lola, then at herself. If she'd done a better job of winning Lola's trust, maybe she'd have confided in Del and been safer because of it. It's not her fault, she reminded herself. Or mine. It's the bad guy's fault.

"What'd he look like?"

Marco squinted in concentration. "Tall, at least six feet. White. Really bad hair, black, stringy. Down to his shoulders. Huge glasses, the big, black kind. Like from the sixties? But he wasn't old, maybe in his thirties or forties. I'm not sure. Phil got a better look, but he doesn't remember anything but the bad hair. I didn't really notice anything but the hair and the glasses."

"Okay. Anything else you remember?"

He put his head in his hands. "God, Del, I don't know. Lola should be able to tell you more. She didn't say much, but she was pretty shaken up. She might have said more if the cop hadn't been such a fucking prick. Oh, sorry, Del."

"That's okay. Listen, you guys did great. Phil kept the guy from maybe really hurting her, and you called 911. You did exactly what you should have done."

"We didn't chase him. We just watched him run away. I didn't want Phil to get hurt." Shame darkened his expression.

"You needed to stay with Lola, make sure she was okay. Chasing him could have made it worse. What if he'd had a weapon? It doesn't help anything to get yourselves killed. Listen, I'm telling you, you guys did the right thing."

Del held Marco's gaze long enough to see him relax in relief. She had perfected this dialogue with so many witnesses and victims that it felt strange to do it with a friend. It was easier following the script of the job. It helped keep her emotions under control.

She promised Marco that she'd check on Lola and was relieved to see him go. She held herself in check until she made it upstairs. She wanted to rush right over there, but she needed to get more control first. She ducked into the shower, not waiting for it to warm up. The cold water was a good distraction. If Lola was alive, Del would need to keep a cool head, and she took the time to brush her teeth, making sure she could maintain a steady voice and neutral face.

She pulled on jeans, boots, and a pullover, as she would have on a workday. She grabbed her keys, her pocket notebook and her cell phone. It wasn't until she was halfway down the stairs that she realized she'd strapped on her duty weapon. Well, she decided, that was probably a good idea.

She downed a couple of aspirin and a handful of antacids. She assessed Marco's account of the incident. He'd been shaken, but he'd seemed credible and clear. He hadn't seemed to exaggerate or minimize anything, and he hadn't tried to editorialize about the victim or the attacker.

While it was possible that some stranger off the street had accosted Lola, it was unlikely. Most of the time, when people got beat up, it was by someone they knew. And with women, it was usually someone they were or had been sleeping with, or someone who wanted to sleep with them. She took a deep breath and pushed away her disgust and frustration and the fact that she would love to live in a world where she didn't spend half her time looking at battered women. And why, for the love of Pete, did Lola have to be one of them?

CHAPTER SIX

Lola's Thanksgiving was her best ever. She cleared her head by walking a couple of miles to volunteer at a local soup kitchen, a new tradition she'd decided to start. Orrin always preached the value of service to others but wouldn't let her actually volunteer anywhere. Working at the soup kitchen was an amazing experience, and she vowed to return and set up a regular shift there. She was no less shy there than anywhere else, but many of the clients seemed as reticent as she.

After several hours of writing, Lola was stuck. There was a part she just couldn't get right. She knew it was pivotal to the rest of the story, and the weight of that knowledge was paralyzing her. She kept playing out the possibilities in her head, refining and reworking it, but she just couldn't make it go the way she wanted it to. As she sat there, frowning at the screen, she heard Orrin's mocking laughter.

"Stuff it, Orrin. Nobody cares what you think." Wow, she thought, that almost sounded convincing.

She decided to follow up on her impulse to start finding more friends and maybe even a girlfriend. It's about time, she told herself. You've wanted to do this your whole life. The fact that she'd let so much time slip by made her angry and sad and frustrated. Why had she been so stupid? Why couldn't she just start over and live her life the right way? She'd lived in a bubble of fear and uncertainty for as long as she could remember, and other people had structured all of the important parts of her life. Well, no more of that. She was living on her own terms now, and she was done wasting time. The first time she'd developed an overwhelming crush on a woman was when she was nine, and she'd been afraid even then.

She'd just been moved to her seventh foster home and had by then grown wary of adults. There were five other foster kids and a middle-aged woman, Aunt Margie, a solid woman with graying hair and a lined face. She wasn't a cuddly or affectionate woman, but she wasn't mean. That and the fact that there were three meals a day, every day, were enough to ensure Lola's loyalty. But there was something else about Aunt Margie that drew Lola to her. Aunt Margie had a secret.

Living in one foster home after another had taught Lola a few things. One of them was the importance of learning the laws of each house. Not the rules, which people told you about and which were easy to follow: don't leave dirty dishes in the sink, never talk back, and don't ever take food without permission. Rules were easy to understand and were often the same from house to house. Lola had no problem with rules.

The laws were harder to figure out and much more important. They had to do with the bad secrets in a house. If the man was a drinker, there were laws about not making him mad when he smelled like beer and not telling people he was home if they called on the phone. If the woman was a pill popper, there were laws about pretending not to notice her mood swings and about not coming into any room when she was alone, because she didn't want you to see her taking anything. If the man liked to hurt you, there were laws about not telling anyone and not crying out loud and not putting your bloody underpants in the laundry.

Breaking the laws always had much graver consequences than breaking the rules. So whenever Lola came into a new house, the first thing she needed to do was to learn the bad secrets, and the second thing she needed to do was figure out the laws that protected the bad secrets.

During the first few months she lived with Aunt Margie, Lola watched and listened, wondering what the bad secrets and the laws would be at Aunt Margie's. Would the older kids hurt the little ones? Would Aunt Margie have a boyfriend who liked to hurt kids? Would Aunt Margie fly into sudden fits of rage and beat or burn her or lock her in the closet? Would she feel a burning need for the violent purification of Lola's soul, by way of a belt or a hot iron or holding her head under water? None of these things seemed to be true, and it was almost scarier at first, not knowing what the bad secrets would be. There was always something, wasn't there? It wasn't that she wanted there to be something bad, it was just easier to sleep if she knew what to expect. Not knowing was scary. How could she figure out the laws, if she couldn't even figure out the bad secrets?

What made Aunt Margie so happy? It wasn't like she walked around smiling and whistling all day. She just didn't seem ready to fly off the handle at any moment. It drew Lola like a moth to a flame. She watched Aunt Margie so closely that the woman started calling her Lola Owl Eyes. But it didn't seem to make her angry. She didn't even get mad when Lola couldn't answer her questions or make a decision about anything. She just waited until Lola mumbled something and went about her business as though she'd gotten an answer.

She clearly had some kind of secret. Maybe, though, it wasn't a bad secret. There might, Lola realized, be good secrets as well as bad ones. Once this idea took hold, it was impossible for Lola to shake it loose. She wavered about prying. Aunt Margie was kind to her, and Lola didn't want to upset her or get sent away. But she had become obsessed.

The secret had to fit into the few hours when all the kids

were in school and no one needed to be taken to physical therapy or speech therapy or social skills training or counseling or supervised visits with their parents. She would have to sneak out of class to find out what Aunt Margie did at those times. This was incredibly daring for Lola, who was a compulsive rule follower and desperately wanted teachers' approval, but she felt it would be worth it. Lola knew that being a Goody Two-shoes and a loner would serve her well. She didn't have friends to notice that she was gone, and she never raised her hand or looked anyone in the eye. She was not someone whose absence would be noticed. She had seven teachers, and they likely didn't compare notes. As the only nine-year-old in the middle school, she should have been noticeable. But because she was so shy and withdrawn, no one seemed to see her. Their eyes passed right over her. She had not made a conscious choice to be invisible, but now it would be helpful.

She bided her time. She spent over a month cataloguing Aunt Margie's schedule in her school planner, laboriously filling in as many blanks as possible, and finally picked her chance one Tuesday morning.

Ducking out of sight during a change of classes, she slipped off campus and ran the two miles to Aunt Margie's house, praying that no one would notice her. As she neared the house, she slowed down. Her breathing sounded loud, and she needed to catch and quiet her breath. After a few moments spent lurking on the front porch and not seeing anyone, she decided it was time to slip in. She snuck from room to room, seeing no one and growing increasingly distressed. She'd risked everything, only to find out nothing! Aunt Margie could be at the grocery store, although she usually went on Thursdays. Or she could be out for a walk or shoe shopping or getting the vacuum cleaner repaired. Suddenly the folly of her plan hit Lola. How stupid, assuming that Aunt Margie would be at the house, just because she had nothing scheduled for Tuesdays! But then she heard voices in the backyard. Lola tiptoed into the bathroom, peering through the open window and hoping that the curtains hid her.

Kneeling on the toilet to get closer to the window, she tried not to fog up the glass with her breath. At first she was disappointed. What she saw didn't seem like any kind of secret. Aunt Margie sat on the back patio with a cup of coffee in her hands, chatting with Mrs. White, a neighbor. Mrs. White sometimes came over for coffee or lunch on the weekends, and she usually brought cookies or muffins for the kids. She was nice. She helped Lola comb out a snarled ponytail one day, and her hands were gentle. She was younger than Aunt Margie, and prettier, by most standards. But she wasn't anything secret. Who cared if a couple of adults sat around and drank coffee? Lola's disappointment was a palpable thing, and it weighed her down.

Mrs. White said something in a low voice then, and she and Aunt Margie laughed. They looked at each other. After a long, quiet moment, they started talking again, but Lola had stopped paying attention. The sound of their voices blended in quiet laughter, that long, shared look—these things had spoken what their words had not.

Mrs. White and Aunt Margie loved each other. Like, really loved each other. Their quiet conversation in the backyard continued, Lola's spying presence unnoticed, and nothing outward betrayed their love. But Lola had heard and seen enough to know that this was Aunt Margie's secret. She loved Mrs. White, and Mrs. White loved her, and drinking coffee in the backyard with Mrs. White was the good secret that made Aunt Margie happy. They would like to be married to each other. And Lola, who wasn't even sure why she was so positive of this, thought she might burst!

She climbed carefully down from the toilet, her legs shaking, and tiptoed to the front door. She eased it open and shut again, careful not to let it bang. She ran back to school and slipped in with the crowd, snagging her backpack from the classroom where she'd stowed it and entering the cafeteria just in time for lunch. But she couldn't eat.

Lola sat staring at her free lunch with sightless eyes. Running back to school, she'd come to a realization that burned her. And in the weeks that followed, this realization continued to haunt her more and more. Aunt Margie and Mrs. White loved each other, but they couldn't really be together. They had to pretend and sneak around and just love each other in their hearts. Lola had heard many words for gay, of course. People used them all the time. But they were ugly words that seemed bad and weird and gross. Aunt Margie and Mrs. White weren't bad or weird or gross, but Lola knew that other people would think that they were, and she felt afraid.

She began to watch Mrs. White, who always looked cool and beautiful and glamorous. Lola wondered if the two women kissed, and what it felt like. She wondered, gazing at Aunt Margie's thin lips late one afternoon, if they weren't tinted just a little bit from Mrs. White's lipstick. What would it feel like to kiss someone? Like, not because they forced you to, but because you wanted to? Perched on the stool she still had to stand on to brush her teeth, she looked in the mirror. Would any woman ever want to kiss her? If she were pretty like Mrs. White, maybe, but she wasn't. She glared at her reflection. Why couldn't she be pretty?

One of the boys at school had called her a troll on the first day of seventh grade, and she'd been called Trolla by most of the kids since then. And next year, high school would be even worse. She would be the only ten-year-old, and all of the girls would be pretty and wear makeup and high heels and be a foot taller than Lola, and no one would like her. Mrs. Fiori, the science teacher, had said that social standards for beauty were based on biological imperatives, that symmetry and proportion mattered more than fashionable clothes or makeup.

But Mrs. Fiori had been talking about boys liking girls. What about girls liking girls? Would girls like her, even if she was too short and too skinny and ugly? Not that it mattered. Girls didn't get to like girls. As much as Lola hated to admit it, Mrs. Borden, the lady at her last foster home, had been right: girls don't get to pick anything. They just have to accept whatever God gave them and pray for the strength to endure with grace.

She felt very afraid for the delicate looking Mrs. White and especially for Aunt Margie, who suddenly seemed much more fragile and vulnerable. Please, Lola prayed over and over, protect them. Keep their secret. Even if it is a sin, like Mr. Borden said. Please don't let anyone hurt Aunt Margie or Mrs. White.

Her prayers, it seemed, were answered. Over the next several months, Lola watched them and loved them and imagined herself their secret guardian. Her love for them grew fierce, fueled by secrecy and fear and envy and hope. She imagined that she was their daughter and that they would love her and never make her go away. They would all be safe and happy and be a family and stay together forever.

And then one Saturday morning Aunt Margie sat the kids down and announced that she was moving out of state and would no longer be their foster mother. Lola hoped but didn't dare to ask whether Mrs. White was moving out of state too. She never knew what happened to them. She was moved later that day to yet another pious family extra fond of the rod.

As Lola sat at her computer scanning the personal ads nearly thirty years later, she felt the same mix of exhilaration and envy and fear she'd felt kneeling on the toilet lid in Aunt Margie's house. Some of the women in the ads were very young, and Lola felt sharp regret that she had been paralyzed by fear for so long. She had known she was attracted to women, but she'd told herself that it didn't mean anything, that all women felt these yearnings and did nothing about them. Men were, she'd concluded early on, an unfortunate necessity, one that couldn't be avoided. She rolled her eyes. No wonder Orrin thought she was such a ninny. She was.

"Stupid, silly Lolly," Orrin crooned, "you'd never survive without me to take care of you."

"But I did, Orrin. I am."

He laughed, that mean laugh she hated.

"Okay," she told herself, "stop talking to Orrin, and definitely stop listening to him. Turn off that record!"

She found that she could use a few keystrokes to refine her online search and weed out the under-thirty-five crowd, and she felt much better. She was surprised by how many women in her age group were "single and looking." Several specified that they did not like bisexual or married women, and Lola bit her lip. Would women despise her because she came out so late in life? Would anyone ever really accept her? She had been married to a man for nearly twenty years. She'd never even kissed another woman. She was like a middle-aged teenager, and she was inexperienced and insecure and distinctly unbeautiful—who could possibly want her?

"The past has passed," she whispered, and she forced herself to read the remaining ads.

CHAPTER SEVEN

After a quick couple of buzzes on the doorbell, Del leaned on it, listening to the chimes echo through the house.

"Try ignoring that, sweetheart." She was electric with tension and rocked on the balls of her feet.

She'd been fearful that she might end up looking for a body, but now that she was here, her gut said Lola was alive and in hiding. Sure enough, after a few moments, Lola unlocked the door with a click and opened it a crack to peer at Del with one eye. The other was covered by hair hanging over half her face. Del had seen this look more than once. Women always thought they could hide black eyes with their hair, and it never worked.

Del pasted a pleasant expression on her face. Don't let this get personal, she reminded herself. She's just another victim, that's all. Her gut cramped again, and her smile faltered. You can't help her if you let yourself get wound up. She nodded. Waiting for the door to open, she'd concocted her cover story. Lola might not ask for help, but she would not refuse to give it.

"Hi, Lola," she offered her best sincere expression. "Listen, I'm really sorry to bother you, but I could sure use a friendly face. Can I come in?"

Lola's eye widened. "Of course, Del, are you all right? Please, come in." She led the way into the living room. She was holding herself carefully, and Del grimaced at her back. She was obviously in pain.

"Thanks." She smoothed her expression.

"Coffee?" Lola offered, gesturing at the couch.

"That'd be great." Though she wasn't sure more coffee was a super idea, with her gurgling stomach already protesting the previous cup, witnesses were more comfortable if you ate and drank with them. It was weird, but it worked.

Del sat down and looked around while Lola went to the kitchen. Nice furniture. Clean lines, neutral colors, a bit worn. Bold, colorful artwork. A few plants. Only the plants looked new. Maybe a moving truck had come, after all, and she'd missed seeing it. Bookcases on both sides of the fireplace were crammed, mostly with paperbacks. Lola came back, her face gray with the effort of holding a heavy tray. Del stifled an impulse to take it from her. I'm not supposed to already know what happened, she reminded herself. Lola set down a large brown tray laden with coffee cups, cream, sweetener, cookies and grapes, centering it on a huge red ottoman. She eased into the chair opposite Del with care.

"Please, help yourself." Lola flashed a bright, brittle smile. Phony. Scared. Del's stomach cramped again.

Del accepted a cup and watched as Lola added cream and sweetener to her own.

"Thanks." She waited to see if Lola would prompt her or wait her out. The silence stretched for a few moments, but Lola didn't fidget. She held herself very still and watched Del. Del was reminded of a little bird, trying to gauge the danger. She swallowed hard and pretended to sip her coffee.

"Del, what can I do for you? Are you okay?"

"I'm okay. Had kind of a rough Thanksgiving, and I guess I was feeling a little blue." She smiled her "trust me, I'm a police officer" smile and held Lola's eye until her gaze dropped.

"I'm sorry it was rough. Do you want to talk about it?" Lola's eye was sympathetic, and Del was surprised to find that she actually almost wanted to confide in her. Lola moved closer and sat next to Del. She could feel Lola's warmth. A strand of Lola's hair tickled Del's arm. Del cleared her throat.

"Well, I'm not sure there's anything to really talk about. Just, you know, holidays. They make everybody kind of shaky, I guess."

Lola murmured assent. "Like they make you face what's wrong in your life."

"Yeah." Actually, that was dead on. Del flashed a wry smile and sat back. "I thought it would be nice to stay home and relax, but it gave me time to sit around and think too much. Maybe it's better to keep busy and just move on, you know?"

Lola nodded. "Okay. But, Del," she paused, and Del felt guilty for manipulating her. "I'm here if you change your mind, okay? People say that sometimes it helps to talk through what you're feeling."

"I appreciate that. How do you like the neighborhood so far?" Del smiled and tilted her head. Lola was the kind who unconsciously mirrored other people's postures.

Sure enough, she tilted her head, which drew her hair away from the side of her face just a bit. Her left eye, slightly exposed now, was swollen nearly shut and housed in a nest of black and purple bruising. Suddenly, Lola seemed to remember, and she straightened her head as though casually.

"Oh, it's lovely. Everyone has been very welcoming." She was looking at the fireplace, as though all of a sudden she'd realized it was there and wanted to study it. Del looked there, too.

You knew she got beat up, she told herself. There's no reason to freak over a black eye. You knew it was there. Still, knowing and seeing are two different things, and she fought hard to control the rage that surged through her when she saw that particular black eye. She took a deep breath and forced an easy smile.

"Thanks for being so hospitable. I don't like imposing on people."

"It's no imposition. I'm glad for the company." Still staring at the fireplace. She was waiting Del out, counting on Del to have the manners not to comment. *No such luck, Lola. I see the dead bodies of the women whose family and friends have the good manners not to comment on their black eyes and broken arms and bruised ribs.* She pointed at her own eye.

"Looks like it hurts."

"Oh." Lola coughed out an awkward laugh and shook her head. "No, it's nothing."

Del waited her out. They were so close that she could almost hear Lola's thrumming heartbeat. She again imagined her as a little bird, but this time she was trapped and beating her wings against the bars of a cage. It was a disturbing image, and Del closed her eyes as though to block it out. Then she felt movement next to her. Lola was getting up. *She's flying away.* The fanciful thought was strangely disconcerting. Lola sat opposite Del again, smoothing her jeans with her hands.

"Just—I'm pretty clumsy."

Yeah, tell me that one. I've only heard it about a million times. She watched Lola for a few seconds, giving her a moment to change her mind. But she didn't. She fussed with the tray of stuff and offered Del the plate of cookies.

Del took one and shrugged. "Marco came to see me."

"Oh." Lola almost dropped the plate. She set it down with exaggerated care, grimacing, and then smoothed her expression. "I didn't realize. Yes, well. Marco is so sweet. He and Phil, both. I need to thank them. I guess you heard about last night."

Del nodded, waiting. She kept her expression blank and munched her cookie.

"Sorry for lying to you. I didn't, it didn't seem necessary to tell you."

"Okay." Del snagged another cookie. She sort of even wanted one and hoped it would settle her stomach. But mostly it gave her the chance to take her eyes off Lola for a second and let the woman collect herself. *It didn't seem necessary to tell me?*

No, of course not. Because I've done a terrible job of making friends with this woman. Because I'm scary. Lola was too scaredy not to be hiding from somebody. And I just looked the other way. Her disgust with herself was a distraction she needed to put aside. She chewed on the cookie and forced it down her throat with a slug of the cooling coffee.

"Did you really come over here for a friendly face?" Lola's eyes were on her knees. Del was surprised that Lola had called her on her ruse.

"Yes. Uh, no." Del gave a small laugh. "No, but you did make me feel better."

Lola's expression was neutral for a moment, and Del had the sense that she was being evaluated. Lola's eye signaled that Del had passed inspection. "It's okay. You're a police officer. You're in the habit of trying to help people. And, I guess, lying, sometimes. If that's what it takes."

Del absorbed this. "How did you know?" Marco wouldn't have said. He knew she preferred her privacy.

Lola shrugged. "What you do for a living? Everything about you says, cop."

What did that mean? Is it obvious to everyone? What does she think of me being a cop? Does it scare her? Or, worse, turn her on? She pushed those thoughts aside. *This isn't about you. It's about that black eye and the way she's holding herself like she's about to splinter into pieces and fall between the floorboards.* She shrugged an assent and gave Lola a second to move past that subject.

"So," she began, "would you be willing to tell me about last night?"

"It's nothing," Lola protested. "They already took a report. It wasn't a big deal, really. I kind of overreacted, and that made Marco and Phil overreact, you know, and it was just one of those freak things." She shrugged, affecting nonchalance, but her eye wouldn't meet Del's. She fussed with the coffee things again.

"Okay." Del slowed her words and masked her face. As she did so, she again wondered what in her demeanor showed that she was a police officer. Or was Lola just more observant than most? She did seem pretty sharp. Del waited a moment to start speaking.

"Listen," she said, softening her tone and her expression

deliberately. "Obviously, you don't have to tell me anything. You're fine, and the guys called 911, and the guy just ran off. It's over, nobody died, you know, so it's cool."

She paused to let Lola nod.

"And, whatever, I'm not going to stick my nose in, okay?"

"Okay." But she was still wary. She wasn't buying it at all.

"I just—you didn't know him?"

"No." That could be the truth or a lie. It was hard to tell.

"I just figure if there's some new bad guy in the neighborhood, it would be good to get rid of him, you know, sooner rather than later. Can you understand that?"

Another nod. Still wary. Del took a second, almost reluctant to press the subject. That wariness was smart. This was a trap, and they both knew it.

"Okay. So, the thing is, whoever this guy is, he knows where you live, right?"

Lola's nod was almost imperceptible.

"And that you live alone?"

Lola's head tilted.

Del continued, "Well, no one came out of your house, right? To help you? It was a neighbor who stopped him?"

Lola nodded fractionally. Her face looked frozen.

Del almost wanted to stop. She hated to play on Lola's fears, but she knew that this was necessary. "I'm not trying to scare you," she insisted, "I just think that a little more conversation about the subject might be useful."

She waited a moment and saw Lola consider this. She had assessed correctly. Pushing would make her back away, but gentle persuasion would work.

"Do you think you could tell me what happened?"

Perfect! Del thought, waiting for Lola to respond. She felt some relief. She usually didn't feel guilty for playing a victim to get to the truth. It was for her own good, after all. But it felt dirty, in some weird way, doing it to Lola.

Lola's voice was low and conversational. "You're very good at your job, aren't you?" She didn't seem angry or annoyed. She genuinely seemed interested in the answer to the question.

Del shrugged. Lola was both smarter and tougher than she

looked. But not tough or smart enough to stay safe, she reminded herself, eying the way Lola's hands were fisted, the knuckles white. She was scared, all right. As Del watched, those hands relaxed. The decision had been made, and she would talk. Del let out breath she hadn't realized she was holding.

"You're right, though," Lola continued slowly. "I would like to know what you think and what you'd recommend." She met Del's eyes, tucking her hair behind her ears. "If you don't mind."

Del shook her head, forcing herself not to react to the sight of Lola's face, bruised along one side from temple to chin and from her hairline almost all the way to the bridge of her nose. Her stomach flipped. The guy had walloped her, and hard. Maybe slammed her head into the stairs or the ground. Had she had a concussion? Her eye was clear now, but it had been almost twenty-four hours. Had he been her lover? Had he been a stalker? She tried to swallow, but her mouth was dry.

"Well..." Lola chewed her lip. Her eye met Del's as if in defiance. "I went online. Uh, this is really embarrassing. I don't know anyone around here very well. I mean, the book club is nice, but— Anyway, I set up a blind date. With a woman. At the coffee shop? The one we meet at, by the park?"

Del nodded, her face blank.

"So, I went, but the woman wasn't there. I waited a little while, but I got embarrassed. I felt like everyone knew I'd been stood up."

Del nodded her encouragement.

Lola smoothed her jeans again and shook her head. "Silly. Anyway, I gave up and started walking home, and a man came up beside me. He'd been in the coffee shop, I think. Maybe. Really, I'm not sure. He asked if I was there to meet Joan. And that was the name of the woman online. So I figured it was sort of a bait-and-switch thing."

Del nodded, making a sympathetic noise.

"Like, maybe he was the person online, and it was a setup. So I lied and said no. He was walking next to me, and I was really getting nervous and uncomfortable. He was asking me a bunch of questions. Like, where am I from, and what do I do, stuff like that. He told me I was pretty. He said he liked the way my hair smelled, and I wasn't sure what he wanted or how to get rid of him. I told him goodbye, and I went into the drugstore, the one on the corner? I figured I could just hang out in there for a while, and he'd give up and go away. Which he did. I mean," she flushed, "I thought he did. He said goodbye, and he kept walking. And after a few minutes, I went out and looked around and didn't see him, and I walked home. I didn't see him at all, and I was definitely looking."

Lola stopped, collecting herself. Del could picture it: Lola trotting home, looking around, seeing no one, and gradually relaxing as she got within sight of her house.

"I got home, and he was just—there. Just like that. He was really mad, and he was yelling, and he grabbed me. I tried to get away, but I couldn't. He was so...he was strong."

Del nodded again. She wanted to interrupt as little as possible and ask questions later. Adrenaline was rushing through her body and putting her on high alert. She masked her building tension as well as she could, but it was hard. Lola's recounting was designed to minimize, that was obvious. It pinged as a red flag, over and over, and Del struggled to ignore that.

"So," Lola continued, "he sort of slapped me, and I fell down. That's all, really. I mean, he was trying to get me to go inside my house, but I didn't want to. I, then I heard Phil yelling, and then the man ran away, that way—" she pointed, "and then Marco came over and said he'd called the police." She paused. "I need to thank them. I didn't mean to upset them. I mean, it was scary, but it wasn't a big deal."

Yeah, Del thought, nodding as though she agreed. I can see that it wasn't a big deal at all. That's why your face is smashed and probably a rib or two. And why you're shaking like that, and why your eye—the one you can open—looks dead from the soul out. Yeah, he "sort of slapped" you. I definitely buy that. Yup. But she just kept nodding until she knew she could control her voice.

"A patrol officer came? And took a report?"

Lola nodded.

"Could I see it?"

Lola rose, guarding her torso with an arm, and pulled the limp yellow complainant's copy of the police report from the top of the nearby bookshelf. Del nodded her thanks and scanned it. It was a brief, unclear, badly misspelled and cursory recounting of events. The guy might just as well have written that some stupid bitch got smacked around, but she probably deserved it, and why can't I ever get any good calls? He had gotten the date wrong and neglected to take down the names of the witnesses. He'd gotten the address wrong, too. Not that it really mattered. His disdain for the unworthiness of the victim and the call came through even in his sloppy writing. The department was full of smart, dedicated officers who actually cared about doing a good job, so why did Lola have to get the one asshole on patrol that night?

Nothing would happen as a result of this report. She handed it back to Lola, mentally noting the number. She wanted to have a conversation with Officer Rob Schaeffer. Unofficially, of course. Could be, she thought, she's minimizing because Schaeffer was a dipshit and humiliated her. Or, she's hiding something. It was hard to tell which. Probably, it was both.

She drained her cup. Lola rose to refill it, one arm held against her middle again, and Del considered how to proceed. Carefully, she decided. Lola's mouth was tight. The pain was getting worse. Definitely bruised ribs. They'd take awhile to heal and hurt like hell until then. She probably had a hell of a headache, too. He'd hit her more than once, and hard. Del was sure of that. Why minimize it? Was it Schaeffer or a secret? Or, she thought, force of habit. If she was used to getting smacked around, she'd be used to hiding it. She was suddenly weary and took a deep breath and forced herself to engage and relax.

"Can I ask you a few questions?"

Lola nodded, and Del noted that the wariness still lingered in her eyes. Well, in the eye that could open.

Del tried to disarm her. "You know, I tried meeting someone online," she lied, "she turned out to be pretty different in real life, but at least she was a chick."

"You think he was the person online?" Lola asked. "Or is that paranoid?"

Del answered, "I don't know. It's a possibility."

"Do you think he'll come back?" Lola leaned forward with her eye pinned on Del's.

Del considered. "Maybe." She was surprised Lola was taking control of the conversation. And glad.

"I just keep wondering," Lola sat back and gazed at the painting above the fireplace, an abstract full of reds and golds and greens, "how did he follow me without my knowing it? Did he already know where I live and just beat me here and wait behind the tree or something?"

Her voice took on the sharp edge of fear. "Has he been watching me? Is he out there," she gestured wildly with one hand, "right now, watching me?" She shook her head and lowered her hand. "I don't want to make a bigger deal out of this than it is."

Del rubbed her forehead. "You're sure you don't know him?"

"Yes." It sounded like the truth. Maybe. Though she was still minimizing. Usually people do that when they know who attacked them.

"But you thought he might have been in the coffee shop?"

"I don't know. I'm not sure if I actually saw him or just wondered if he'd been there. I was looking for Joan, not a man."

"Okay," Del continued. "What did he smell like?"

There was a long pause.

"Oh." Lola's voice was small. There was another long pause. "Clean," she said. "He smelled like soap and toothpaste and shampoo. And something else. I don't know how to describe it. Like, plastic or something. I don't know," she finished lamely. "I thought you'd ask what he looked like."

Del nodded.

"He was wearing a dark blue, long-sleeved shirt, like a T-shirt. Jeans. Boots. Brown boots with black soles. The clothes were cheap, but the boots were expensive looking."

"Good," Del murmured, nodding.

"Um, he was really tall, taller than you. Well over six feet. He was in very good shape, I think. He had big muscles, but he wasn't big overall. His hair was gross, really long, really dark, really dirty looking. Weird, because he smelled so clean. Glasses, the big, old-fashioned kind—um, like Martin Scorsese? Big and black and heavy-looking. Blue eyes. Good skin, kinda tan. Perfect teeth." Not surprisingly, Lola's description was significantly more detailed than that in the report, which read, "WM, 6', avg. bld., dark clothing." The glasses, the weird hair— a wig, a crude disguise?

"What did he say?"

Lola bit her lip. "Well, he didn't say much other than what I told you at first, but here, in front of the house, he was really, really mad."

Del nodded.

"He said I was a, well, a whore. He said I should have played nice with him instead of trying to hide in the store." Lola's voice had dropped to a whisper. "He was trying to pull me up the stairs. I figured he wanted to get me into the house, and I was scared of what would happen. He kept yelling and saying that I was a bitch and a whore."

She paused, and Del saw she was trying to decide whether to open up. She waited, forcing the muscles in her body to relax. This was the moment a good interrogator would either get the truth or not, depending on whether or not she'd built a strong enough rapport with the witness.

Think about it later, she coached herself. Think about Lola trying not to get dragged up the stairs and into her own house and raped or killed or beaten or tortured. Don't think about how much you hate this guy. That doesn't help her. Her face and body were still and looked relaxed, and she was conscious of how naturally she masked her feelings. Was that a good thing, aside from its usefulness on the job? Probably not.

Lola cleared her throat. "I don't know if it matters, Del, but I wonder if maybe it could be about my, uh, my book?"

"Book?" Del was nonplussed.

"Well, I wrote this book, and it was kind of a little bit controversial. I used a pen name, but maybe he knows it was me." Lola flushed. "My agent said I might get some hate mail or whatever, but that hasn't happened. Honestly, not that many people have even read it! This guy, I doubt he has anything to do with that, but I just can't be sure." Her next words came in a rush, "Please don't tell anyone, please? I don't want people asking me all kinds of questions and, you know, looking at me, and everything."

Del frowned. "What book?"

Lola refused to meet her gaze. "*I Thought All Women Were Lesbians*. I don't know if you've heard of it."

"Oh." Del sat back. Of course she'd heard of it. Mostly because some Jesus freak was getting famous by ranting on television and radio and online about how this book was the work of the devil. The mysterious author, whom the press had discovered was hiding behind a pen name, was a minion of Satan, a godless whore, a destroyer of families and America and puppies and marriage and whatever.

Del had heard the story and wondered if the publisher created the whole campaign. Surely book sales were driven by controversy. She leveled her gaze at Lola and tried to keep her face impassive. This was going to be more complicated than she'd thought. Her head was whirling with too many emotions and thoughts. She needed to cool it.

"Okay," she finally said, her voice soft and even. She pulled out her notebook. "So, I'll check it out, if you want. I think I'd like to, okay? Just in case it's more than some random thing?"

She waited for Lola's nod before continuing.

"I'd like you to work with a sketch artist down at the station. Can you do that?"

Again, she waited for the nod.

"And I'll talk to the people at the coffee shop. Maybe some of the neighbors. See if they saw anything. And the clerk at the drugstore. See if they have a camera outside." She was writing as she spoke. "Um, I'll need your agent's number. Anybody threaten you since the book came out?"

Lola shook her head.

"Is there anyone from your past who might want to hurt you?"

Lola's eyes clouded over and then cleared. "No."

Hmm. Del wasn't sure if she believed that. Lola seemed like a pretty terrible liar. Del could almost believe she didn't know her attacker. Maybe. But was that just because she'd rather think Lola hadn't lied to her?

"Okay," Del said, resolving to dig into that later. "I'll check in with you every day, just in case. Odds are, this was a random nutcase thing, but let's err on the side of caution. Sound good?"

Lola nodded. "Thank you so much, Del. I really appreciate your taking the time to check this out. I don't want to make a big deal out of it, you know, but I don't want to have to look over my shoulder, either."

She sat back, as though talking had worn her out. Del had more questions but decided they could wait. She needed to give Lola time to trust her. There might be more to this story that she wasn't yet ready to share. And she needed to give herself time to calm down. She was too fired up, and sitting here staring at Lola's bruises wasn't helping. She needed to step back from the situation and assess things more calmly. She took a long, slow breath and relaxed her shoulders.

Lola was as guarded as Del had expected, but she occasionally showed a sharp mind and a surprising directness. Del wondered what Lola's story was. The expensive house, the cheap car, the new clothes, the new hair—the seemingly disparate aspects of her personality all served to whet Del's appetite. The woman was a puzzle, and Del had always found puzzles irresistible.

CHAPTER EIGHT

Lola closed the door on Del with a mixture of dismay and relief. As she tried to rub some of the chill from her arms, she wondered if the chain of events that had led to her new life hadn't also led the attacker to her. For the first time, she was able to feel the measure of how safe and comfortable she'd begun to feel, because that safe, comfortable feeling was gone. She might as well be back in Orrin's house.

When she first woke early one morning and sensed Orrin's absence, she wasn't alarmed. He often woke early to work in his home office, which she knew actually meant watch pornography on the computer. She pretended not to know this, of course.

She waited until the alarm on her bedside clock buzzed to rise, make the bed with perfect hospital corners, and head to the kitchen to make Orrin's breakfast: two eggs, hardboiled, a neatly cut half of a grapefruit, and exactly six ounces of tomato juice, with no splatters of tomato juice on the sides of the glass.

She stood at the stove with her head down and rolled her shoulders, wishing for coffee. But Orrin didn't allow it. She tried to think of a time when she had been in charge of her life and didn't realize she was crying until a teardrop fell into the gurgling egg pot.

Recalling herself, she wiped her eyes and went back to watching the timer. When Orrin heard it go off, he would time how long it took her to turn off the stove. How he heard the little snap of the plastic dial as it went to the off position, she would never know. As she watched the eggs dance in the warming water, Orrin barked her name. She hesitated a moment. Should she turn off the eggs and start them again later, or should she hope she could get back before the timer went off? She glanced at the clock. If she turned them off and then on again later, she wouldn't have his breakfast ready by seven. Orrin snapped his fingers, and the decision was made. Eggs, off.

She hurried to the office, smoothing her hair into a tidier bun. What had she done wrong? She'd dusted and vacuumed the office the day before. Maybe she'd made a mistake. The carved legs on his desk took forever to dust, and he could smell if she used too much furniture polish as a shortcut for getting the dust out of the little crevices, which she usually did.

She held her breath and knocked. The door flew open, and she tried not to recoil as he reached for her. He was mad, he was so mad, and she shut down.

He yanked her past his huge mahogany desk in the center of the room, and she banged her thigh into a corner of it. Where were they going? To the sewing table in the corner. To his old computer, the one she'd started to think of as her own. Orrin grabbed her by the hair and pushed her to her knees. He shoved her forward until her face was smashed onto the keyboard. She held in a cry of pain. It would only excite him.

"Read it!" He was screaming. "Read it to me!"

But she couldn't see the screen. He seemed to realize that and pulled her back and up by her hair. There on the screen, her words stared back at her in giant black clarity. He'd enlarged the text, because his eyesight was worsening. Lola opened her mouth but couldn't read the words to him as he'd commanded. She mouthed them: "She looked into Tanya's eyes and knew that they would kiss."

Her breath caught in her throat. She was paralyzed by panic. She'd hidden the love story in a file called "Laundry Tips" for the last three years. Why would he look in there? Had she done something to make him suspicious? She had been thinking more and more about finding some way to escape, and she must have given something away.

Orrin was pulling her again, trying to make her go somewhere, but she wasn't sure where. Why was she thinking about stupid things right now? It didn't matter why or how, the important thing was that he had found it, and now she was in big trouble. She could almost see the letters marching like a parade in front of her: BIG TROUBLE!

What would he do? What would he do? She tried to speak and couldn't, tried to get up and couldn't. She couldn't look at him and curled up on the carpet. He was screaming at her, pulling on her, but she couldn't make out the words, couldn't move when he tried to make her, couldn't think. Then her legs were burning. He was dragging her toward the hallway. She didn't think. In her panic, she grabbed for the doorframe as they passed it.

Even as her fingers curled around the wood, she knew this was a mistake. Defiance only made him much, much angrier. She tried to unglue her fingers, but they acted as if of their own accord to claw at the white painted edge that was sharp and slick—she'd cleaned it the day before. Using more polish than necessary, of course, because that made it faster and easier and left her more time for writing. A helpless laugh escaped her and turned into a sob. The letters marching in front of her eyes changed: OH, NO! SHE'S DONE IT NOW!

Orrin hesitated only a moment. He sputtered like Porky Pig, so surprised was he by her defiance, and this made her moan—she couldn't say if she was laughing or crying or something else—in helpless despair. The letters screamed: OH, YOU BAD GIRL! She thought she might pee her pants, but if it got on the carpet, oh, there'd be hell to pay. HELL TO PAY! She gaped up at him. What would he do?

She wished he had a gun. Then he could just shoot her and be done with it. Maybe he did. Maybe he had a gun in his den. She wasn't allowed in there, not even to clean, so he could have anything in there, and she'd never know it. This seemed absurd, all of a sudden. He was gone for hours every day. She'd never once considered violating the sanctity of his den.

She heard a voice ask, "What about my sanctity? What about that, Orrin? What about my sanctity?" Was that her own voice? It hardly seemed likely, but it wasn't Orrin's. She swallowed hard. This was getting so bad it almost felt unreal.

That was defiant move number two—strike two, folks: She's Ooooouuuutt! Because Orrin had the home field advantage, he always had the home field advantage, and that meant strike one, and you're out, Lola, you're always out, haven't you been out for nineteen years?

Then she remembered that being "out" meant being openly homosexual, and she burst into a sob that shook her whole body and forced her bladder to let go. She felt the warm, then cold, wetness spread under her, and she could only say, "Oh!"

Orrin actually let go of her for a minute, more flummoxed— or, perhaps, disgusted—than angry, and he looked down at her as though she were some strange and repulsive new species of insect. Then he howled in fury and slammed her head into the doorframe. It didn't hurt that much. It was just a sharp knock to the side of her head and a stinging in her ear. She gaped at him. That was just a warm-up.

Orrin's fist drew back and paused and came looming toward her and smashed into her nose. She saw it coming, but then it was flying at her, into her, through her. There was a long moment when she couldn't process anything, and when she could think, she wondered if he'd punched a hole through her head, like a doughnut. Maybe, she thought, with a thrill of hope, she would get lucky, and he would kill her.

Blood flooded her throat, and she couldn't see or get any air, and she vomited blood for several seconds. It wasn't ever going to stop, and then it did, and she could breathe, and Orrin was gone.

What would he come back with? He kept his hurting things in his den. Did he go to the den? She couldn't see now, there was too much blood to see, but she could hear him coming again. What was that sound? Was he slapping a belt against the wall? Was it only a belt, or something worse? She hiccupped and felt blood run into her mouth. She went away then, slid into the dark, quiet hole in her mind where she was safe.

She came to as she was being pushed out the door, and by then the sun was high overhead and hurt her eyes. He gave her the keys to the car he'd bought for her sixteenth birthday, a heavy suitcase, and what he explained was three thousand dollars in an envelope. It wasn't until later that she wondered why he'd had that much cash on hand, and how he'd arrived at that particular figure. Almost twenty years, and he felt she should get a used car, a suitcase of rags and three thousand dollars?

She was wearing clothes that she didn't remember putting on, but she could walk and see and move, so she figured she must not be hurt. There were sunglasses on her face, too, and they hurt. They were huge and heavy. They weren't hers. She wasn't allowed to have sunglasses. Whose were they? Why had he put them on her? Then she remembered that her face must be a mess. She started to take the sunglasses off, but Orrin started to step forward, and she stopped.

He pointed at the car, parked at the curb, and she didn't resist. She plodded in a daze to her car, the suitcase banging against her legs. It was hard to see. Her eyes wouldn't open all the way, and the sunglasses sat funny on her face. Was it because she wasn't used to sunglasses? She was scared to drive without being able to see very well and scared to stay still and make him angry. She finally started the car and drove blindly for a few blocks and pulled over and sat in the idling car, trying to figure out what to do. Was it a trick? It had to be, didn't it? Would he come and find her and be angry? Sometimes he liked to test her. Was this a test? What was she supposed to do? She couldn't think. She wished she could think.

Finally, she started driving again and found a cheap motel a few miles from the house in nearby Rancho Cordova. She checked in, paying cash for one night, and walked up the stairs to the dim, musty room. She sat on the bed for a couple of hours and waited for Orrin to come and tell her what to do. Was this right? Was this what he wanted her to do? She couldn't be sure. What if she'd already done things wrong? What if she was already in trouble? What if, dear God, what if he meant it?

Hope was too risky. It was probably what he was counting on. He would let her think she was free until she seemed to believe it, and then he would come and get her. It would hurt ten times more if she let herself hope that she was free for real. Her chest hurt. She needed something to do. It was getting hard to breathe and to see. Ice. There was an ice machine on the ground floor. She put the sunglasses on and took the trash can with her. It took about ten minutes, but finally there was a sizable mound of cloudy cubes to take back up to the room. She wrapped a pillowcase around the ice and lay on her side, inching the makeshift ice pack toward her face. She wouldn't be able to see or drive at all, if she didn't get the swelling down.

She fell asleep for a while. When she woke up, she was wet. The ice had melted. She went to look at her reflection in the bathroom mirror but didn't recognize herself and turned away.

She didn't want to believe. She knew better. She knew that this was a test. What else could it be? Still, no matter how much she tried to fight it, as night began to fall her hope grew. She held herself very still. Maybe if she stayed very still, it would be real. She got more ice and filled the bathroom sink and eased her face down into it. It hurt, but she needed to be able to drive. A plan had formed itself while she'd been sleeping.

The next morning, she was parked down the street from Orrin's house, wearing the oversized sunglasses and feeling silly and scared. She'd given in. She would behave as though he were really letting her go. She couldn't stop trying to believe it. If he killed her, so be it. If he didn't kill her and didn't let her go, she would kill herself. Whether it was a sin or not was no longer something she needed to worry about. Hell couldn't be any worse than life with Orrin. It would all be over soon. That thought was such a relief that she repeated it to herself over and over: "It'll all be over soon. It'll all be over soon. It'll all be over soon." After a while, the words didn't mean anything at all.

At exactly eight, Orrin emerged from the garage in his giant black SUV, making the engine roar and the tires squeak, and sped off toward his office. He would be gone until six, at least, if he followed his usual routine. And if there was one thing she knew about Orrin, it was that he liked to follow his routine.

Lola scurried up the front walk and let herself in. As she'd suspected, Orrin hadn't bothered to change the lock. She wasted no time, heading straight to the office. She disconnected the computer she'd used, the slow one that Orrin had discarded when he got his fancy new desktop with the giant screen (for porn, she'd noted silently at the time) and carried the heavy load with all its wires and accessories clumsily to the car. She snuck back in one more time and headed for the master bedroom.

She reached into the top drawer of her nightstand. In it was the music box Orrin had given her on her sixteenth birthday. She rubbed it for luck, the way she used to, and had to fight a sob. She stuffed it into her giant purse and headed out. She hesitated at the door. What if this was the test? What if he caught her coming out? She felt like a child stuck on a bed because the boogeyman might be hiding in the closet or under the bed. She shook the thought away. Now was not the time for woolgathering.

Taking a last deep breath, Lola pulled the door shut and looked around, half certain that Orrin was right there, waiting to catch her. But he was nowhere in sight, and she tried to believe in that. She knuckled her mouth and scurried, head down, out to her car. She didn't look back at the house she'd lived in for nineteen years. It never occurred to her to do so.

Could he find her? She'd used cash and a fake name to check into the hotel. She had no credit card for him to trace. She had no cell phone for him to call. She thought that maybe, maybe, she was safe. Still, she found herself glancing around like a criminal as she took a circuitous route back to Rancho Cordova.

She stopped on the way and bought her very first cup of Starbucks coffee and loaded it up with sugar and milk. She took off the sunglasses in the store, unable to see the signs with them on. The strange looks she got reminded her of the state of her face, and she hurried enough to spill both milk and sugar all over the counter.

One of the employees, a young woman, told her not to worry about it and stood a few feet off, waving a rag as if in surrender. Lola nodded and ducked her head, too embarrassed to offer thanks or apologies. She slunk out of the store and waited until she was in the hotel room to drink the coffee. Even if it hurt to open her mouth to drink it, even if it had been humiliating to be stared at like that, the coffee was the best thing she'd ever tasted.

She whispered to herself, "I am not a criminal. I am not a child. I am a grown woman. He doesn't own me. He does not own me. He never did! I have rights, don't I? I should get the rest of my things." There were books she wanted, and a thick, warm sweater that she loved.

She tried to talk herself into going back to Orrin's house and stood at the motel room door with her keys in her hand for nearly an hour. In the end, she couldn't make herself do it. She went to bed, chilled and sickened. She felt like a coward and a weakling. It was two blurry days later that she finally crawled out of bed and took a shower. I'll go back tomorrow, she decided.

She was hungry, but it was too late to go anywhere, and she was too restless to sleep. She finally turned on the television. A local news show was on, and the anchor was excited as he announced the latest scandal: local physician, Orrin Beckett, had been killed in a tragic car accident.

Lola stood in front of the television with her mouth hanging open. She couldn't process this information. Had she imagined the news story? She must have, right? Her ears didn't work for a moment, and she shook her head to clear it. Orrin, dead? It couldn't be! Could it?

She jumped from station to station, trying to glean more details. The crash had occurred late the night before, and there had been someone else in the car with him, a woman. The car had careened into a tree for some reason and had caught on fire. Because the crash had been on an isolated road, the scene hadn't been discovered until sometime during the day. There appeared to be no survivors.

Orrin is dead, she told herself. Orrin is dead. Really. But her mind refused to accept this as a possibility. Orrin couldn't die.

He was far too powerful to be killed by a mere car crash. God couldn't just die, could he?

On the news, they showed a picture of the girl, and she was lovely. She was "burned beyond recognition," that was what the reporter said. Lola sank onto the edge of the bed, transfixed. She gaped at the image of the beautiful young girl who was beaming at the camera. The sun glinted off her golden hair, and her heavily made-up eyes sparkled. She was the very image of youth and beauty and glamour. Lola instinctively rose when the image of the photo went away, as though she could grab it and bring it back, and in doing so bring back the girl herself. She shook her head, wishing she could change what had happened and knowing that she could not. She retched and ran for the bathroom and was sick.

I should have called the police the first time he hit me. The first time he drugged me. The first time he raped me. I should never have pretended that it was okay to hurt me. He got tired of me, and he found another girl to take my place, and I might as well have killed her myself.

She went into a strange kind of dream world for weeks. All she did was write. She couldn't have said what day of the week it was, or when she'd last eaten or slept. She just wrote. She finished the first draft of her book before she started getting worried about money. She wasn't sure what to do. It occurred to her to just go back to the house, but somehow she still couldn't make herself do that. What if it had all been a trick? What if Orrin was waiting there for her? She knew that this wasn't a rational fear, but she also knew that there was no way she'd ever go back to that house, not ever.

She called a lawyer, one whose name she found in the battered phone book in the motel's lobby. They met in his downtown office, a glittering steel and glass showplace full of sharp edges and cold surfaces and ugly sculptures. After a week or so, she got a call from the lawyer. There was some kind of problem with Orrin's business partner. She hadn't even known about a business partner.

Orrin didn't like to share his jar of grape jelly. How could he share a business? It must have been a junior partner, she thought, though she said none of this to the lawyer.

She didn't like him. He seemed like a giant blond peacock, strutting around and snapping orders at his staff. He looked through her. Talked at her. Ignored her questions and only called her to demand information or paperwork or question her judgment. If she'd had any courage left, she'd have fired him. But she didn't. There were other lawyers who wanted to talk to her, and the peacock talked to them for her most of the time.

In the daze of the next few weeks, Lola found it hard to concentrate on all the complicated things that were happening. According to her lawyer, the authorities believed that Orrin for some years had been taking money out of his regular accounts, both business and personal, and putting it somewhere else. He and his partner had two sets of books, according to a forensic accountant from some federal agency. She didn't know what to say.

She read every word she could find about the accident. "Tami Holden," she whispered, over and over. Why couldn't I have found a way to leave? If I had, maybe that girl would still be alive. The image of the young beauty danced in Lola's mind and blocked out everything else. When the lawyers got mad, Tami Holden's lovely young face crumpled and blackened and turned to ash, and Lola knew that it was her fault. She had been too selfish and too weak.

"I'm sorry," she said, rubbing the edges of a newspaper photograph of Orrin's young girlfriend. "I'm so sorry. I should have been the one to die. You should never have been anywhere near him."

One of the men showed her some pictures of Orrin. He was sitting in a bar, arm around a woman with long red hair.

Lola stared at the photo. "Is that Tami Holden? She looks different."

The man laughed. His laugh was nasty, dirty, mean, and Lola recoiled and looked at his face. Most of the time, she tried not to look at the angry people, but this man was scary. He was handsome, she supposed, with perfect newscaster's hair and bright blue eyes, but he had a shark's smile. He and Orrin would like each other, she thought. After that, she tuned them out and waited for it all to be over.

The lawyer sent her to a therapist, a woman named Lauren. She asked if Lola identified herself as a "battered wife." Lola shook her head. Later, she formed those words with her mouth, feeling them and wondering what they meant, exactly. She dreamed that night about Tami Holden in a wedding dress, hung from a clothesline and being beaten with a broom handle. Her hair and the big white dress danced when the broom handle hit her middle. Her face crumpled and burst into flames. Lola wrote a letter to Tami Holden's family, apologizing for her part in their daughter's death, and her lawyer promised to give it to them. He read the letter, opening it right in front of her and making a copy. She shook her head, not sure what to do. He sent her to the therapist again.

Lauren also asked about Lola's writing—she had taken to bringing a notebook with her everywhere and writing in it whenever she was stuck waiting at the Laundromat or the lawyer's office or Lauren's waiting room. Was she writing a book? Would she try to get it published? Lola didn't know how to answer that. She wasn't sure what she was doing from one minute to the next. But the thought stuck with her even after she stopped going to see Lauren. This, because one day the receptionist told her that she was no longer covered under Orrin's insurance.

She wanted to share her book with other people. Why, she couldn't have said. She found a website where she could put it online for free, and all she had to do was type it in. The problem was that the Internet service at the motel was very, very slow, and her computer was very, very old. So she could only load it on the website a few hundred words at a time, and that took hours. She knew it was silly. The odds of someone running across her story were very bad, and the odds that anyone would bother to check back and read the thing little bits at a time were even worse. Still, she kept at it, and she imagined some sad, lonely, confused woman out there looking for just this kind of story so that she'd know she wasn't alone.

She checked on the computer every day, and there was a place to click on and find out how many people had read the story. When there were more than a hundred people who'd read it, she felt that she'd achieved her goal. She clicked on it one day and thought there'd been a mistake. It said that over a thousand people had read all of the parts she'd uploaded so far!

She danced around the motel room, delighted to know that a thousand people had actually taken the time to read some of her story. There was a place for people to leave comments too, but she avoided clicking on that. What if people said her story was stupid? What if people said she should never write another word? She knew that would be more than she could stand. She kept putting in a few hundred more words every day, and over time, her curiosity got the better of her. It was a month before she clicked on the comments section and started reading. There were a lot of comments, hundreds, and Lola waded through them. She'd decided to skip anything negative, and that saved a lot of time. She could only find a few dozen positive comments, one of them from a woman who said she was an agent and wanted to represent Lola.

It took Lola a week to call her, and then suddenly things were moving very quickly. The agent told her to stop putting the book online for free and publish as an eBook.

"Would anybody really pay to read my book?"

The agent assured her that they would. And she turned out to be right, though not for the reasons Lola would have anticipated. A televangelist had read and gotten angry about her book, and his followers bought copies of the digital book by the thousands. One day the agent called Lola and said that a publisher wanted to offer her a contract. Was she, perhaps, interested in putting out a printed edition? Suddenly, there was money, more than she could have ever imagined, and she was a real author.

Eventually, she moved out of the motel and bought a house. She was free for a year after Orrin's death until one day a stranger followed her. He appeared in front of her house and called her a whore, and he hit her, and she felt like all the changes she'd made were window dressing, and that, underneath, she was still Orrin's mousy, pathetic, fat, stupid, worthless wife.

She tried to forget about that and spent the day cleaning, doing laundry and paying bills. It was hardly exciting stuff, but it kept her busy until long after dark. She jumped when the phone rang just as she was climbing into bed.

"Hey, Lola." Del's voice sounded tired. "You okay?"

Lola murmured her assent.

"Remember, you hear any little noise at all, or just feel like something's off, call me, right away, okay?"

"I will, Del, and thanks so much. I really appreciate the way you've stepped in and helped me. But I'm sure that nothing will happen."

"Great." Del sounded unconvinced. "Sure you don't want me to crash on your couch?"

"No, thanks. Good night."

"'Night."

Lola turned off the lamp and sat up in the dark for a moment, listening to the sounds of the house. The cats were curled up at her feet for now, but she knew that soon they'd begin their nightly patrols of each room. If something were wrong, they would be restless, nervous. Everything was fine. The alarm was turned on, and it silently guarded her home. Nonetheless, as on the previous nights, she closed her eyes only to see The Creep's intense stare.

She'd seen that look, or some version of it, dozens of times before, and it always presaged some horrible nightmare of violence and humiliation. She shivered and burrowed deeper into the blankets she'd piled on the bed. She couldn't get warm, and she couldn't erase the image of those eyes from her mind. Hot tears scalded her skin as she gave in and cried herself to sleep.

CHAPTER NINE

Del hung up and stood looking out her front window at Lola's house. She felt like there was something dark and sinister creeping around the outside of the place and poking around to find a way in. It was a silly thought, one she wanted to dismiss as nonsense but couldn't.

She wished suddenly and with great surprise that her daddy were around to advise her, to help her figure out a plan. He'd been smart, once. He'd been "slicker than spit," according to Nana. He'd have known how to soothe Lola and make her smile. Once upon a time, he'd been able to "read people like picture books and play them like fiddles," another Nana-ism.

Del smiled, thinking of him, the way he was in the old days. He drove an old Ford pickup, the same one her entire childhood. It was a dinosaur, the kind of truck that could pull a stump out of the ground or jounce with ease down a muddy, potholed dirt road. It was more like a tank than a truck, sturdy and tough and unbreakable. Not like today's cars—they all looked like plastic toys to Del. That truck was the one thing about her daddy that never changed, and she was surprised by the lump that filled her throat and made her eyes prick. She rubbed at them with rough hands and cleared her throat. It was just a truck, wasn't it?

He took her hunting, only once and only after months of begging on her part. She hunkered next to him, silent and watchful, not daring to mention her full bladder or to scratch her itching nose. At seven, she would sooner have died than done some foolish thing to earn his disapproval.

She cut her eyes at him and was struck by how relaxed he was. He seemed like a timeless thing, rooted more comfortably in the forest's damp, cold ground than in town, where he often seemed oversized and restless. Here, shaded by towering trees and overgrown scrub, alert to the small noises of the animals and sniffing with flared nostrils as the wind shifted, he seemed more animal than man. She strove to emulate his stillness, his alertness. She tried to see the forest with all of her senses, the way Daddy had told her to the week before.

"Injun' blood," he said. "That's what makes us good hunters."

That was how he got Momma to agree to let him take Del.

"It's her heritage," he said, and Momma laughed. She grabbed Del's face with one bony hand and pointed at Daddy with the other.

"Yeah," she muttered, her eyes bright with either anger or humor—Del wasn't sure which, "honey, I surely can tell. Yessir, that Injun' blood shows up real nice in them nice blond curls and pretty blue eyes she got from her daddy."

Once upon a time, Daddy would have laughed at that and grabbed Momma up in a swinging hug, and they'd have kissed until Del looked away in embarrassment. But now he narrowed his eyes in that new way he had, and Momma flounced away with a nervous laugh before he could get good and mad.

But that was far away from the forest, where Daddy seemed like his old self again. Del realized that she could think about that and still keep aware of the little sounds around her. A small thing, squirrel or mouse or rabbit, hesitated in its path some twenty feet behind her, and she could all but see its wide eyes and trembling chest as it tried to assess the danger. The wind shifted again, and that drove the little thing back into its hidey-hole.

Del would not have believed that she could sense such a thing before that moment. She felt as if she had learned about a third arm or second head inside herself. She eyed the rifle Daddy had given her for her birthday, and for a moment felt only a child's delight in its newness and specialness.

But the gun was heavy on her legs, and she was afraid. What if she messed up? What if she missed? What if she got the hiccups or something? But these feelings faded, and she slowly drifted outside herself and into some quieter place where she was not a girl or a person or seven years old, but an animal that belonged here and was a part of the world. She was legs and arms and eyes and belly and mouth. That was all. And the rifle, only moments before a strange and wondrous foreign thing, was as naturally a part of her as a cat's claws or a dog's nose. She was only distantly aware that she'd managed to forget her bladder and her cold feet and the way her shirt was too tight across her shoulders.

That awareness faded away, and she was again attuned to the life stirring around her. Some large things, deer or something like deer, pranced lightly down by the river. One, then two, then maybe four eased down in near silence to drink. She didn't actually hear these sounds as much as feel them. There was a smoke smell coming from far away. The farmhouse a few miles down the road had a woodstove. She wasn't sure how she knew that. There was something important out there somewhere in the gathering fog, and she strained to find the quiet inside her that would let her figure out what the important thing was. Finally it clicked—something big was hunting, and it was near.

She felt more than heard a large snake slither toward the river, and she peered up at her daddy. He nodded, as though he could read her mind, and she felt connected to him by a million invisible lines grown through the air and the scrub and the animals and the trees and the fine mist that left tiny, sparkling droplets glistening on the tops of everything. She could almost imagine the weight of the drops of mist on the million lines that ran between her and Daddy. It didn't weaken them, though. Somehow, it made them more real.

She smelled that there would be more rain soon, but not until dark, and the big thing that hunted nearby wanted to feed before that happened. She looked at her daddy to see if he sensed that, too. He didn't look at her but nodded again, a barely perceptible dip of his chin that she mimicked unconsciously. Had the snake been the menace she'd sensed? She doubted it. The other predator was bigger and more dangerous and somewhere nearby, and she flashed her eyes at Daddy, but he cut his eyes past her and to the right. Her hands tightened on the rifle at the way his nostrils flared and eyes went hard.

She turned to look with him and sensed something—she couldn't name it, except that it was dangerous and big—making its stealthy move down the hill and toward the river and what she thought might be deer. She held her breath as the hunting thing glided down, down, not even slowing to look at them. Then it was too far down for them to sense, and she looked a question at Daddy, but he was tense and still and ignoring her. There was a sound and then a small splash, and she understood that the thing had missed its prey and was moving across the river toward something else now. The deer had taken flight in the moment before the splash, and they were long gone already. She let out breath she hadn't even realized she was holding.

She smiled at Daddy, and he smiled back for a second and then winked at her. You and me, the wink said, we're special.

Even now, decades later, she felt a child's thrill at that wink. *He* would have been able to sit on her front steps and sense whether there was danger afoot over at Lola's.

She felt foolish, all of a sudden. She hadn't been able to rely on him for squat in decades. And she'd known better than to look to him or anyone else for help or for anything since she was, what, eight or ten? She was acting like a big baby, wishing for her daddy. She snorted at her own foolishness.

Lola's face, filled with shame and fear and pain, flashed into her mind, and she tried to shake it away. If she'd been thinking about how the deer felt, she'd have been too distracted to see the mountain lion, or whatever it had been. It was more important to focus on the predator than the prey, hadn't Daddy taught her that? She needed to regain her focus.

"Where are you?" she whispered, as she leaned forward on her chair and peered into the darkness. She wasn't sure if she was asking her daddy or the bad guy.

CHAPTER TEN

Lola had bad dreams again that night and gave up on sleep long before dawn. She decided to do some writing as a distraction, and it wasn't until the loud protests of the cats alerted her to the lateness of the hour that she stopped working, and she was surprised to note that it was nearly eight. The sun had come up without her noticing it. There was a lot she should do, she knew that, but she smiled, feeling suddenly reckless. I'll go shopping, she decided, and felt a small thrill of guilt and glee at the indulgence of it. Orrin felt that vanity was unbecoming.

"Go to hell, Orrin."

She'd thought it would be funny, but her voice sounded shrill and ugly. She whirled around, sure that Orrin would be behind her, his eyes glinting and his mouth drawn tight. Of course, he wasn't there. She closed her eyes and decided to go ahead with her plan, though some of the fun had already gone out of it. She had felt like a whole new person after going to the salon, and she wanted to re-create that feeling and remember what freedom from fear had felt like.

Lola started at thrift stores but ended up driving several miles to a suburban mall, having decided that it was not a mortal sin if she wanted to buy a few brand-new things. If she got enough clothes, then she probably wouldn't have to go shopping again for years.

Gawking at a dressing room mirror, surprised to find herself not entirely repulsive in a pretty blue camisole and French knickers, she wondered for a moment if Del would like the way she looked in them. She reddened and turned away. "Who cares?"

Smiling with relief as she reached her new home, Lola felt a kind of lassitude steal over her. She was safe. She was fine. No one would hurt her ever again. The stranger who'd attacked her was surely gone for good—why would he come back? There was no reason to be afraid anymore. While she was lugging her purchases up from the garage, her mind wandered back to that errant thought in the dressing room, and she was startled into running for the phone when it rang.

"Hello?" she said breathlessly.

"Finally! Dammit, Lola!" Del's voice burst through the phone. "Where the hell have you been?"

Lola froze. She couldn't think. The anger in Del's voice paralyzed her. Her chest tightened. Panic flooded her, and she didn't notice that she was shaking her head.

"Lola? You okay? Lola?" There was a long pause. Del's voice was softer. "Hey, I'm sorry. I didn't mean to yell like that. It's just, I was worried that something happened. Is everything okay?"

Dumbly, Lola nodded. She rolled her eyes and cleared her throat. "Yes. Sorry. I'm sorry." She looked out the window and had a moment of anger. Who was Del, to yell at her like that? But then she heard the anxiety in Del's tone and was flooded with guilt.

"I called your house and your cell a bunch of times. It's been, like, five hours."

"Sorry. I'm really sorry. I didn't—I'm sorry."

"No." Del sounded frustrated. "I just, with what happened the other night, you know—"

"No, of course," Lola rushed in. "It was stupid of me. I'm sorry. I didn't think about it. I left my cell at home. I haven't been using it much. I never had one before. I—" she stuttered lamely, "I went shopping. I'm sorry, Del. I'm so sorry." Please don't be mad at me, she wanted to say, but her throat was closing despite her efforts not to cry, and she couldn't speak any more.

"Cool." Del sounded far away. "Well, anyway, I'm glad you're okay. Call me if you need anything." And she was gone without waiting for a response.

Lola swallowed with a gulp. She had bungled things badly. Del had been kind enough to try to help her, and she'd acted like an irresponsible airhead. Orrin was right, she didn't think. She just did whatever she wanted and didn't think about anyone else. She was so selfish!

Tears stung her eyes as she gathered up the silly, too fancy things she'd bought and carried them to the kitchen. The items from the thrift stores couldn't be helped, but she would pick through and choose a few necessities from the new things and take the rest back. She'd been spending money too freely for weeks now, and it was time to get back to being sensible. Orrin was right. She had no self-control. That was why she ate too much and exercised too little and never got anything important done. She just dithered all the time. Why did she have to be so stupid? She was very, very tired. She dropped onto a chair and sat there as the afternoon faded into the darkness of evening.

CHAPTER ELEVEN

"Crap! Crap, crap, crap!" Del slammed her fist into her thigh.

She couldn't believe she'd done it again. Every time she saw Lola starting to trust her, she'd say or do something to scare her. Wasn't she going through enough right now? *Stupid. I scared the hell out of her.*

She overreacted, a part of her carped.

No, she didn't. I did. I made her scared, and I acted like an ass, and it's my fault, not hers. Her stomach hurt, and she rubbed it. *Put it aside. Do something useful tomorrow.*

She got permission from her captain to pursue the attack on Lola, though he acted like he didn't really care what she did. She spoke with everyone she could think of, arranged for a sketch artist to meet with Lola, and poked around in Lola's life.

What she found was depressingly predictable. Lola Bannon grew up in the system, birth parents unknown. She was found as a toddler, abandoned in an Amtrak station in LA. Del counted thirteen foster homes, three group homes and emancipation at sixteen. Scholarship to a small private college at sixteen. So, very, very smart. Got married to Dr. Orrin Beckett right at eighteen and dropped out. So, not smart about everything.

Then, nothing at all until the husband had a fatal accident. A girlfriend, a missing partner, some missing money, a messy tangle of an investigation. It was hard to tell who exactly had their hands in this little pie. The reports had all been redacted, and thick black lines obscured most of the words. But there was no stamp identifying which agency had redacted them. Who would spend that kind of time on something like this? Didn't they have terrorists to catch?

Enough! It was time to go and make peace. But as she was heading over to Lola's, the phone rang. Another murder. Another domestic. By the time she reached the crime scene, the media had gotten wind of the story and now trampled all over the front lawns of a row of Victorians in the affluent Pacific Heights neighborhood. Del's first act was to pull a couple of patrolmen off what she thought of as "standing around gawking at the body" duty and onto crowd control.

Once the perimeter was established, Del took a second before heading in. It wasn't any warmer up here on the hill than down below, but the sun shone brightly and made the whole place look like a postcard. She hadn't ever been on a call up here and was struck by how pretty it all was—a chorus line of perfectly maintained mansions basking in the sun and gazing down on the churning sea of humanity below. It looked more like a movie than real life.

But inside the house, real life intruded in rude Technicolor. The victim's blood was everywhere. Del, bootied and gloved, sidestepped bloody footprints and tiptoed around broken pieces of furniture. The furniture was nicer, and the rooms were bigger, but the scene here was eerily similar to the one she'd walked into two months before. Oh, and the victim was a guy. But being a man and having a nicer house and more money hadn't saved him from his soon to be ex. Preston Daniels was cold and headed for the morgue just like Ana Moreno had been.

Del was completely occupied for the next several days. She managed to call Lola every day, and it felt good, talking to her, even for just a minute or two and even though there wasn't any news to share.

"How's your day?"

"Well," Lola said, laughing, "Buttons ruined another one of my shirts. I swear, I need a lock on my closet door!"

Her laugh was lovely. Lovely Lola, she thought, hanging up. Lovely, lovely Lola.

Not everyone seemed thrilled with Del as the lead, but her new temporary partner, Tom Phan, didn't seem to mind. She soon found that she liked him more than she'd expected to. He didn't act like she was an interloper or a flunky or an airhead. He treated her like a partner, and she realized that it had been a very long time since she'd experienced that. He was also smart and observant and thorough. Nothing seemed to be beneath him, either. By the end of the week, thanks to a combination of hard work and luck, they felt confident arresting the victim's husband.

"All our bases covered?" Phan stopped outside the station door, his hand hovering just in front of Del's arm.

"Pattern of abuse, physical evidence supports our theory, neighbor as a witness to two different attacks. Phan, I'm not worried."

"Well, then, after you." He smiled and tipped an imaginary hat, and Del smiled in spite of herself.

She went home Friday night in a better frame of mind than she'd been in for months. She'd done good work with a good partner and was reasonably sure that the murderer would spend the rest of his life in prison. She thought maybe Phan hadn't minded working with her and that maybe he'd be willing to work with her again.

Phan had gone through some trouble with his partner the year before and had apparently been persona non grata ever since. Maybe the two outcasts would end up being a team. That she hadn't had a really good partner in a long time reminded of her first partner. Jack Halloran had been a smart, tough, mountain of a man, and she'd measured every other partner in the years since against him. Every single one had fallen far short. She had learned a lot from Halloran: how to talk, how to read people, how to assert authority without abusing it.

Most of all, he'd taught her the importance of emotional self-control. She'd gone on patrol those first years like any other rookie—fired up, reactive, impulsive. She'd been a hothead with a chip on her shoulder, according to Halloran, and he'd been right.

"You know what separates us from civilians?" He'd asked her this one night on patrol, and she'd laughed.

"We have badges to go with our guns?"

He pulled over. She frowned and looked around. What was he reacting to?

"No, Mason. The difference," he peered into her eyes, "is that we keep our cool and our focus. That's what makes us cops."

He'd pulled back into traffic and said no more, but Del had taken his words seriously and never forgotten them. Her ability to keep her cool had served her well, long after Halloran's retirement party, and she still kept his advice in mind. She got so in the habit of masking and controlling her emotions on the job that she wasn't able to stop doing so in her personal life too.

Elise, a pretty blond veterinarian Del dated for almost three years, summed it up when she complained, "It's like falling in love with a robot. You say all the right things, you do all the right things, but it's all a show. Your heart is locked up somewhere I can't reach it."

Del wanted to argue the point, but she had to admit that Elise was pretty much right. She liked Elise and enjoyed her company, but, like every other girlfriend before her, Elise would be easily replaced and almost as quickly forgotten.

Then along came Janet. Del had always been able to trust her instincts, and being so wrong about Janet had shaken her confidence deeply. She wanted to go back her to old ways, being able to maintain emotional distance from everyone in her life. That was best. She obviously couldn't trust her own judgment. She let friendships fade, she ignored the interested looks of women she should have pursued, and she locked her heart away for safekeeping once more.

Lola, who was a victim and therefore off limits, and who had more baggage than a goddamn cruise ship, had somehow changed everything. Del felt completely unbalanced again. She frowned as she rode home, wondering if she would ever regain her equilibrium.

CHAPTER TWELVE

"Don't tell me I don't know what the fuck I'm saying. That's total bullshit!" The woman in front of Lola in line hollered into her headset, gesturing with her hands for emphasis, jabbing the air with her long, elaborately decorated fingernails.

Lola tried to tune her out, but it was impossible. She settled for avoiding eye contact with the loud, angry woman. Meanwhile, the beer-soaked man behind her kept shuffling closer and closer to her, never touching her, but exhaling his hot, foul breath into her neck. She hated the smell of beer, and the man smelled like he'd bathed in it a month earlier and not washed since then.

After several minutes of trying to avoid the shuffling beer man and the yelling phone woman, Lola lost patience and whipped around to confront the man. But she saw at once that he was broken. His eyes were red and rheumy, sunken in a nest of wrinkles barely recognizable as a face. He looked more than homeless, he looked like a walking corpse.

Her sudden turn startled him, and his eyes darted to her face. Well, one of them did. The other drifted to the upper right corner as though contemplating some skyward heavenscape. Lola instantly felt guilty. She smiled at the man, hoping to avoid upsetting him. But her smile seemed to frighten him, and he backed away from her as though she'd sprouted horns and a tail.

He crossed his arms and shook his head, and Lola made things worse by bursting into nervous laughter. She turned back around, still giggling, and the loud woman on the phone shushed her. Lola tried to look abashed, but the woman yelled into her headset for a good three or four minutes about how trashy the people were down at the police station.

"You see all kinds of crazy freaks down here," she intoned, glaring at Lola and raising an eyebrow.

Lola got the giggles again. She stifled them and sneaked a glance around the phone woman. There were three people in front of her, all waiting for their turn to harangue the petite, pretty desk sergeant.

It was strange, walking into Del's world, seeing all the activity and hearing all the voices and ringing phones, knowing that this was where Del worked. Most of the police seemed to be men. Was it hard, being a woman cop? Did they give her a hard time? Did they know she was gay? Did it affect how they treated her? How did Del feel about it? How in the world did a person get used to this hard world?

She glanced around with a sudden desire to flee the station. She should never have agreed to meet with the sketch artist. It wasn't like she could really say much about the man except that he was mean and scary and his fists were hard. What good could she do? The glasses must have been a disguise. And it had worked. They were the only things she could remember clearly.

Her cell phone rang.

"Hello? I'm here. I'm sorry, Del, but there's a pretty long line to get inside." She glanced at her watch. She'd come twenty minutes early, but she'd been in line a good while. She heard a sound on the phone, and Del was gone.

"Del?" Lola flushed and put the phone away. Now Del was mad at her again.

But then Del was coming toward her, gesturing at her and sketching a wave at the woman behind the counter, who flapped a hand at Del and went back to nodding at the couple yelling at each other and her.

"Hey. Next time, not that there's going to be a next time, just call me when you get here. I should have told you. That line takes forever."

Lola scurried to follow Del, who gestured at an open door and made a face, pointing to her watch.

Lola nodded and smiled, but Del was already striding away. Obviously, she was busy. Lola stalled for a moment and watched Del enter a small room. There were three other officers in there already, and one of them said something that made Del and the others laugh. Del said something, and then they all started talking and sifting through the tall piles of paper in front of them.

Lola couldn't stop watching. Del was so at ease! She seemed a part of things here. Del thought of this as comfortable, this overwhelming place full of noise and people and ringing phones. Lola was relieved, and ashamed of that relief, when the sketch artist, an older woman in a shapeless gray suit, came over and led her to a quiet room away from everyone. In there, it was easy to pretend, as the woman told her to, that she was just describing the man to a friend over coffee.

After an hour, the drawing could have been of nearly anyone, and Lola knew that she'd failed. She fled the station without saying goodbye to Del, unable to face her or the way everyone in this place scared her.

Lola had been home only moments when the doorbell rang. She looked out to see a group of kids clustered on the stairs.

"Hold on," she yelled through the door, punching in the numbers. "Sorry." She smiled uncertainly at the nearest youth, who beamed at her with bright eyes. " Uh, hi. What can I do for you?"

They were delivering her rented Christmas tree. The kids overwhelmed her with their chatter and questions and jokes and energy, and she was glad she'd taken the time to put on makeup that morning, and her fading bruises didn't show. They set up the tree with a flourish, and she realized that she needed to offer them something. Money—a tip? Food? She wasn't sure what to do and floundered. Suddenly, it was too late, and they were gone, and she was alone with the tree. She looked askance at it.

The poor tree didn't have any lights or ornaments on it and looked naked. She'd never had a real tree before, a live tree, much less one that would live on after Christmas. Now that it was here, it seemed like a good distraction. Maybe it was silly. Del would think it was silly, maybe.

"So what?"

The silence seemed to mock her.

"She's not the boss of me."

Orrin would think it was silly.

"He's not the boss of me, either."

Tucking her cell phone into her purse, not wanting to make the mistake of again worrying—and angering—Del, Lola headed toward the shops. She was overwhelmed by the wide variety of choices and ended up just grabbing whatever pretty and charming and completely random ornaments caught her eye. It was fun, seeing the decorations and hearing the music. Lola began to feel like a part of things, carrying her lights and ornaments and exchanging smiles and nods with other shoppers. Maybe she could get presents for Del and for Marco and Phil. That wouldn't be weird, would it?

At home, she turned on the radio and sang along to Christmas carols as she worked on the tree. After almost two hours of fussing over the meager decorations she stepped back to survey the results and was pleased. Orrin would have been horrified. It glowed with lights and was weighed down with ornaments. It was beautiful.

Kneeling to pick up the small pile of wrappings, Lola wondered why the kitties hadn't come to investigate. They'd probably been scared away by the noisy kids—just as well, she thought. Buttons had a habit of biting things that weren't food and making herself sick. Queenie wouldn't deign to engage in such silliness, but she did like to kick around anything that fell on the floor. Not to have fun, mind you, but to teach it a lesson.

Lola smiled at their very different personalities. How could those little animals have become so important to her? Maybe it was just her loneliness, but she thought of them as having deeper thoughts than even some people. She rolled her eyes. They liked to eat and clean themselves and chase invisible prey—they were not contemplating the state of the universe. But they were good company, and she wanted to see how they would react—surely they hadn't ever seen a Christmas tree?

The mess cleared up, Lola started to worry that the kitties might have gotten out when the kids had brought in the tree. She'd kept an eye out, of course, but there'd been a lot of kids, and she'd been distracted. Two slinky cats could easily have slipped out in the confusion.

"Okay, don't panic," she told herself, and she checked their downstairs hiding spots before heading upstairs.

"Kitties," she called, "kitty, kitty, kitties!" At the door to her bedroom, she stopped, mouth open to call for the cats. She was frozen in place by a bitter, metallic smell she recognized as blood. It was too dark to see, and she was suddenly sure that she did not want to turn on the light. Still, her hand fumbled toward the switch and flicked it.

"Oh, oh, no," she heard a faint voice cry out. She heard it whimper too. She forced herself forward even as she wondered who was making those sounds.

"You are, Lolly," Orrin said. "Look." He was whispering almost tenderly. "Open your eyes and look."

There, in a tableau that drew the air from her lungs in a whoosh, were Buttons and Queenie. They were on the bed, lying on their backs. The cats were almost unrecognizable with their bellies sliced open. Blood was dried on and around them, and their eyes were open and unseeing. She felt her body shaking, she heard her breath rasping through her throat, she felt herself sliding into the hole, and she was gone.

CHAPTER THIRTEEN

There was an alarm going off in Del's mind, had been ever since she'd gotten home from a quick run after work. She'd called Lola and gotten no answer, and she'd been sure there was something very wrong. She unlocked Lola's front door, glad she'd gotten a key from her, and crossed over to the radio that was perched on a pile of books. She snapped off the sounds of "Silent Night"—she shouldn't, not really, but it was making her crazy.

The house was very, very quiet, then, and Del uncoiled her senses and tried to read the house. Her whole body quivered with adrenaline. Her nostrils flared, her ears strained for any sound. Nothing. Nothing at all. Lola's purse was on the entry table, keys, too. Shoulders dropped, knees soft, Del settled into a crouch. She was light on the balls of her feet, and her invisible feelers stretched out, listening, smelling and searching—for what, she couldn't have said. A bad guy? A body?

She felt the weight of her backup and duty weapons. She kept her hand near her waist as she checked each downstairs room, noting that all of the lights, save those on the tree, were off. Living room, clear. Kitchen, clear. Laundry room, clear. Powder room, clear. She opened the door into the garage and squatted down to look. Nothing but the car and a couple of recycling bins. She locked the door from the garage into the house and eyed the open part of the upstairs hallway. All the lights were off up there too.

She eased up the inside edge of the stairs with sweat tracing a cold line down her back. She checked each room as she passed it. Guest bedroom, clear. Hall bath, clear. Office, clear. One room left. She slowed as she headed toward the master bedroom at the back of the house. There was something on the ground, and she tried to see it, but it was just a lump. In the dark, it could have been a blanket, a jacket, anything. A body, maybe. Lola, dead because Del was too late.

Headlights from a passing car flashed light across the hallway, and she saw that the lump was Lola. She looked like a deflated balloon, twisted and lifeless on the floor. Del's heart jigged in her chest. Cool it. She fought the impulse to dart forward. Was the bad guy still in there? Was Lola alive? She didn't look it.

She had a bad moment then. If Lola was dead, if the guy had killed her, Del wasn't sure she could control herself, wanted to control herself. She was hoping that he was still here. Her trigger hand twitched closer to her weapon, and she forced it away. Her breath was too fast and too shallow, and her body tensed and flexed. She was losing control, losing focus.

What if Lola was alive, and Del was standing here, hyperventilating and letting her bleed out? She'd never lost control in a crisis like that, and it shook her. She took a second to catch her breath, look around, ascertain the wisdom of moving forward. She didn't let herself move an inch until she was sure that she could do so with calm and control.

She pulled her weapon and crept down the hall until she

was standing over Lola. When Lola inhaled, Del let out the breath she'd been holding. She was alive. Unconscious, but alive. No obvious injuries. Del looked up and saw dead animals and blood. She saw giant letters scrawled on the wall over the bed. She cleared the room, trying to take in every detail. Drawers had been opened and dumped. The closet was open and looked empty. She cleared the bathroom, then checked the victim for injuries and carried her down the stairs. She put the victim on the couch and turned on the light.

The victim was cold and motionless and white. Breathing was shallow but regular. Del grabbed the lamp and held it close with one hand while pulling up the eyelids with the other. The pupils contracted appropriately. Del pulled the blanket off the back of the couch. She chafed the wrists and lightly slapped the cheeks.

Finally Lola came around. She was groggy at first and seemed confused by Del's presence. But she was Lola. She was alive, and she was herself. Then Del saw the memory hit—she must have seen the dead animals. Her eyes widened, her mouth stretched to form a giant O, and the little bit of color she'd started to regain drained in a moment.

"I know," murmured Del. "I'm sorry. Did you see him?"

Lola's mouth snapped shut, and Del watched her. Lola appeared to be okay. Shaken and disoriented, but okay.

She shook her head.

"Listen," Del said, when she felt Lola's pulse regulate and saw her eyes return to normal. "I need to know. Are you sure you didn't see anyone? Are you hurt? Were you drugged? Did anyone hurt you?"

Lola looked at her blankly. Then she looked down at her limbs and felt her head and face, like she was taking inventory. Finally, she shook her head.

"I have to call it in. Do you need an ambulance?"

Lola shook her head.

"You sure? Huh?"

A wordless nod.

"Okay. Stay here. Just rest here for a minute while I make the call."

Lola grabbed her hand, her eyes huge and pleading.

"I know, just give me a minute. You'll be able to see me the whole time, okay?" Lola nodded with clear reluctance, and Del pulled her hand out of Lola's cold fingers. She backed away, unable to tear her gaze from Lola's eyes. They were dark with pain and fear. They burned into Del, and she couldn't look at them and turned away.

Del shook her head. Her emotions were running wild. She was angry and scared and worried and guilty and confused. Those eyes were killing her. What she wanted to do was take Lola in her arms and warm her and reassure her and stop her shaking. But it was work time, not friend time. She cleared her throat. She could certainly make the call right here, but she needed to get away from those eyes.

"Just wait here." *I'm breaking my promise*, she thought. She shrugged and made the call.

She snuck a glance at Lola, who was staring off into space. Del looked away from her. She needed to do something. She couldn't just sit around, holding Lola's hand.

She got the first patrolman on scene to take Lola outside. An EMT was just pulling up, and she wanted Lola checked outside, away, somewhere else. She needed to think. She drew diagrams of the rooms. She tried not to think about Lola, about what might have happened. About how she went for a run to relax after work and was therefore gone instead of checking on Lola first thing. She watched the EMT through the window.

Finally, the exam was done, and the EMT waved her out. He recommended a more thorough medical exam, but Lola panicked at that. At least she was talking now.

"Del, I swear, I'm fine. Please, I really, really don't want to go to the hospital. Please?"

The EMT looked to Del to work her, but it was too hard to look at Lola's scared, pleading eyes.

Del shrugged. "I guess she's okay, if she says so."

Not professional. She knew it. But it was too hard to insist on something that would upset Lola. Del wished she could go back to the person she used to be, the one who could just stop feeling things when she wanted to. But it looked like that person was gone, and seeing Lola scared and sad and lost didn't help. It made her feel crazy inside.

Del called Phil and explained the situation, asked if Lola could sleep in their guest room. Phil was still on the phone, hesitating, when Marco ran over, carrying a blanket. Phil groaned and hung up as Marco bundled Lola up and led her like she was a sleepwalker. Phil passed by them when he came over to ask if she thought it was the same guy who'd attacked Lola before, if it might not have been random.

Del hesitated. "Maybe, and maybe," she replied, worried that he'd refuse to let Lola stay.

He eyed her with a speculative look. "Any chance he'll come back and look for her?"

Del waggled her hand. "I'll be here and keeping an eye out, but, uh, you know how to shoot, right? You still have that pistol?"

He nodded and headed back without another word. He would spend the night perched on a chair with his dad's loaded pistol in his hand. That was obvious from his face and demeanor. Phil was a nice guy and almost a friend, but Del was more than willing to sacrifice Phil's night of sleep for Lola's safety.

The night passed in a blur. A two-man forensic team covered every inch of the house, and Del took pictures, notes and statements from the neighbors. Nobody had seen anything. Nobody had heard anything. There were no fingerprints, no footprints outside. No obvious points of entry.

Was it the same bad guy? What did he want? He'd been looking for something. What was he looking for? Lola had said that the guy who jumped her tried to get her inside, and Del had assumed that this was so he could hurt her in private. What if he was trying to get her inside to show him where she'd hidden something? What was Lola hiding?

CHAPTER FOURTEEN

When Lola met Marco at the base of the stairs, he folded her in his arms without a word. She tried to keep her cool but didn't struggle when she started crying again. She felt like she could cry for a week and still be full of tears. But finally she pulled away with a wry smile.

"Sorry about your shirt."

He shook his head. "Want some coffee?"

Phil insisted on making breakfast for the three of them, though Lola just played with the food and gulped down a scalding cup of coffee. It was only after breakfast that she finally remembered to thank them for their hospitality.

"I didn't remember where I was when I woke up," she admitted, "I don't remember coming here."

"I'm not surprised," Marco murmured, shaking his head.

"It was so kind of you—I'm sorry for imposing like this. I swear, I'm not usually this much trouble," Lola said.

Phil had been using a piece of toast to sop up the last of his egg yolk, and his eyes darted to Marco's face. Marco shook his head slightly.

Lola put down her cup and took a deep breath. What was going on? Phil was pleasant, but she got the sense that he was unhappy with her presence. Did he not like her? Did he worry that she was bringing danger to him and Marco? She realized that whoever had killed Buttons and Queenie might not be done. He might want to hurt her, and he might be willing to hurt other people to get to her. She should never have allowed them to bring her home. What if something terrible had happened to them?

"I should go," she declared, standing up and ignoring her wooziness. "I have to go now."

They protested, of course, but she saw that Phil was relieved, and she thanked them again, resolving to send flowers or cookies or something, with a thank you note. And not put them in danger again. Marco and Phil had helped her twice now, and she'd barely acknowledged it. She needed to do something nice for Del, as well. She should already have done so.

As she stepped through her own front door, Lola saw Del standing near the Christmas tree, just looking at it. Even from the entryway, Lola could see her weariness and worry. Had Del stayed here all night? She flushed, feeling that she should have reacted more calmly to the situation, instead of zoning out and leaving the whole mess to Del.

"Del," she began, "I'm so sorry. I just kind of fell apart last night. I don't really remember too well, but I—"

Del held up her hands. "Don't apologize. You had every right to be upset. Did you get any sleep?"

Lola nodded. "You?"

Del shook her head.

"You must be exhausted!"

Del grimaced and shrugged. "Not my first night without sleep. I had a team dust the place and take some pics. They were pretty thorough, but I wanted to make sure. I had them sample the blood, but it'll take forever to get it back."

"The blood?" Lola was confused. "You mean, like, to see if they were drugged? Maybe they didn't feel any pain?" She heard the hope in her voice and felt childish for it.

"Well, maybe, I guess, but..." Her voice trailed off as she saw Lola's confusion.

Del looked speculative and softened her expression. Lola saw her decide to do so and was struck by how transparent Del's moods and thoughts were sometimes. She'd seemed inscrutable, at first. Was Del letting her guard down around her more, or was she getting better at reading Del?

"Why don't I go ahead and take your statement, now, is that all right?"

Del's voice had taken on the tone that Lola had learned meant she was on the job. It was professional, warm and cool at the same time. It worked, she noticed, as if from a distance. She felt calmer and more focused.

They sat at the kitchen table for over an hour, with Del taking notes and asking Lola questions. They went over everything, and Lola was surprised to find that she remembered many small details about the day, like the name of the leader of the Christmas tree kids, and what time she'd left for the store, and what she'd eaten for lunch, and what time she'd noticed that the cats weren't nosing around her legs like they usually did.

She did fine until she got to the hard part, the part about going upstairs, and then she stopped talking. Del waited and said nothing. She wasn't impatient or irritated or mad. She just waited. Lola took a deep breath and described what she'd seen on the bed as dispassionately as she could: the cats, their eyes, the blood, the bloody blankets. There was a long silence as Del looked down at her notes.

"Okay, Lola, that's good. You've done a great job." She paused, and Lola tensed. Del's tone was deliberately casual, and that made her nervous. "So, was there anything else in the room that caught your eye?"

Lola frowned. She went back over the memory as though it were a photograph. She remembered smelling the blood and looking in the room and seeing them there, dead and bloody and defaced. She forced herself to linger over the memory for another minute and shook her head.

"No," she said finally, "I'm sorry. I don't remember anything else." She searched Del's eyes, wondering what was wrong. Had she forgotten something important? Had she missed something?

"Okay." Del smiled at her, and it was a professional smile.

"Why are you looking at me like that?"

"Can we go take a look at your room? It's not as bad as it was. Just a little empty."

Lola nodded, too nonplussed to do more than follow Del up the stairs.

Her room looked foreign, somehow, not at all like the one she'd decorated so carefully and come to feel at home in. She paused for a second, wishing that the whole thing had been just a bad dream. The white mattress drew her eye, though there was no blood. Somehow the whiteness made the room ghostly. She forced her eyes away from it to find out what she'd missed.

"Oh!" She was shocked out of her dreamy state. "Oh, my God!"

She couldn't tear her eyes away from the ugly letters defiling her pretty lavender wall. The large watercolor painting she'd chosen with such care was gone, and in its place was the word "whore." The painted letters were huge and dark and squared off. The word looked official somehow, like she'd been tried and found guilty by some tribunal.

"Oh," she repeated, unable to form any more coherent response.

It felt like Orrin was shouting that word at her, calling her that ugly name. She could hear his voice in her head. She could smell his stale breath and feel his hot, dry skin and the ropy muscle beneath it. She was hit by a wave a fear and revulsion and staggered against Del.

"Do you want to sit down?" Del offered, but the only place to sit was the bed, and Lola never wanted to touch that thing again.

"God, no! I mean, sorry, no, thank you. I'm fine. I'm sorry."

She stood swaying, her eyes skittering around the room.

The dresser was a mess, the drawers upside down on the floor in a sloppy heap on top of her clothes. The closet had spilled its few shirts on the floor. A half-dozen hangers hung empty on the rod, abandoned and white in the darkness of the closet. There was the painting, the one from above the bed, propped against the wall near the closet door and ruined—slashed through.

Just like Buttons and Queenie, she thought, and tears burst from her eyes. Violence had stalked her for as long as she could remember. She had thought she'd escaped it for good, but it came and found her again. Would it always find her? Despair wrapped itself around her and weighed her down. She would always be afraid. She would always be weak. She shook these thoughts away. Grow up! Just stop thinking like that! But the despair stayed with her. She watched Del look at her and knew that she'd seen her falter again. She was flooded with self-loathing and shame.

"I'm sorry," she whispered. "I don't want to be like this, you know? I want to be strong."

"Okay, it's okay. Come on, let's go."

Del led her as one might an invalid down the stairs and to the living room couch. She eased Lola into a sitting position and tucked a blanket around her shoulders. Lola worked to pull herself together while Del made coffee. She came in a few minutes later with the tray. It was crammed with cups and with plates of food. She sat opposite Lola and gestured at the tray. Lola shook her head, but Del handed her a cup of creamed coffee. It was sweetened.

Leave it to a cop, Lola thought, to notice how you take your coffee. She couldn't swallow the coffee but pretended to. Then Del rubbed her thumb against the inside of her palm, and Lola saw that she was nervous, which made her nervous. Del gestured at the coffee.

"It'll warm you up."

Lola pretended to swallow some more. The cup did warm her hands. Del snagged an apple slice and munched in silence for a few moments. There was something very normal about eating apple. It made all the bad things seem far, far away. Del's breath smelled like apples when she spoke, and it was such a wholesome smell that it almost cleaned the remembered smell of blood from

Lola's mind again. But this lasted only a second, and Lola tried to shake herself out of her lapse into whimsy. It wasn't helpful. It was childish. She had to stop being so childish.

"Was it there last night?" Del's quiet voice broke the silence.

Lola forced herself back to the moment. "That word? Honestly, I don't know. I mean, I saw the, you know, and I just kind of went—fainted. Really, it might have been there, and I just didn't see it. Or maybe not. I don't know. I'm so sorry, Del. I'm sorry. I wish I could be sure."

"No problem," Del answered lightly, but Lola could tell that it mattered.

Why, she wasn't sure for a moment. Then, the truth hit her like a hard slap. She set down her cup too hard, slopping coffee. She had been alone in the house, and the cats had been dead, and she hadn't seen that word on the wall. Maybe it wasn't there, then. Maybe she wasn't alone at all.

Lola swallowed hard. She needed to focus.

"Was it him?" she asked aloud. "The Creep? The man who—followed me? Or a different man? When you said about the blood, I didn't—those letters, they're written in blood? Buttons' and Queenie's blood? Oh, my God!"

She wanted to check her body for injuries, even though she felt no pain or achiness to suggest she'd been hurt. It was the uncertainty, the not-knowing feeling, that was so scary. Like she'd left her body vulnerable and unprotected and wasn't sure whether it had been safe or not. Like she was a bad caretaker.

She'd felt this way dozens, maybe hundreds of times before. Every time she went away, she came back feeling like she'd lost her mind. Sometimes she wondered if one day she'd slide into the hole and not come back again. This was both a terrifying and an oddly enticing thought. Imagine, she thought with a shiver, never having to be afraid again. Never hurting again.

Then she looked up and saw Del's blue-green eyes darken and change. She seemed inscrutable again. I would never see her eyes again, Lola thought. I would never smell apples again, or read a book, or taste coffee, or listen to music. I would never feel the soft fur on Queenie's belly, or—and the reality of so much death, the kitties's and Orrin's and young Tami Holden's, hit her again. She bit her lip.

"Was he in here, do you think, when I fainted?"

Del waited a moment to answer. "I'm not sure. I think it's a possibility." She paused again. "The thing is, I bet it'll come back to you. You know, if you just relax and give it some time. You'll remember whether those letters were on the wall when you fainted or whatever, or if they weren't." She pushed Lola's cup toward her. "But if you don't remember, it's okay. We'll just operate under the assumption that he might have been the same guy or might not, and that he might have been here when you got back from the store or might not have been. I'll investigate every possibility, and we'll figure it out."

Lola wasn't fooled by Del's too soothing tone. She chewed her lower lip. What was happening? Why was this happening? And what was she supposed to do?

"You're scared. I get that. I don't like all this uncertainty, either. But I'm here, Lola, and I'm going to protect you, I promise, and I'm going to find this asshole, and I'm going to lock him up, okay?"

Lola nodded. Poor Del looked so upset. *Why did I have to go away like that?* She frowned at Del, wanting to apologize, to say, hey, you shouldn't have had to deal with all of this. But Del already seemed pretty wound up. And she always seemed a little irritated when Lola apologized.

Del shook her head in disgust. "This is so sickening. What's wrong with people?"

She stood abruptly, her hands clenched into tight fists, her face splotched with anger, and Lola involuntarily flinched, her head hitting the couch's back. She saw Del take in her reaction and ease slowly back into the chair, her eyes clouded. Lola flushed, embarrassed by her overreaction, and tried to shrug an apology.

When Del spoke again, her voice was soft. "Sorry. I didn't mean to—upset you. I just don't like the idea that he might have been here when you were. And I don't like being unsure of so many variables."

Lola nodded and forced a wan smile onto her face. She was

thinking about how to say something and was reluctant to start. The last thing she wanted to do was to alienate Del. She was more than a little cowed by what she thought of as the prickly pear part of her new friend.

"Del," she began, "I appreciate everything you've done for me. I want to thank you so much. You've gone way beyond the call of duty here, and I'm feeling guilty. This isn't your problem. Let someone else take care of it. You've had enough to deal with."

"Like what?" Del's voice was too controlled.

Lola almost stopped but forced herself to finish. Del was too good a person to get dragged into Lola's mess. What if something bad happened to her? Lola had let Marco and Phil and Del all put themselves in potential danger, all because she had been weak and stupid. She'd let Tami Holden die. She'd let the kitties die. She'd let Orrin die, for that matter.

The flashes of pain and frustration she'd seen in Del's eyes had scorched her. She didn't want to be the reason Del was in pain. That was the one thing she could give her friend—the opportunity to bow out of a dangerous, upsetting, frustrating mess. She'd been a coward and a weakling and let Del shoulder the burden, and that was wrong. She didn't want to do that anymore.

"Oh." Lola was unsure how to proceed. "No, I just mean, what if something happened to you? What if you got hurt or even killed? I couldn't take that." Her eyes filled. "You're my friend, my only friend besides Marco. I can't stand the thought of putting you in danger."

But Del just looked at her, and she didn't know what to do. In her nervousness, she kept babbling, hardly knowing what she was saying, "I was thinking, I mean, I'm kind of controversial, I guess, because of the book, and maybe you don't want to, you know, tarnish your reputation by being connected with me. What if the other cops made fun of you? What if they lost respect for you, and that put you in danger later? I wouldn't want that. I don't want anything bad to happen to you because of me. Please, I—" Her voice trailed off.

Del's face was a mask of rigid control, and Lola felt lost. She shouldn't have said anything. Her resolve to be independent and to look out for her friend were lost in the dark blankness of Del's eyes, the way her mouth was tight and hard. Lola's mind swam in uncertainty. She shrank into the couch. Her mind was blank, her breath shallow. She held herself very, very still.

"So." The level tone in Del's voice set off even more warning bells in Lola's head, and she shook her head.

"You're worried about me? You think I can't handle myself? You think that *freak*," she gestured upstairs, her voice rising steadily, "is smarter than me? Or maybe you think a man would do a better job? Or maybe anyone but me. Oh, and what was the other thing? You don't want me to get 'tarnished' by being associated with you? Why, because you're a dyke?"

She spat the word, and Lola flinched and gaped at her. Del's eyes were so dark that Lola didn't recognize them. She couldn't breathe. She couldn't think. Del was so angry! She heard a small exhalation escape her, and it sounded like a whimper. She despised herself in that moment, maybe even more than Del did. She was miserable. And Del wasn't done. She was burning with anger, and her body looked like it was about to explode. Lola tried not to look at her, it hurt to look at her, but she couldn't drag her eyes away from Del's. They were hypnotic in their flashing intensity.

"Is that it? You think I don't know how to do my job? And I should scurry into the closet like a fucking coward?" She huffed and shook her head, taking in the room. Her gaze returned to Lola's face and burned into her.

"Well, Lola, *I'm* not ashamed of who I am."

Her tone was acid, and Lola tried but couldn't stop crying. She blinked the tears away and saw that Del's face was granite.

"But you don't have to worry about that. You think you can take care of this yourself? Be my guest. You and your bullshit and your stalker can go straight to hell!"

She stormed out of the house, and Lola stared after her, unable to do anything but let what felt like endless rivers of tears stream down her cheeks and down her chin and down her throat and down and down and down.

CHAPTER FIFTEEN

"Ohhh," Del groaned aloud, startling a passerby. She strode down the street, trying to regain her equilibrium. She imagined she could see herself as from a distance, red-faced, hair wild— she looked nuts or drunk or both. No wonder Lola had looked so scared. Lola was like a dog that's been kicked too many times. That was one of the first things Del had noticed about her. She would surely never trust Del again. How could she protect Lola if Lola was afraid of her? And how could she look into those big, beautiful eyes and face the pain and betrayal and fear she would surely see there?

Don't be a coward. She needs help. Del squared her shoulders and marched up to Lola's door. It was already open when Del reached it, and she stood wordlessly looking down at Lola, who stared at her feet for a moment before she finally met Del's gaze and held it.

"I want to help you." Del spoke without thinking. "I want to find the guy who attacked you, and the guy who killed your cats. Whether that's the same guy or not. I want you to be safe."

Lola looked at her as though from behind glass. Del debated addressing the things she'd said and decided not to. It was enough that Lola hadn't slammed the door in her face.

"I think I should stay here." She waved in the direction of the couch. "I think you're in danger. Okay," she finished lamely, "uh, I'm gonna check on some stuff. I'll be back here at around seven. Will you be all right till then?"

There was a long moment when Del wondered if Lola had heard her, but then she nodded. It was like she was underwater, and Del wondered how much of that was the bad guy and how much was her. Too much was her.

Del hesitated. "I'm sorry," she said, turning away and escaping to her own house.

She showered and went to the station. By then she had managed to shelve her guilt and frustration over losing her cool with Lola. She would beat herself up over that some other time. Now, the priority was finding the bad guy.

Del tried to press a manager in the lab into moving her stuff up the line, but he refused, explaining that he couldn't move up an animal cruelty case above homicides and assaults and rapes. She thought again of Lola's too-still body on the floor and her blank stare and her cold hand, and she shuddered. How long before something happened that made this a high priority case? Not long at all, if her gut was right. She sat at her desk, looking over her notes and talking to herself.

"The writing on the wall—it's signature behavior, something extra, the kind of compulsive shit only a certain brand of freak does." She got a few weird looks from a passing group of civilians, but she ignored them. She logged on and searched the database, sure that the guy was an experienced destroyer of people's lives, someone who'd been popped before. Her fingers flew over the keyboard, and her eyes scanned the endless, tangled webs of information that crawled with agonizing slowness onto the screen. She also needed to consider the possibility that the writing on the wall was a red herring.

That's what I'd do. I'd get the investigation off on the wrong foot. I'd find something distinctive, forensically clean, and visually and emotionally evocative. Something like writing "whore" on the wall in blood. That would keep everybody all frothy and focused on the wrong shit. She wished she knew which of the two it was, signature or bullshit. She had to investigate both possibilities equally.

It was starting to feel like one of those books she'd loved as a kid. If the guy turns left, turn to page eighty-nine. If he turns right, turn to page ninety-six. Only in real life, it was a hell of a lot more frustrating. And she could go down the wrong path just long enough for the bad guy to hurt or take or kill Lola.

It was several hours later that she noticed the time. She should have been tired, but she was wired and restless and only reluctantly kept the bike at the crawl required in the city. She loped up Lola's stairs like a kid late for curfew, but the door opened before Del could even knock.

Lola was composed when she pulled the door open. She looked like she'd just gotten out of the shower. Her skin was damp, her hair still wet and a little wavy. She wore an oversized hockey jersey and sweatpants, and Del couldn't help but smile. She looked like a little girl dressed up in her big brother's clothes. Except for the fact that her skin was pale, and her eyes were ringed with deep purple. Del felt the smile slide off her face.

"Hi," she said, lamely.

Lola nodded, her face still and expressionless.

Del started to say something innocuous, but Lola cut her off with a quiet voice.

"I thought you might be hungry." She led the way to the kitchen, which smelled heavenly. Del nodded her thanks and sat down to a heaping plate of salad and pasta and garlic bread. She ate steadily, too hungry to watch her manners, and had polished off the whole plate before she noticed that Lola wasn't eating. She had a cup of coffee in front of her and sipped from it occasionally, silently watching Del.

Del cleared her throat. "Listen," she began, "about earlier. I—"

"No, please." Lola reddened and shook her head, and a strand of hair danced near the top of her cup. "I'm the one who's sorry. I offended you, and I honestly didn't mean to. I didn't say it right. I just don't want anything bad to happen to you." She sighed in frustration. "I still haven't figured out how to say it right." She turned her head and frowned.

Even frowning, she looked soft. Sweet. A pang of something sharp and undefined made Del suck in her breath. Was it desire? That, and maybe something else, something that made her stomach hurt. Del was struck again by how vulnerable Lola looked, all round cheeks and big doe eyes and soft-looking hair. No makeup, no artifice, no flirting, but she was somehow the picture of desirability.

She pictured Janet—her always-painted nails, always-reddened lips, always-lacquered hair. In contrast, Lola was all softness, warmth, realness. She made Janet look hard and plastic and cold. Del couldn't believe how much she wanted to stroke that soft hair, kiss those full lips, hold Lola's soft, warm body against her own. She shook the thought away. It was inappropriate. Completely inappropriate.

"Lola..." Del searched for words. "You didn't do anything wrong. You were trying to be a good friend. And that's what I'm trying to be, too. I don't know why I flipped out like that. I care about what happens to you, and the last thing I want is to hurt you." She paused. "I'm sorry for being such a jerk."

Lola's laugh startled Del.

"'I'm sorry.' 'No, I'm sorry.' 'No, I'm sorry.'" She used her two hands like little puppets and smiled at Del with brilliance that was only a little forced.

Del felt an answering smile spreading across her face. The two women broke into loud, snorting laughter. Only someone listening very closely, thought Del, would hear Lola's creeping hysteria. It sobered her, and she saw the moment when Lola heard the change. She didn't say anything, and they just looked at each other across the table for a long moment.

Something was happening, Del felt it. What it was, she couldn't say, but she was reminded of the hunting trip with her daddy. A million invisible nerves stretched between Lola and her and bonded them, and the feeling was strange and scary and somehow right. She knew that Lola felt it too, and she saw her own wonder and uncertainty and fear mirrored in Lola's wide eyes. Had she felt the same thing with that nasty old man? Del cleared her throat, suddenly desperate to end the moment. Lola offered her a small smile and jerked up out of her chair to clear the table. So, she too had felt the restless need to escape.

Del rose and tried to help, but Lola didn't seem to notice her. She worked very quickly and quietly, her movements efficient. She looked tired, all of a sudden. Del had the urge to pull Lola toward her and just hold her. She would nestle in, her head just under Del's chin. She'd be warm and real and round and soft. Del's arms itched to reach out and snag her jersey and pull her in and kiss the top of her head. And her soft, sweet lips. It wasn't a sexual urge, but a warm, family kind of feeling. A softness. She hadn't felt like this since she was a kid, when she'd loved this or that stray dog or feral cat, and maybe even her parents, once upon a time. It was damned confusing, feeling all these things.

Lola turned, a damp dishtowel in her hands, and peered into Del's eyes. "You okay?"

Del gave a half smile. She must have shown more of her feelings than she'd meant to. Once again, she was aware of how little clarity and focus she was able to maintain around Lola. "Just tired, I guess."

Lola immediately offered tea, a bed, a shower. Del declined all three, explaining that she wanted to be downstairs in case anything came up. Lola nodded in apparent relief, and Del realized that Lola was planning to sleep in the guest room. She'd bet good money that Lola had showered in the second bathroom rather than her own. She couldn't blame her. As Lola headed upstairs, calling her thanks and good nights, Del went around the house, checking the windows and doors. She went upstairs while Lola was brushing her teeth (in, Del noted, the second bathroom) and did the same check up there. The alarm was on, but it was better to be sure.

Del had planned to catch up on her sleep, but she was still too keyed up. She wandered through the circle of rooms on the lower level, peering out uselessly at the dark, and found herself back in the living room, facing one of the bookshelves. Turning on a lamp, she scanned the titles in the one near the window. Lots of different authors, many she'd heard of, some she hadn't. Some good contemporary novels, some science fiction, several classics, a few biographies and histories, lots of women, several well-known lesbian writers, a few anthologies of poetry. Del assessed people by their books or the lack thereof. By this standard, Lola was one of the coolest people Del had ever snooped on. The other bookcase was very similar, but for one thing. Two hardbound and two paperback copies of Lola's novel were tucked into the bottom shelf. She'd used a pen name, but Del recognized the title and snagged one of the paperbacks. Would Lola mind her reading this? Well, she decided, flopping onto the couch, if she did, she shouldn't have put it there. Besides, maybe something in here is what turned the bad guy on. This is *research*. She stretched out her legs and settled down to read.

CHAPTER SIXTEEN

The next morning, Lola was halfway down the stairs before she remembered that Del was there, and she stopped, taking in the sight of Del's long legs sprawled over the ottoman. Her eyes were closed, her mouth was soft, and her arm was stretched out with her hand palm up, fingers curled. Lola held her breath. Del seemed so vulnerable, asleep. She looked like an exhausted puppy, the way her limbs were flung out so carelessly. The blanket Lola had given her lay in a puddle on the floor. Del's hair was tousled, her shirt rumpled. The hard planes of her face were softened now and pink with the warmth of sleep.

Orrin had looked many years older asleep than awake. Animated, his face had been handsome, even as he'd gotten older. But relaxed, face slack, he'd looked weak and vulnerable, something she suspected he'd known and hated. It had been very confusing, pitying the powerful man who ruled her life. She'd hated herself for being so weak and helpless that she could be bullied by a failing old man.

Del shifted her leg, and Lola's thoughts of the past receded. Del's sleeping form inspired a sharp and aching tenderness in Lola that she could hardly process. She wanted to wrap Del in a soft, warm blanket and tell her that everything would be all right, though she knew Del would hate being babied. She bristled the way Donny—one of Lola's long-ago babysitting charges—often had as a toddler. He'd only wanted to be cuddled when it was his idea. Del was like that, maybe. She'd get edgy at the first sign of unwanted affection, but she'd need it desperately when it was on her terms. This was not a good thing, Lola reminded herself.

Del frowned in her sleep, and Lola watched her leg twitch again. What was she dreaming about? What was happening in that head of hers? Was she being chased by a bogeyman? Was she climbing a mountain? Dancing with some phantom lover—maybe that awful woman who hurt her so badly? How anyone could worm her way into Del's tender heart and then break it was beyond her. Del was special. Anyone could see that. Whatever agenda the woman might have had going in, hadn't she been tempted to abandon it and just love Del? How could she have walked away from such an amazing woman? If she were mine, Lola thought, I'd cherish her. I'd let her know how much I treasured her, every minute of every day.

"But she isn't yours," Orrin reminded her, his voice surprisingly low.

Going soft, Orrin? Maybe death had tamed the demons that had raged in him. Maybe death had set him free. She rolled her eyes at her fanciful thoughts. *He doesn't exist anymore except in your head, remember?*

Del gave a small sigh, her lips parting for just a moment, and Lola wondered what it would be like to just once taste those soft lips. They were Del's most feminine feature, pink and full and lush. She didn't seem to wear lipstick or anything. She didn't need to. To adorn them would have been sacrilege. To kiss them, heaven. Lola realized that she was actually clasping her hands at her breast, like some winsome heroine in a nineteenth-century romance. She gave a small laugh and forced her hands to her sides.

She tiptoed down the rest of the stairs, trying not to make any noise. As she crept past on her way to the kitchen, she noticed a book on the floor next to Del's blanket. That's right, she remembered with delight, she's a reader. She snuck closer, curious to see what book Del had chosen. Her breath caught sharply. *My* book?

She was horrified. She had never imagined anyone she knew reading that book. She had never imagined having to look someone in the eye, knowing that they had read her words. The story was fictional, but Lola had flayed open her heart during the process of writing it. She felt violated. She knew that this feeling was absurd. She knew that even as she felt it, but it was still true. She felt humiliated.

When she reopened her eyes, she saw Del looking back at her. At least Del had the decency to flush and look away.

"Good morning."

Lola nodded, unable to speak.

Del gestured at the book. "Hope it's okay I grabbed this. Couldn't sleep." She yawned hugely and stretched.

Lola nodded again and headed to the coffeemaker. That's it? She grabbed the coffee, slammed the fridge closed, and huffed. That's all you have to say? I poured my heart out in that book, and all you have to say is that you couldn't sleep? She quivered with outrage.

Del heard Lola banging around and smiled. Good, get mad. I'd like to see that. She felt as though she'd somehow violated Lola's privacy, but she was glad she'd stayed up to read the whole book. It was about a woman who stays married to a man out of a sense of duty and only realizes the futility of this at the very end of her life. The story was clearly fictional, but the uncertainty and guilt and confusion that fueled it were just as clearly not. It had been hard to read, sometimes. The sense of loss, of waste and frustration and regret, all felt painfully personal. She wished she could think of a way to broach the subject without hurting or embarrassing Lola. She decided instead to lie. Cop's habit, she told herself. I've already done enough damage.

Strolling into the kitchen, where Lola was abusing some pancake batter with a wooden spoon, Del plunked into a chair.

"Don't take this the wrong way, but I didn't make it too far. Too tired, after all, I guess." She widened her eyes in a show of innocence and watched Lola's reaction.

"Really?" Lola's eyes searched Del's face. "Well, that's okay. It's not very good. I'll find you something better to read tonight."

"Hmm." Yawning and stretching, Del jumped up. "Gotta go." She headed for the front door and punched in the alarm code.

"Don't you want breakfast?" Lola still held the mixing bowl in her hand.

"Can't. Gotta shower and get to work. I've gotta protect a friend."

Lola smiled at her, and Del felt warmed. Whatever damage her temper and snooping had done, Lola's good nature had overcome her hurt feelings.

"See you tonight, maybe around seven again."

Lola nodded and waved the wooden spoon at her, and Del laughed, sprinting across the street to her own house.

Lola headed back to the kitchen. She knew that Del had probably lied about not reading the book, but she appreciated being able to save face. She decided to make Del something special for dinner and pulled out a cookbook. Del had done so much for her, and she didn't know how else to thank her. Maybe, Lola thought, as she flipped through the pages, I'll eat with her. Maybe she won't mind.

She chose lasagna, since Del had liked the pasta, and started a shopping list. She'd always wanted to learn how to make lasagna, but Orrin disliked different kinds of foods touching each other. Lola decided to make cookies too. That way, when Del was reading herself to sleep, she could munch on a snack. She looked up that recipe too, and added to her shopping list. She thought that maybe she'd wait to shower until after she'd finished cooking. That way she'd smell nice when Del got home.

"You're like a puppy," she told herself aloud, "she's nice to you for five minutes, and you chase after her, wagging your tail."

CHAPTER SEVENTEEN

Del spent most of the day trolling through various databases, trying to find something that would help her narrow the search. She'd finally gotten the hate mail from the publisher, and her captain agreed to give her two guys to sort through it. There were three huge bags of it, and the captain raised his eyebrows. Three guys. Del would go over the ones they sorted into the "Second Look" category. She wished she could do it all herself, but there was just too much.

The rage in some of the letters seemed to burn her fingers when she held them. The writers all had three things in common: they wrote anonymously, they loved Jesus, and they wanted to kill "Lisa Miller." She finished one particularly vitriolic missive and had to go to the bathroom to wash her face and hands. She had to get the sick off of her body, if not her mind.

Finally, late in the afternoon, she decided to check in with a friend in the computer crimes division. Well, she hoped he was still her friend. After last year, she wasn't sure she had any left in the department. But Anton Jones seemed glad to see her. He was tucked into a tiny cubbyhole, off by himself, and Del felt like she was visiting the department's resident wizard. His wall was completely covered with comics and math formulae and Hubble images. His lanky frame was folded into an undersized chair, and Jones nudged it back to make room for her.

After a minute of small talk, she filled him in on things.

He rolled his eyes. "Oh, God."

"What?"

"People are so naïve." He picked up a pen and started rolling it in his long fingers. "If I stood here and told you I was a sixteen-year-old blond girl, you'd know I was lying. But I say it online, and it's true." He tossed the pen at her. "As far as you know."

"Yeah, I know. But did he pick her, you think, or was it just a random thing?" She tossed the pen back.

Anton shrugged. "Need more data." He tossed the pen at her again.

"Is there any way to track him down? I mean, could you look at her computer and tell where he e-mailed her from?" She tossed the pen onto the desk.

"Would you do it from your computer at home, if you were a dark hat?"

Del shook her head.

"Odds are, he went to a library or a café, used cash or a stolen card." He eyed her. "The vic is a friend?"

Del nodded, her face bland, and he laughed.

"Maybe more than a friend?"

Del shook her head. "My neighbor. And I want this guy out of her life. I think he's escalating fast. He—I think it was him, anyway—broke in and cut her pets open like fucking baked potatoes, left 'em for her to find. She's freaked. And I can't seem to make any headway."

Anton nodded, making a face. "Tell you what, I'll look into it. Gimme your friend's info, get her to send me screen shots if she can, and I'll see what I can do. I may need to see her actual computer, though."

"I really appreciate this, Jones. I want this asshole."

"You owe me, just remember that." He grinned at her, rubbing his fingers together.

She pretended to fish in her pockets and then shrugged.

"I will." She straightened up and looked into his eyes. "Thanks. I mean it."

He called after her as she walked out, "Oh, and Mason? Say hi to your 'friend' for me." He brayed with laughter.

Del rolled her eyes, but she was glad that at least one other person—and one of the smartest guys she knew—was looking for the bad guy. She sat for a moment trying to choose her next move. She could re-interview the neighbors again, go to the coffee shop and the drugstore again. Harass the forensics team again. Then an idea struck her.

"Hey," she called Jones on the crackling phone at her desk. "What about a decoy?"

She heard him scratching his cheek before he answered. "Yeah, why not? Try to duplicate her wording as much as possible. You have a laptop? Use that and send it to me. I'll reroute it for you. Don't use a department machine."

"Okay, thanks. I'll get back to you with whatever."

He was already gone. Del snagged her jacket and helmet, headed home to grab her laptop and overnight bag, and went to Lola's. She realized that she was humming as she rapped on the door and reminded herself that this was not a social call but an emergency intervention. It didn't help. She was still humming.

"Hi, Del." Lola opened the door, damp from the shower again, and Del was distracted by her light cotton pajamas. Her damp hair had made it nearly see-through at the shoulders, and Del let go a nervous laugh.

"Turning in early?" Her voice was hoarse. She felt like an awkward teenager!

"No." Lola smiled. "I decided to be comfortable and lazy."

"Good for you." Del thought Lola should wear pajamas every minute of every day, but she refrained from saying so.

She explained what she wanted to do, and Lola listened

carefully and nodded, then asked if she wanted to eat dinner first.

"Later."

Lola nodded. "Okay."

Del felt a flash of irritation at Lola's obedient response.

She followed Lola to her office. Focus, she told herself, forcing her eyes away from the sight of Lola trotting up the stairs in front of her. Tiny waist, she'd noticed that before. Long legs. Amazing ass—round and plump and perfect. *That's* why I'm not thinking clearly. I've gotta stop thinking about her like she's mine. She's not, and she never will be. She was glad to focus on their task as they entered the office, a bright, sunny room with yellow walls and a huge, L-shaped desk.

They sat next to each other, and Lola warmed up her desktop while Del turned on her laptop.

"So, let's pull up the chat history, okay?"

Lola was blushing. "I know you have to see this, but it's a little weird, you know?"

"Don't think about that. We're trying to set a trap, that's all. I need to know what it was about you that drew him."

She saw Lola's mouth tighten and wished she'd found a better way to say that.

"Okay." Lola tapped on the keyboard.

Old computer, thought Del. Half-million dollar house, and she writes on a piece of ten-year-old crap? She remembered the ancient Buick. She'd been struck the first day by how incongruous the car had looked pulling into the garage of the expensive house.

Del leaned over to look at the screen.

"Single? Lesbian? Like to take long walks? Love coffee, books, &
movies?
"Me: 40s, smart, fun, active, honest. Drug & Drama free. No
smkg.
"You: 30-50, see above.
"I'm looking for a friend first, maybe more if it works out.
"No pressure, just meet at a coffee shop. Live in the city? Email
me!!!"

"Okay." Del felt rather than saw Lola's discomfort. "Well,

I can see why you responded. She seems very normal." He, she thought, remembering Jones's words. "And you emailed her?" Him.

Lola nodded and opened it up.

"Hi. I'm new to the area and am looking for friends.
Maybe more, later. I've never done this before and am a bit shy.
My name is Lola. I live in the Eureka Valley neighborhood.
I am a freelance editor and love coffee, books and movies."

"And what did you get back?"

"Hi, Lola. Pretty name. I've never done this before either.
It's weird, isn't it? I'm new to the city too,
and this holiday weekend is making me lonely.
I'd love to meet you, say at The Café?
Tomorrow night at six?
If we enjoy each other's company, great.
If not, no big deal. But I'd love to hear all
about your favorite books. I work for a publisher.
Oh, my name is Joan. See you tomorrow?"

"No red flags there, either," Del noted, and Lola pulled up her response.

"Joan,
Sounds good. See you tomorrow.
Lola"

"After I sent that," Lola confessed, "I almost sent another one canceling. I still can't believe I went to meet a stranger like that!"

"Hey." Del shook her head. "There's nothing wrong with reaching out to people. It should have been fine. You should have gone to the coffee shop and met some nice woman and hit it off and made a new friend. Or girlfriend, or whatever." She paused, considering. "I need to try and figure out what about your response got her—his—attention. Was it just that you answered? The fact that you're new to the city? That you live in the Castro? Your name? Your fake job?"

Lola looked up at Del and shook her head. "I shouldn't have said so much. I was stupid!"

Del rolled her eyes and scanned the screen again.

"Okay," she said, sitting down at the laptop and opening the ads. "Do I respond to an ad that looks like 'Joan's'? Or do I write a new one and hope he responds?"

She and Lola spent the next two hours scanning the personal ads, looking for one that seemed similar to 'Joan's'. There were seven possibles, but none really pinged for Del.

"Enough!" she said, unintentionally startling Lola, who'd been engrossed in an ad comprised mostly of abbreviations and text-speak.

"I don't know what half of this means!" Lola leaned back and stretched, arching her back and rolling her neck.

"Me, either." Del's eyes swept over Lola's body appreciatively before she caught herself and turned away, turning the feint into a real stretch that made her groan. Her shoulders ached from hunching over all day. She looked out of the window and saw that the sky was dark. How had that happened so quickly?

Lola heard Del's groan and felt guilty. "Del, you can't work twenty-four hours a day! Come on, please eat some dinner."

She hurried to the kitchen, pulling lasagna out of the fridge to reheat it. With the microwave churning and the table set, she held up a bottle of beer in offering to Del, who was washing her hands. She had run into Marco on the way to the grocery store, and he'd mentioned that Del liked beer.

"Sure." Del sniffed the air. "What is that, lasagna? Did you make it from scratch?"

Lola nodded. "My first," she crowed. Then she felt silly. Lasagna had turned out to be very easy to make, and she'd started wondering what other easy things she'd never learned to do in her stunted life.

They sat down, and Lola watched Del eat in silence for a few moments. She seemed to think it was okay. Lola wanted to eat with her and see how that might be, but she still felt strange about doing so. She fiddled with her fork and tried not to stare at Del's mouth.

"You didn't put something in it, did you?"

"What?"

"Well, you made two plates of food. It smells and tastes

amazing, and you haven't touched yours. So, I have to wonder, did you just poison me?"

Lola smiled and shook her head. She played with her fork.

"So?"

"What?"

"Why aren't you eating?"

Lola wasn't sure how to get out of answering. She was still thinking of a lie when she heard herself tell the truth. "I'm not used to eating with people."

"How come?"

"I was married. Before, I mean." She met Del's eyes and saw that this was not news to her. "You already knew that?"

"When I started looking for your attacker, I had to check you out. In case there was some old boyfriend or girlfriend or whatever I should look at. Most people don't fess up to nasty exes until it's too late."

"Oh." Lola's voice was small. "What else did you learn about me?"

Del's gaze was level. "Okay. Foster kid, married at eighteen. No record. No family. Dead husband. Car crash. Feds all worked up about Beckett's dirty money, which they never found. Wrote a book. Bought a house. That's it."

Lola nodded, her eyes unreadable.

"You mad?" Del sat back, tipping her beer into her mouth. *Shouldn't be drinking*, she thought. *Gotta be alert. That's why I'm here, right?*

Lola shook her head. "It makes sense, I guess, that you'd have to do that. I just never thought of it."

"Dr. Orrin Beckett."

"Yes." Lola's eyes skittered away, roamed the kitchen. Del saw her mouth tighten and was tempted to drop the subject. But curiosity drove her on. She told herself that she needed information to keep Lola safe. She knew it was a dirty lie and pressed on anyway.

"You were gonna tell me why you won't eat in front of me."

"Was I?" Lola's smile didn't touch her eyes. "Or are you interrogating me?"

Del met her gaze and said nothing.

"Well, I—Orrin—" She searched for words, licked her lips, started again. "He liked things to be a certain way. I wasn't allowed to eat in front of him. I mean, unless he told me to. I guess it sounds, maybe, a little weird." She hoped that Del would say, of course not. That's not weird. It's perfectly natural.

"Yeah. It sounds very fucking weird." Del drained her beer, and Lola rose to offer her another one. She wished her face didn't show her every feeling. How had Orrin come up? Why had she let it? She should have lied, said she'd already eaten, anything.

"I'll get it." Del waved her down, grabbed and opened her second beer, and kept her face as neutral as possible. She was pinging all over this—Dr. Beckett was a bad guy. She could tell. And Lola had been afraid of him, still was, maybe—did that mean he wasn't really dead, or was she that messed up? Her fear was still written all over her face, her posture, the quaver in her voice.

Del fought a flush of rage and frustration. Why do so many men want to hurt women? And why do so many women let them? She flashed on her father's face, contorted with rage, and adrenaline flooded her body. Darkness pushed into her gaze and narrowed it. She felt rather than saw Lola taking in her reaction, and she again masked her face.

Cool it, she told herself. Don't freak her out. You already did that, remember? Put on the badge and stop acting like an out-of-control kid. She took a deep breath. She pushed up her sleeves. She sipped and gazed out the back window. It wasn't working. She was still fired up, and she could feel Lola's antennae twitching. She was prey, always watching for danger. I don't want to seem like danger to her. Don't want to *be* danger to her.

Another sip. Shouldn't be drinking, she thought again. But anger was seeping through, spreading its black stain on her thinking, and the beer would help with that. I'll finish this one and be done. She pushed ahead, knowing it was the wrong time and not able or willing to stop.

"What else?"

"What do you mean?" Wide eyes, small mouth. Sitting very, very still. Playing dumb. Badly.

"What else? You said he liked things to be a certain way.

What things?" Del took a long draw from the bottle and eyed Lola over it, making her eyes crinkle like she was smiling.

"Oh." Lola shrugged with as much nonchalance as she could muster. "I don't know. Nothing very different from most people, I guess."

Del just looked at her.

"I'm not that easy to live with, I think. I do a lot of irritating things. Make a lot of mistakes. I mean…" She cleared her throat. "I don't mean to, of course. But I'm not that good at a lot of things."

"So he didn't like how you did things? Or what you did? I don't get it. What kind of things?"

It was a trap. Lola knew that, but she didn't know how to get out of it. She shook her head. "You know, things. He didn't like change. He didn't like inconsistency. Or mess. Or, I don't know," her hands waved around her head, "noise or dirt or upset, you know, stuff like that. He just wanted things to be done right."

She wished Del would look somewhere else, but she kept staring and drinking her beer. Her stomach was starting to hurt. The last thing she wanted to do was to talk about Orrin. Ever. Especially with Del, whose eyes were dark and snapping. She was electric, all lit up like she was mad. Lola swallowed hard. She wanted to leave, to hide, to stop the conversation, but she didn't know how.

"You married him when you were, what, eighteen? He was forty-something?"

A shrug. A vague shake of the head. Who knows? Who cares? It was clear that Lola wanted her to stop asking, but Del thought maybe she could probe a little further before Lola shut down completely. She would answer even if she didn't want to. She was *obedient*.

"What if things weren't 'right'?"

"What do you mean?"

"If you didn't do things right? If you didn't, I don't know, make his toast the way he wanted it, did he throw a fit? Did he lay on the ground and cry?" She pantomimed a toddler throwing a fit.

Lola forced a weak, polite laugh out of her mouth. She shook her head and started to get up, but she sat again when Del shook her head and waved her back down.

There was that obedience again. How long, she wondered as she watched Lola squirm, did it take him to break you? To get that automatic, mindless, rabbity fucking obedience drilled into you? He's been dead for months, but you're still obedient. If I told you to jump up on the table and dance, you would do it. You wouldn't want to, but you'd do it. She felt acid churn in her stomach, her throat. She put down her beer.

"Did he get mad?" Her voice was too loud, even over her too-fast breathing and the ragged pounding of her heart.

Lola shrugged, desperate to run away but trapped. *Stop it! Leave me alone! Stop asking questions!* She wanted to run, but she sat quietly, her hands fisted under the table. She tried to keep her breathing normal, but she felt her chest tightening. She knew she was bright red, but there was nothing she could do about it. She stared at the table and silently pleaded, Please stop. Stop asking questions. Please!

Her eyes flickered to Del's face, and something broke inside of Del. *I won't bully her.* She made sure that her voice was soft this time, that her face was a mask of calm. "We don't have to talk about it." Finishing the bottle, she rose and started rinsing off her dish. "It's okay to say you don't want to talk about it."

Lola tried to speak and found that her throat had closed. She finally stood and scraped her lasagna into the trash and put the rest of the pan in the fridge. She rinsed out Del's beer bottles and put them in the recycling bin in the garage. She took a moment alone there, waiting for her cheeks to cool and her eyes to clear. She hated feeling like she was always on the verge of falling apart. She hated letting Del see her as weak. She hated to think that Del looked at her the way that lawyer had, like she was a type. Like she was broken.

When she returned, Del was in the living room, plugging in the Christmas tree. They stood next to each other looking at the lights and ornaments.

"It's a little random, I know," Lola said, feeling defensive.

Orrin snorted in her ear. "A little random?"

"Huh? I think it's great." Del fingered a small snowman. "I haven't even gotten a tree, yet."

"Why not? Too busy hanging out with your neighbor?"

Del's smile made Lola's heart jump. In the gentle glow of the holiday lights, Del's face looked soft and vulnerable again, the way it had early in the morning. Lola wanted to touch Del's golden hair, look into her beautiful eyes, kiss her gorgeous mouth. She could almost taste Del's lips, feel her warm skin. She would smell like the sun, Lola was sure. She would smell like summertime. Knock it off, she chided herself. You're like a horny teenager!

She snorted with laughter at her inner monologue's word choice, startling both of them. Del was unsure what to think, but the laughter was infectious, and she was glad to see Lola relaxing.

"You have a great laugh," she whispered, and they both sobered.

Del could see that Lola was thinking of a graceful exit, and she decided to forestall it. She sat on the couch, patting the seat next to hers. Lola sat, and they gazed for a while at the tree.

"Lola—" she began, and she was interrupted by the sound of breaking glass. The alarm started wailing, and Del jumped into action. She pushed Lola to the floor, covering her and pulling her weapon at the same time. She saw no one, heard nothing but the scream of the alarm. Peering carefully out the front window, she yanked the plug that kept the tree lit. In the sudden blackness, she grabbed Lola's arm and dragged her to the front closet.

"Stay here," she hissed, and pushed her in and eased the door closed. She crept silently toward the back of the house.

She was just entering the kitchen when something exploded with a BANG! It was in the laundry room, maybe ten or twelve feet from her—she should go in the other direction.

Right now, she thought, as she stumbled, caught herself, and ran toward the explosion, I should grab Lola and take her out front and call it in. But her feet moved toward the laundry room as if of their own accord. She eased forward, peered in, and cleared the laundry room. The window was smashed in. There was something dark all over the floor, the walls, the ceiling. The dryer was dented. The washer too. Debris, everywhere. She edged over to the window. The yard was dark, and she turned on the floodlights but saw nothing. She cleared the rest of the downstairs, the upper floor and the garage. Finally, she called dispatch.

She pulled a pale, shaking Lola from the closet, dragged her out into the street, and held her until she saw the red-blue flash of a light bar coming at the house. Lola pressed her face into Del's chest. She was cold enough to chill Del's skin through her pullover. Del wanted to hold her until the shaking stopped, but she pushed her into a sitting position on the curb, pulling her hands free.

"Just sit there for a minute, okay? I need you to stay here. I'm sorry, I can't handhold you right now."

She wanted to take it back right away, but she didn't. She walked toward the patrol car instead. A rookie with wide eyes stood with his weapon drawn and shaking in his too-tight, nerve-rattled grip. *Great.* Gotta love rookies. Maybe his momma will let him start shaving someday soon. She tried out an easy smile on the kid.

Her thinking was all black and smoky, and she needed to be cool right now. She set her weapon on the ground and stepped back from it. She explained that she was on the job, and she let him pull out her badge himself. She was worried he would kill himself, Lola, and her, and maybe a couple of the neighbors, too. He might, if he didn't get calmed down. Finally, he seemed to believe her, and she talked him into holstering his weapon.

By the time the guards from the security company showed, two department techs were already in the house, taking pictures and scribbling in their notebooks. Del stood back and let everybody run things for the time being. She was on fire with impotent rage. He'd been right there, yards away from them. He'd been close enough to shoot, maybe close enough to chase down and beat into a lifeless pulp, and she had been useless. She'd been distracted and unprofessional and drinking, and she had been absolutely useless.

CHAPTER EIGHTEEN

Lola was alone in the darkness of the closet. Mrs. Simms used to put her in the closet. For a few seconds she wasn't sure if she was grown-up Lola or little girl Lola, and she had to recall Del's face to be sure. Little Lola didn't know Del, did she? So that meant that she was grown-up Lola, and Mr. Simms wasn't going to come and drag her out and hurt her. For the first time, she realized that Mrs. Simms knew that her husband would hurt Lola when he let her out of the closet and took her to her room. That it was all a setup. How many little girls did they do the same thing to?

"Why didn't I stop them from hurting anyone else?" She chewed her lip. "It's just like Tami Holden."

She knew she should be quiet, but she couldn't remember why. It was the same reason for being in the closet in the dark.

Del! Be quiet because of Del. That was it. Her side hurt, but she didn't pay attention. She tried to listen for Del, for any sound, but it was hard to hear over her own breathing and the high-pitched screech of the alarm. Then she wasn't able to hear anything. She sat down, feeling a little lost for a second. She dug her fingernails into her palms, trying to make sure she didn't go away—Del might need her.

How can I just sit here, she thought wildly, and leave Del alone out there? What if he hurts her, what if he kills her? She started to rise twice, stopping herself both times and easing back onto the cold floor. Her side hurt when she did that, but it wasn't important. It was a level two injury and could be dealt with later.

Del had a gun. Del was smart and strong. She knew what to do, and Lola didn't. If she made a mistake, if she did something that caused Del to get distracted or confused, Del could get hurt. She strained harder to hear and held her breath. She felt completely helpless and weak. She felt like a child. Tears ran down her face and chilled her.

When the door burst open, she shrank back, but Del's gentle hands pulled her up, Del's strong arms held her, and Del's warm face was in her hair. She heard Del's heart beat and felt her breathe, and she began to feel safe. They were moving. Del wanted to go outside. Lola couldn't understand why, but she didn't really care. She inhaled Del's clean scent and felt her warmth and solidity. She concentrated on feeling, smelling, hearing Del. And then the other police were coming, and Del pushed her away. Lola tried not to mind that.

Del waved at the young cop, and he guided Lola back inside and sat her on the couch. Del was on the phone, pacing around the living room, yelling at someone. Well, not yelling, but talking really loudly through clenched teeth. Lola shivered. Two men from the security company arrived, took one look at Del's face, and slinked back out the front door. Lola smiled sympathetically at their retreating backs.

Del wouldn't look at Lola. She hadn't looked at her once since she'd pulled her outside and pushed her onto the curb. She probably blamed Lola for this whole mess. And it was my fault,

Lola thought. I acted like an irresponsible nitwit and went online and got myself in trouble.

"Oh, Lolly," Orrin whispered, "what have you done now? Can't you do anything right? I tried to teach you, didn't I? But you're just not smart enough." He sounded regretful, pitying. Lola swallowed hard. She would not cry. She didn't have the right to cry. This whole thing was her own fault, and now everyone was upset because of her. Del must hate me, she thought. I can't blame her.

The young officer gave her a glass of water, and she pretended to drink some of it, mostly because his anxious, unlined face and thick brown curls reminded her of the twins. Funny, she hadn't thought of the boys in years, and they'd been on her mind a lot lately. They would be about this boy's age, maybe. Imagine, Curty and Donny being old enough to be police officers, college graduates, maybe even married! Of course, they wouldn't be Curty and Donny now, would they? Curtis and Donovan. Grown men, serious men with important work to do, and they wouldn't remember her. How could they? She'd been their babysitter only until they were, what, two-and-a-half? And then she'd met Dr. Beckett, and the twins's family had moved away, and then it had all been bad, bad, bad things until Dr. Beckett died. And now things were bad again.

Her arms throbbed from when Del grabbed her and pushed her into the closet. Del was so fast! Lola barely registered the sound of glass breaking and then she was under Del, in the dark, being dragged on the floor.

The boy who looked like Curty and Donny was asking her questions, and she tried to focus. There was writing on the wall outside. Did she know what it was? Had she seen anyone? Heard anything?

Lola shook her head and fought a wave of nausea. More writing? Was it the same word? She felt vague and dreamy, a state that she was loath to leave. But Del needed to see that she was okay, she could tell, and she forced herself to snap to attention. The glass in her hand was tilting, and she leaned down to put it on the floor

That movement reminded her that her side hurt, and she

looked down and saw blood all over her pajamas, all the way down one side of shirt and on the inside of her sleeve and down her pants all the way to the floor and on her sock, too. This reminded her of the kitties, of the blood and how they'd been slit open like purses, and she wondered if she could have been slit open like that and not have noticed it.

"Did I go away?"

The boy who was not Curty or Donny eyed her with wary concern.

"Did I go away?" Lola repeated the question, but then she remembered that the boy wasn't in the closet with her. Did she go away? She didn't think so. She had a little lost moment in the closet, but it was only a moment. And then the pain hit, and she felt woozy again. I'm falling asleep, she thought, but it was the hole. She couldn't go away, not now, not when Del was so upset.

"I fell apart when The Creep killed Buttons and Queenie," she explained to the young officer, who looked at her like maybe she was going around the bend. That was such a funny expression, going around the bend.

"Like it's a road," she said, which didn't improve the boy's faith in her sanity one bit, she saw that. "Which seems to suggest inevitability, doesn't it?"

"Ma'am," he said, his voice actually cracking, and Lola smothered a laugh. Wow, that hurt a lot, and she gasped.

"Maybe it's more than a level two," she explained. He didn't know what that meant, did he? She'd come up with the code when she was a little girl, as a way to determine how serious an injury might be—levels one through five, five for an injury that could maybe kill her. It was important to know how bad an injury was.

"Because of the laws," she said to the policeman. "Because of the bad secrets."

"Ma'am?"

"Don't ever," she whispered, shaking her head, "ever call any woman ma'am, okay? I don't care if she's a hundred and twelve, it's miss or miz, every time."

"Okay, m-uh, miss." He frowned at her, clearly unsure how to respond, and Lola realized that she wasn't going away after all. Well, she thought, how about that? I didn't go away. I didn't want to, and I didn't, so there.

When Del looked over and saw Lola bossing the rookie, she fought a smile that fell when she stepped closer.

"Holy shit, what the hell happened?" There was blood all over Lola, and Del cursed softly—how could I not have seen that, felt that?

I held her, Del thought, looking down. There were smears of drying blood on her jeans, her shirt. I didn't even notice she was hurt. I pushed her, made her sit down on the curb like a fucking perp.

"I'm sorry," she said, helplessly.

Lola made a face. "I forgot—it didn't hurt until just now."

"What do you mean?" Del was frowning at her, but Lola didn't know how to explain it.

"I don't know." She shook her head. "I'm sorry, Del, but it was just like that. I thought it was a level two. I still think it's a level three, at the most."

Del couldn't respond for a minute. *What the hell does that mean?* "Yeah, okay. Lift up your shirt."

"I didn't go away at all. I mean, I think."

"Okay." Del frowned at her. "Either you lift up your shirt, or I will. Which is better for you, Lola. You decide, okay?"

"I—Del, I don't want to. Please?" Lola gave the rookie a look, and he made an exasperated noise.

"So, officer, did you notice that the victim was bleeding out, or were you too busy sitting on your ass watching me do your job?" Del didn't bother to even look at him.

"Del!"

"What?" Del looked from the sullen rookie to the indignant, bleeding Lola. "What?"

"It's not the boy's fault! It's dark in here. And I didn't remember, or I would have said something. Be nice." She was breathless by the end.

Del shook her head. "Yeah."

Lola frowned. She looked a little lost.

Del barked at the rookie to call for an ambulance. She kneeled in front of Lola and pulled up her shirt, exposing a ragged, five-centimeter gash maybe two inches below the ribcage. It didn't seem all that deep, but it was still bleeding and would need stitches, at least. The gut was a dangerous area for a laceration, and she was reluctant to do anything at all. She looked up at Lola's face, trying to gauge her blood loss by her mental state.

"You don't know what happened?"

Lola shook her head. She actually looked embarrassed, and Del smiled in what she hoped was a reassuring way.

"Well, it doesn't look too bad, but I bet it hurts like hell."

"A bit."

Del narrowed her eyes. She'd bet the farm it hurt a hell of a lot more than a bit. Lola's breathing was shallow, her color bad. But her eyes were clear, and the bleeding was a trickle, not a flood. She stood, tucking the bottom of Lola's shirt into the bottom band of her bra to keep it out of the way. It was a strangely intimate thing to do. She'd never have done that with any other victim, and she couldn't meet Lola's eyes after that. Was it inappropriate? It was practical, that was all. She knew the EMT would need to be able to access the wound. She sent the rookie upstairs to find a clean towel, snatched it from him, and pressed it firmly against the gash.

"I know it hurts, but I want to stop the bleeding." She put Lola's hand on the towel. "Can you hold that? Huh?"

Lola nodded.

"Well, let's figure it out, okay? Let's figure out how you got that cut in case you need a tetanus shot or something." She didn't look to see if Lola responded.

She turned on the lights and looked around. There was a small trail of blood smears leading from the living room to the closet. "I'm gonna retrace my steps, see if I can figure it out."

Del barely had time to take a single step before saw a small flash of something shiny under the armchair the rookie had just vacated. She grabbed an evidence baggie as an automatic reflex and lifted the shiny thing. It was a Christmas ornament, a star maybe, and it was broken and bloodstained. She fished around under the chair with a pen and batted out the other half, also tinged with Lola's blood, and put both pieces in the baggie.

"Well," she said, turning to Lola, "this must have fallen off the tree, and when I tackled you, you must have landed on it. Sorry about that."

Lola was smiling. "Del," she giggled, "what are you going to do, arrest it?" She pointed at the baggie and really laughed, but that hurt.

"Oh. Oh, hmnn." Lola pressed her lips into a thin line.

"Whoa," Del said, leaning over and peering into her eyes. "Take it easy. Just breathe nice and easy for me. Can you do that? Just sit there for a minute and try to relax. I know it hurts, and I'm sorry, but they'll be here in a minute. I'm gonna flag them down."

Lola nodded, her eyes wide and dark, and Del escaped to stand in the doorway. She stood frozen, not wanting to let Lola out of her sight and not wanting to look at her. She'd never been squeamish, not ever, but looking at Lola's soft skin and seeing how fragile it was, how that little plastic thing had torn through it so easily, was disturbing. She didn't want to think about it. Didn't want it to have happened. She glanced over and saw Lola watching her and looked away again. Finally, an ambulance arrived. She waved them in and stood back. Lola called out to her from the gurney.

"Del?"

"I'll come see you in a bit, Lola. I have to stay here." She turned away, not wanting to see the hurt and disappointment on Lola's face. By the time she looked back, Lola's eyes were closed. Had she fainted? Del tried to assess the blood loss. A pint, maybe a bit more? Not enough to kill her.

She called Tom Phan and begged for his help. She called Jones. She called her captain, who surprised her by authorizing a full-scale investigation. Yes, she could have a forensics team. Yes, she could have Phan as a partner. Yes, she could do whatever she needed to. Yes, this was a priority. She hung up the phone. She was relieved to finally have some support and the tools she needed, but she was shaken by the fact that Captain Wonderbread, as she privately thought of him, considered the situation dangerous enough to warrant priority status.

She wandered the house, gloved and bootied now, not sure

what she was looking for. Something was off. She was missing something. Was it Lola? Was Lola playing her? It wouldn't have been hard to scratch herself with the ornament and draw attention to her injury. Getting hurt made her seem less like a suspect. Del played through the possibility, watching the scene unfold in her mind with Lola as the bad guy: she'd have had to bring the ornament with her, in her pocket or something. She'd have had to anticipate that Del would push her down or cover her. She tried to see it, but it just wasn't there. *Am I at all objective?*

No, she wasn't. But she was pinging all over, and it wasn't on Lola. Not right now, anyway. She let her gaze wander aimlessly over each room of the house as she made her way through it, taking it in as though she'd never been in Lola's home before. She noted the orderliness of each room, the worn look of the furnishings. Everywhere she looked, things were neat and cozy and organized. Nothing was out of place, but it wasn't compulsively clean, either. It was in Lola's bathroom that she got her first major thrill of hyperawareness—something was wrong in there. She turned in a slow circle and took in every detail. The rug was slightly askew, and she resisted the urge to straighten it with her foot. The curtain was hung at an angle. Maybe Lola had tried to do it herself. Del smiled faintly. There was a large print on the wall opposite the large, mirrored medicine cabinet. A Kandinsky, bright geometrics. It too was hung slightly askew. Everything in the room that Lola had put there was a little imperfect. Somehow, that was cute. Just like everything Lola did. Del again ran her gaze over the sink, the shower, the toilet, the print, the medicine cabinet.

Something was wrong, something was off. She slowed down even more, aware of her breathing, of her stomach growling, of the sound of her bootied feet slowly rotating on the tile. There! The shadow cast by the medicine cabinet on the wall behind it was off somehow. This was an older house, and the light came from the globe in the center of the room. In a newer house, there would be lights over the mirror. Del fought her first impulse, to reach up and see what was up there. Instead, she closed her eyes for a second. What could it be?

And then she knew. It was obvious, really. What would a

bad guy hide in a woman's bathroom? A camera. Of course. She pretended to nose around in Lola's medicine cabinet for a minute, long enough to give a surreptitious glance that confirmed her suspicion. She went from room to room again, finding a camera everywhere but in the upper hallway.

She was still considering what to do when Wonderbread called to tell her that she was off the investigation. She was both a witness and a personal friend of the victim, which made her a liability. Phan would lead, and Dominguez, a decent detective Del had worked with a few times, would be his partner. But he understood that she'd want to stay involved, which wouldn't be a problem unless she made it one. They would move Lola to a secure location. Did she want to handle that, go with her? Del fought disappointment.

What changed his mind? She filed the question away for later. Del's foolishness with Janet? He probably thought she and Lola were more than friends. Hell, half the department probably did. Whatever.

She shifted Lola's purse, which she'd grabbed on the way to the patrol car, to her other shoulder. Jesus, the thing was heavy. Ugly, too. How did Lola lug this monstrosity around? And why? She got the rookie to give her a ride to the hospital. Then, halfway there, she redirected him to the station and called Phan. Would he pick up Lola? And could they talk later?

***

"Just relax, miss, we'll take good care of you," the man in the ambulance said, and Lola closed her eyes. He was nice, the way he smiled at her and tried not to hurt her when he put the thing on her side. He saw that the thing under her was bumping her neck, and he fixed it, smoothed it away and nodded when she smiled her thanks.

"Okay? We'll be there in a few minutes, and you're gonna be fine, miss." His warm brown eyes crinkled at her, and Lola tried to smile again, but she couldn't remember how. She was a little woozy, and the lights were too bright, and she tried not to think too much about the blood and the kitties and the way Del had looked at her like she was broken again. There was some jostling, and then she was inside, and the air was close and still.

"Wake up, Lola."

Lola opened her eyes to see a man with piercing blue eyes staring at her. He wasn't the man who was nice and told her to relax. This man leaned closer and closer until he was only an inch away from her. Why was he doing that? He sniffed her hair and smiled a bad smile. Fear slithered through her, and she shuddered, which hurt her side. Lola could smell his toothpaste, his shampoo and some other smell, something familiar—she frowned. Who was this man? Why did he seem familiar?

"Hello, there. You remember me, don't you?"

It was The Creep! It was the man who attacked her and killed the cats! She tried to scream, but his hand was hard over her mouth by then. She made a small, useless noise against his palm and stared at his wide, hypnotic eyes in horror.

"I'm so glad we got this time alone together, my pretty little whore. I've missed you."

She tried to bite his hand, to scoot away, to twist her head to the side, but he was impossibly strong. Every movement hurt her side, but it didn't matter. That was a level two injury or maybe three, and this man wanted to make a level five injury, and she had to get away. She squealed and bucked uselessly.

"Knock it off!" He was angry, hissing at her. "Stupid bitch! Listen! Damn it, you stupid little slut, listen to me."

Her head was swimming, and she grasped for clarity. She was in an ambulance, and she was strapped to the gurney, and The Creep was alone with her. Where was the nice man? The Creep put his hand on her throat, and she tried not to cry. He was very, very angry. His eyes glittered, and she tried to convince herself that he wasn't going to kill her, that he wanted to talk to her, but her body didn't believe it.

She flailed uselessly against the restraints and his hands. She didn't want to go away. If she did, he would kill her. She was sure of this, and she knew with a surprising certainty that she wanted to live. She wanted to live, and she would not live if she went away. But the hole opened up, and it drew her away, and she was gone.

***

When Del finally got to the hotel just after dawn, she peered at Lola from the doorway, unsure of her reception. Lola looked shrunken, except for her wide, wide eyes. She looked drugged. Her face was white. She shivered but didn't seem to notice it. She was staring at nothing. Thank goodness, her eyes cleared when she noticed Del. She sat up straighter, licked her lips. Was she glad to see Del, or was she bracing herself?

"How you feeling?" Del was slow in closing the distance between them. Lola might be afraid of her, might associate her with the bombing. Might blame her for being useless. Might blame her for tackling her. Might be, probably was, had every right to be hurt about how Del had pushed her away and not even noticed that she was hurt and then ignored her and let her go off in the ambulance alone. And let her get stitched up alone and got Phan to bring her here.

Lola made a face. "Okay. Hurts a little."

"I'm gonna wash up. Out in a minute."

She took her time and stood facing the mirror without really seeing her reflection. Instead, she mentally reviewed the crime scene. The appliances were toast. The dark substance on the floor was mostly dirt and laundry detergent, but the pipe bomb had destroyed the linoleum. It looked like a nightmare in there, but there was no structural damage. There was no real damage done on the exterior, except the window and the paint, but it would be a bitch to paint over those letters. Sanding, cleaning, priming, repainting—thank God the house had been painted only months before. Otherwise the whole thing would be faded, and she'd have to paint the whole damn house to make it match. Or someone would. Lola could probably afford to hire a painter.

Del wanted to go over the house from top to bottom. How long had he been there, in the backyard? Why hadn't the motion-activated floodlights gone off? They worked. She'd checked. Had he been able to see them in the kitchen? There was a camera in there, of course, but had he been watching? Had he seen her down two beers in a few minutes? She couldn't drink, at least until this was over. It had been careless. Her reaction time had been slowed down, her senses dulled. She couldn't afford to be careless like that anymore. She hoped she'd covered her discovery of the cameras well enough. She'd told Phan about them, and she was hoping maybe the two of them could come up with a way to use them against the bad guy. Maybe. It was about time she got ahead of this guy. He'd been playing with Lola. The image of a cat toying with a little mouse danced in Del's head, and she shook it away.

Lola was asleep by the time Del came out, and Del didn't examine her relief over this too closely. She folded the rough bedspread over Lola, careful not to wake her, careful not to touch her.

Del left a note for Lola and jogged a couple of miles to South San Francisco, then rented a car and drove to a discount store. They would need a lot of supplies, and she went over her list with exhaustive care. Everything from medical supplies to ammunition to food to clothes. A laptop, backpacks, a duffel bag. She watched the charges add up and slid her credit card across the counter with a rueful smile.

She drove back, rubbing her eyes at a stoplight. She'd move Lola to a different hotel every night or two. Phan would go along with that. While he and Dominguez ran the official investigation, she would run her own. She'd set a trap for him. She'd draw him out and kill him. The fog in her head dissipated as she focused on this. She could see it as clearly as any movie, and she could feel her weapon, solid and steady in her hand. She could feel how she would regulate her breathing and focus her eyes and plant her feet wide apart.

She finally had a mental picture of him, though she knew it was hardly accurate. He looked like a cartoon of a bad guy: long lanky hair, comically large black glasses, a dark blue shirt and jeans, a leering grin on his twisted face, creeping toward what he thought was Lola. Del could see herself draw her weapon and look straight into his eyes. She wanted him to see her. She wanted him to know that he was going to die. Would he try to negotiate? Would he try to beg or bargain or trick her? She hoped so. She would like the chance to talk with him a little but recognized that this was unlikely. When the time came, she would end it. She was a good shot. It would only take one bullet.

I won't need a gun. She forced her fisted hands back on to the steering wheel. Killing him would be easy. She only had to picture three things: Lola's scared face, Lola's blood, and the black words painted on the back wall of Lola's pretty yellow house: "DIE WHORE." Yup, Del thought, as she pulled into the parking lot and started hauling bags up the stairs and into the room. I'll be able to kill him, no problem.

CHAPTER NINETEEN

When she opened her eyes early the next morning to see Del packing food and clothes into a couple of overnight bags, Lola was dismayed. That meant Del thought they would be hiding for a long time. Del seemed very preoccupied. What was she worried about? Was Del mad at her for sucking her into this mess? Surely Del had a life of her own, one that she was putting on hold in order to help out. Should she try to talk to her? Del might appreciate being let off the hook. But Lola hesitated. The last time she'd tried to let Del off the hook, it had made Del angry. She didn't want to do that again.

Lola murmured a good morning, and Del smiled at her briefly before returning to her packing. She chewed her lip, trying to decide what Del wanted her to do. Del was so quiet! Lola sat up and waited to see if Del would tell her what to do.

She handed Lola a small pile of clothes and things and nodded at the bathroom. "You first."

There was a package of plastic food wrap on top of everything else, and Lola frowned at it. "What's this for?"

"Your stitches need to stay dry."

"Oh." Lola nodded. "Thanks." Her side hurt a little when she got up, when she undressed, when she leaned over to turn on the water. Maybe Del was annoyed with her for getting hurt. Who else but Lola would fall on a Christmas ornament and need stitches? Orrin was right, she was a clumsy cow.

Lola felt like a stranger in her own skin, showering in this impersonal place, her whole middle wrapped in plastic. She smelled different, because of the soap and shampoo. Even her mouth tasted different, because of the new toothpaste. She slipped back into the bedroom, and Del passed her without a word, holding her own bundle of clothing and sundries. Again, Lola couldn't help but worry that Del was mad at her. Maybe she wished she could go home. Maybe she felt that this was all Lola's fault for going online. She probably thought Lola was stupid and reckless and promiscuous. Maybe Orrin had been more right than Lola had cared to admit. Maybe she was too stupid and selfish to do anything right. It was starting to look like Del thought so, anyway. Lola tried to push these thoughts away. They didn't do any good.

Maybe Del wasn't even mad. Maybe she was just tired. She'd been busy while Lola had slept. There was a brand-new laptop charging on the other bed and a pile of plastic bags and tags and wrappers on the other. An empty duffel bag and several bottles of water sat alongside an assortment of snack foods on the floor between the beds. She packed the food and waters in the duffel, leaving it on the floor. Hopefully that was what Del wanted. All of this stuff had cost plenty of money, and she'd find a way to pay Del back for it. How, she asked herself, will you pay her back for putting her life on the line for you?

She tidied up, made the beds carefully so as not to disturb the laptop, and tried to find a hair band in her purse, which she found on the floor near the door. Del must have grabbed it, she thought, or had someone bring it. She pawed through it and was appalled by the amount of stuff she'd left in it. She grabbed one of the empty plastic bags—apparently they were outside of the city—and started cleaning out the garbage.

There were tissues and gum wrappers and breath mints and empty lip balms and cough drops. Three of Orrin's lists. A broken watchband Orrin had told her to get repaired two days before he'd kicked her out. A receipt for the vet in Folsom where she got Buttons and Queenie. She hesitated over that one, then pushed it into the garbage bag. She went through the small pile of things worth keeping—her wallet, a few odds and ends, her old music box. She rubbed the top for luck, and it was smooth as glass under her finger. *How many times did I rub this thing for luck?*

For nearly two decades, Orrin was The Enemy. But once upon a time, long ago and far away, he was her best and only friend. She had loved him, and she had lost him a long time ago. But there had been, maybe, a tiny part of her that had been waiting for her friend Dr. Beckett to come back and smile at her and tell her that everything was going to be like it was before. That he would be nice again and be her friend again.

Dr. Beckett only really died for her when Orrin died in that car crash, and she hadn't mourned him yet. It surprised her how much it hurt to know that Dr. Beckett was never coming back. He was gone forever, now. She opened the box and refrained from pulling out her treasures. This was silly. With everything that was going on, pawing through her old things was a waste of time and energy. But in that tiny box was her whole history. She'd taken off her wedding ring months before and put it in the box. *Almost my whole life so far*, she thought, *nearly the whole first half of my life fits into a three-inch box.* She closed the box and put it back into her much-lighter purse. She set the trash in the tiny bin and sat on the bed and waited.

***

When Del stepped out of the bathroom, hair dripping on her neck, she saw Lola turn expectantly to her and suppressed a frown. She was feeling riled up and had been ever since she'd come back into the room. Lola had been crying in her sleep, tears running silently from her eyes, and Del had wanted to gather her in her arms and promise her that everything would be all right. She couldn't do that, she had to focus. She had to stop thinking like a lovesick idiot and start thinking like a cop again. How had this woman become so important to her? When had this happened?

She felt a sudden and unwelcome rush of resentment toward Lola and wasn't sure why. Irrational though it was, she was angry with Lola for putting herself in danger, and at herself as well for being so careless. Who in the world trolls the Internet looking for a date? Predators, that's who, predators and stupid, naïve, silly little girls. Grown women know better. Grown women know that they shouldn't go traipsing off to meet a stranger at night in the city by themselves. She felt Lola's eyes on her and twitched her shoulders. She could see herself turn and grab and shake Lola till her teeth made music. For a second, this image was so vivid that it almost seemed like a memory.

She took a deep breath. Where'd *that* come from? *This isn't Lola's fault. I'm not mad at her, not really. I just feel—what?* She couldn't name it. But it made her restless and edgy, and she wished she could go for a run or something. Anything to work off some of her tension. She didn't want to snap at Lola and hurt her feelings. She shook herself back to the present, to Lola watching her in the hotel room they'd fled to because someone wanted to hurt her.

"Do you think you could sleep a little?" Lola asked, her eyes warm and concerned. She stood up and stepped toward Del. Her voice was tremulous. She was being careful. She'd noticed Del's edgy mood, and it had made her nervous. Del didn't want to think about that. She looked around the room and shook her head. Lola had cleaned up.

She'll do that, Del thought, she'll clean up after me and cook for me and take care of me. She's been somebody's little wifey forever, and that's all she knows how to be. Do I want that? Does she want that? Does she even know what she wants? She's a child. She has no ability to take care of herself or to decide anything. She's looking to me to figure this all out for her. Again, she backed away from her thoughts. There was too much going on that she didn't want to think about. Dark clouds swirled through her thinking and got darker and darker. She was losing it, just when she needed to *not* lose it.

"Del, maybe you could sleep a—"

"Some of us don't get to just go nighty-night when we feel like it," she shot out.

Lola backed up a step. Her gaze dropped. "I'm sorry." She started to hug herself, but she must have bumped her cut, because she went white and dropped her hands to her sides.

Del rubbed her forehead. "Listen," she began, "sometimes I get a little wound up. And right now, I'm pissed off. Not at you. People snap at other people when they're pissed off. It doesn't mean anything. I don't want to do that—"

"Then don't." Lola's quiet voice cut off Del's words, and Del stared at her.

"What?"

"Don't. Don't snap at people. At me. I mean, if you really don't want to."

Del barked a short laugh. "Well, okay, then. There you go, problem solved." She rubbed her hands together in an all-clean motion and laughed again.

"Don't laugh at me." Lola's voice quavered. "I mean it. You aren't some helpless child. You have a temper. So, fine. You don't have to give in to it. You can decide how to handle your feelings like a grown-up instead of a spoiled brat. You don't get to yell at me." Her voice rose and grew sharp. "You don't get to call me names. You don't get to tell me what to do, and you don't get to—"

Her voice broke, and she backed away again, sitting on the bed with a plop. It must have hurt like hell, because she gasped and held her body stiff and straight. She closed her mouth and looked deliberately away from Del.

Del stood frozen in front of her, unable to move or speak.

"I'm sorry," Lola whispered. She was still pale, her eyes dark.

Del was rooted to the floor until she forced herself to move and squat in front of Lola.

She waited until Lola's eyes met hers. "I'm sorry. Okay?"

Lola nodded.

"You're right, you know." Del was glad that her voice was cool and smooth. No shaking. No emotion. Cooled off. The way it should have been all along. She stood back up.

Lola shook her head, but Del stopped her with a gesture.

"No, what you said about not giving in to my temper." She drew a deep breath. "I say things I shouldn't say. I expect everyone to jump when I snap my fingers. I like being in charge." Her eyes dropped to Lola's.

"You don't say."

Del grinned her daddy's slow grin, and Lola's answering smile was a real one. She was so beautiful when she smiled like that. Del held her gaze and saw a flush stain Lola's cheeks. A fissure of energy ran between them.

Del heard herself saying, "We're all wrong for each other, you know that, right?"

Lola nodded. Her wide eyes were fixed on Del's, and Del felt like she was on fire.

"Neither one of us is ready for this. You're a victim, you're a witness. It's inappropriate."

Lola nodded again. Her eyes were wide, her mouth, soft and inviting. Del saw her cheeks flush even brighter and her breath quicken. She was oriented toward Del—her curved thighs, her generous hips, her lush breasts. She stood, her whole body an invitation.

Del swept across the small space between them and crushed Lola's mouth with her own. She felt Lola flinch in shock and then soften and slowly, slowly start to kiss her back. Her mouth searched and probed and devoured Lola's, and she pressed against Lola's body with her own, careful to avoid her hurt side.

God, she was soft! Her skin was smooth and warm and inviting. Del could feel Lola's pulse threading in her throat. Her chest rose and fell quickly, and her breath was sweet in Del's mouth. Del's hands were on Lola's face, her still-wet hair, her damp shoulders, and her warm, round hips. She felt Lola press back against her, her hands clutching Del's shirt, and she groaned again. *Stop!* she yelled at her body. It ignored her and kept kissing and pressing into Lola's yielding warmth.

Lola's hands roamed lightly, tentatively, up around Del's shoulders, her neck, into her hair, and Del exhaled loudly. She grabbed at the slippery fabric of Lola's shirt and struggled with the buttons. The bra Del had bought was too small, and Lola's breasts strained against the fabric. Del kissed the warm bounty of skin in her cleavage and let her tongue flick at the deep crease with greedy hunger. Her hand grazed something, the bandage on her side. A flash of anger distracted her for a moment. Was she in pain? She glanced at Lola's face, but she seemed to be okay.

Del wanted all of this flesh, every sweet inch of it. She wanted her naked. She wanted to own her and see her exposed and vulnerable to her alone. The underpants she'd bought for Lola were plain white cotton, unbeautiful, utilitarian, but she wanted to see them. She wanted to rip them off and tear them into pieces. She was trying to slow herself down, to cool off, to think this through, but Lola's skin was singing out to her— touch me, kiss me, own me, explore me, make me your own. She shook with desire. She was dizzy, drunk on need. Lola's mouth was open and soft, her skin rosy and warm. She wants me too, Del realized. She wants this as much as I do.

This realization erased what little self-control she'd managed to hold onto up to that point. She launched herself at Lola, kissing her breasts, pulling Lola's body toward her own, her hips grinding into Lola's. She pushed her thigh between Lola's, forcing her legs apart. Lola's whole body immediately tensed. Her eyes flew open. This time they were too flat, dull with fear. Del froze and slowly pulled back, wiping her mouth with the back of her hand. Her heart bounced painfully against her ribs. What was wrong? This, all of it—God, it was totally wrong. It was predatory. Unprofessional. Inappropriate. Just *wrong.* Lola pulled her shirt closed, and Del turned away.

Lola reddened, ashamed of her childish reaction. She'd been so drunk on Del's kiss one moment that she'd hardly known where she was, and the next moment, she'd panicked. She wasn't sure why. She wanted to explain to Del that she'd liked the kissing, that she'd never felt so alive, ever, that she wanted Del to kiss her again, that she hadn't meant to pull away. But she didn't know how, and Del's back was to her. She was looking out of the scummy window.

"Del?" she forced the tremor from her voice. "I'm sorry. I don't know what happened. I—"

Del turned around, and Lola wanted to cry. Del's face was contrite and somehow also blank and politely neutral. "No, you didn't do anything wrong, Lola. I'm the one who should apologize. I don't know why I did that. It was totally inappropriate. I've never crossed the line like that before, and I'm sorry. It won't happen again."

"But—" Lola watched Del stride out of the room and let the door slam behind her. Her body tingled with longing and her mind with fear and shame. "What's wrong with me? What's wrong with me?"

CHAPTER TWENTY

Del strode around the parking lot, struggling to keep her emotions in check. She'd lost control and taken advantage of a vulnerable, confused, frightened woman who clearly didn't know her own mind and was, Del reminded herself, both traumatized and in danger. She needed to focus on that and on nothing else.

There was no doubt in her mind that the attacker and the cat killer and the pipe bomber were the same person and that he would try to get to Lola very soon. Whether he wanted to kill or kidnap her was a question Del wanted to answer and couldn't. What was his game? Why had he put cameras all over the house? What was he hoping to see?

She called Phan and jumped in without preamble. "Bad guys follow patterns. They fixate, start out friendly and nice and then escalate."

Phan grunted. "This guy doesn't follow any kind of pattern. He seems completely disorganized, but his forensic countermeasures are fucking exemplary."

"Why 'whore'? All three times, that's the only consistent thing."

"Yeah. And what about the cameras?" Phan made an exasperated noise. "Is he a peeper, or is it something else?"

"How can we use them?"

They debated various options for using the cameras, but each involved getting approval from the captain, who was unlikely to approve any of their ideas.

"So," Phan muttered, "we wait."

"Unless there are exigent circumstances," Del said, and Phan snorted a laugh.

"Right. Unless there are exigent circumstances."

"I'm not convinced that Beckett's definitely dead. And where's the money?"

Phan's voice was soft. "And who else is looking for it? The partner?"

"Why didn't the Feds track him down?"

"Why," his voice was almost a whisper, "didn't they hit Lola harder?"

Del didn't have to look up to know that Lola was watching her from the window. "Yeah," she whispered back. "What am I missing here?"

***

Lola was quiet as they packed up and moved. Her eyes followed the black weapons duffel when Del took it out of the closet and out to the car before coming back for Lola and the rest of the stuff. She didn't ask any questions, though, so Del didn't have to lie. She also didn't ask where they were going, but she did shove her credit card at the desk clerk of the next hotel. Del grabbed it and slid it back at her.

"Not yours."

Lola frowned, about to protest, and Del explained, "What if he's tracking you by them?"

Lola put away the card without a word.

Del checked the rooms before gesturing Lola into the one further from the stairwell and heading into her own. If Lola had any comment about the change to adjoining rooms, she didn't share it. Del dropped her stuff on the chair, used the bathroom and opened the door between them to find Lola curled up on the bed. She left the door open and lay down for a moment on the rough bedspread on her own king-sized lumpy mattress. I'll rest until Phan gets here, just for a minute. She closed her eyes and was gone.

In her dream, she saw her daddy's face. He had been handsome once, tall and blond and dimpled. He was, her momma said, an even better version of Robert Redford. Women always looked at him with hunger in their eyes, especially Momma, and he had a slow, knowing smile that made just about every woman swoon.

Little Del followed him around, copying his swagger and his smile and his rich, warm laugh. She adored him, wanted to hear him laugh and feel his giant hand rough up her curls. When he looked at her with pride, she was fit to bust with happiness. When he called her his best pal, she felt she must be the happiest kid in the world.

She would perch happily in his lap, see the sun shining through the golden hairs on his strong arms, feel his legs, solid beneath her. She would feel the rumble in his chest as he spoke and laughed. She could smell his cologne, his sweat, the beer on his breath. Not a sour smell, not like later, but a warm, robust smell. Back then, he was her superhero, golden and shining and powerful and good—the most important person in her world.

Things changed somewhere around the time Del turned seven. Her daddy lost his job for reasons Del never knew. He sat around brooding, and he was easily irritated by her, by Momma, by everything. She didn't know what she was doing wrong and tried harder and harder to get his attention. One day he casually backhanded her for walking in front of the television, and she felt a shift inside of her. This was not her daddy, this sullen man who smoked and drank endlessly and never smiled or said anything that wasn't a grunt or a holler. That daddy was gone, and this man who looked like him was a stranger. She hated this man for taking her daddy away. She watched him for signs that he'd turn back into his old self, but they didn't show.

The sheriff beat on the door one morning, and that made Daddy really mad. They moved into a trailer park, where he started drinking even more. He became grimy and bearded and bloated and sour. Her momma, who had always seemed little more than a dim shadow attached to Daddy, grew even more brittle and thin and worn. She took to wearing bright makeup and tight clothes and high heels. She got a job in a bar and was gone most of the time.

Daddy had by that time stopped even pretending to look for work and would sit on a lawn chair in the gravel center of the trailer park with a rowdy group of men Del watched with wary eyes. None of them worked. None of them took care of the packs of kids who ran around in the dirt. The men never seemed to move unless it was to cuff one of the kids or kick at a dog or grab at a woman. They started the days bleary and sullen and grew loud and raucous as afternoons yielded to evenings.

Del sometimes hunkered down under the rotting wooden steps of what her momma jeeringly called the veranda—a thin strip of tacked-together plywood scraps that hung off the side of the trailer. She hid and watched and listened as the men her momma called "the peanut gallery" shared rude comments about the girls and women in the park. What had happened to her daddy? What had she done to make him into such a hateful thing? She grieved for him, though she didn't know the word. She ached for things she could not name—affection, kindness, approval? She ached for the hero she'd once worshipped.

Late one night, she watched from under the veranda when Momma came home from work and tried to get Daddy to come inside. He waved her off, and she shook her head and asked when he was "gonna start being a man again and get a job."

Del gasped in shock. What was she doing?

Del's momma continued, her bony, scarlet-taloned finger drooping in his face. "You can't even get it up, you fat pig! Show me you're a man. Show me!"

Momma's sharp words sounded like a mosquito's buzzing, and Del shook her head, covered her ears. Her daddy smiled his old, easy smile. Del's eyes lit up, and a small spark of hope flared in her chest. Was he back? Was he coming back, finally? Her breathing was too loud, and she moved her hands to cover her mouth and quiet it.

Slowly, casually, Daddy rose, turned to face his pals, and muttered something she couldn't hear. There were a few quiet chuckles, and Daddy hitched up his pants, which immediately sagged again under the weight of his protuberant gut. He smiled before he slapped Momma twice, quick, almost careless slaps. The men burst into jeering laughter, and Daddy waited for Momma to lift her head. He again muttered something over his shoulder that made his friends cackle, and then Daddy swung around to face Momma again.

This time he backhanded her hard enough to make a loud cracking sound and send her to the ground in a boneless heap. For a moment, Del thought Momma had disappeared, leaving behind only her clothes and shoes. There was a moment of silence. Del held her breath and saw movement in the heap and let the breath out with a sigh. Daddy's gaze drifted over, and Del realized that Daddy knew she was there all along and didn't care. She let out a sob, and Daddy just hitched his pants up again. He stood for a moment before easing back into his chair with an ugly laugh that was echoed and amplified by the jeers and howls of his cronies. Del curled her hands over her face, unable to face Daddy and unable to look away.

Del watched her momma struggle to her feet. Momma lit a cigarette, blew blood-sprayed smoke into the air, and turned to stagger over to their trailer. Del ducked her head as her mother passed over her, listening to her stiletto heels dig into the spongy wood of the steps and the veranda. A drop of blood fell between the boards and splattered onto Del's knee. She waited until Momma had wrangled the door open and gone inside to grab a handful of gray dirt and rub it on the blood.

She'd seen Daddy and Momma fight before, but this was different. They weren't a couple of drunken lovers wrangling in that wrestling-match-lovemaking-fighting-flirting way she'd become used to. They *hated* each other, something she'd never realized before. Why? How had that happened? She was sure that it was her fault, though she couldn't have said why. She felt guilty and scared and in the way. If she'd never been born, they maybe would still love each other. If she were a good girl, instead of a "mouthy little brat" as Momma sometimes called her, maybe they wouldn't hate each other so much.

Del held her breath and waited until the men had turned their attention to one of the scantily clad teenagers sauntering by. It felt like there was a rock in her chest, and she wiped her face dry before she snuck out from under the steps and crept into the trailer. Daddy would never see her cry; she swore it to herself in that moment, and it was a vow she never broke. Not when Daddy broke her arm, not when Momma threw a bottle at her and it cut her head open. Not ever. She was cold inside and still, and she knew suddenly that someday she would be big enough to leave this ugly place and these ugly people, and when she did, she would never look back.

It was dark inside, and she crept on cat's paws past the living room and the strange shadows in there to the hallway, dancing her fingertips lightly, soundlessly along the smooth, notched paneling on the wall. She hesitated before entering her parents' room. It was a sacred place, somehow. A place where she didn't belong. She smelled smoke and heard a tiny squeal of mattress springs. Don't be a chicken, she scolded herself. She's hurt, so see if she needs anything. A good person takes care of somebody who's hurt.

It was the first rule she recited to herself, but not the last. Over the next few years, she would develop a list of things a good person does, a code of ethics that would define her as an adult, but she didn't know that then. All she knew then was that the rule felt right, sounded right in her head. She squared her shoulders and pushed open the accordion style door with a steady hand.

"Ma'am?"

Silence. The room smelled like smoke and perfume and sweat and beer. Momma seemed broken, hunched over on the mattress that sagged almost to the floor under Momma's bony hips. With her black boots and black stockings, she seemed to float in the dark like a wraith. She was a thing that existed only within the cloud of smoke that encircled her bowed head. A swirl of teased blond curls made a denser cloud inside the smoke, and it almost looked, there in the darkened room, like there was no solid part of Momma, just smoke and then hair and then some unknowable, untouchable, denser cloud of anger and blood and vodka.

"Y'all right?"

Silence.

"Ma'am?"

"Whadda you want, huh?" Her mother finally tipped her head up and blew a stream of smoke her way, but Del had long since learned how to duck away from that. "Wanna rub it in? Maybe y'all wanna take a picture?"

"No, ma'am." Del wanted to make things better, but she didn't know how.

"Listen, here, girl." Her momma's watery gray eyes skittered around Del's face. "Ain't no man on this earth better'n your daddy, you hear?"

An hour earlier, this statement would have made Del swell with gladness. Now it was just a bunch of words that meant nothing. She nodded. "Yes, ma'am."

"Yeah. Damn straight."

Del waited for more, thinking her momma must have some kind of answer for how things had gotten broken. Maybe, some small part of her dared to hope, it hadn't been Del's fault, after all. Then she thought, a good person doesn't think about herself when somebody else is hurt—this became one of the rules too.

"And one more thang." Momma's voice was slurred—when she drank, she sounded like Nana, who'd lived with them in Texas until her death. "That's my man. He's mine."

Del frowned, nodded.

Momma fixed her gaze, steadying her voice and narrowing her eyes. "Y'all remember that, Adele Savannah Mason, you hear me?"

"Yes, ma'am."

"You better, girl. I'll whup your ass—you got that? Huh? I'll whup yo' narrow ass, you don't watch it."

Del backed away. Momma's face was twisted with rage and wildness and smeared with blood and makeup. Del felt and tried to hide a wave of revulsion, but she must have hidden it badly, because Momma popped up quick and grabbed Del's shoulders and shook her hard and pushed her. Del hit the wall with the back of her head and fell onto her bottom with a thump. Momma snorted and again sat and hung her head, her straggly hair covering her bloody face.

Del scrambled up and backed away quicker now. Sometimes, she told herself, a victim isn't a good person. So you don't turn your back on the victim, either. But you don't treat them bad. Another rule.

By the time she was ten, there were over fifty rules. She wrote them down in her tight, neat block letters in a little notebook given her by a teacher she didn't remember. She had memorized them by then, of course, and it was only a few months later that she threw the notebook away. She'd added a final rule: the rules are a part of a good person and can never be forgotten or ignored.

At fourteen, she was looking for a way out and met a woman who let Del stay with her until Del tried, unsuccessfully, to seduce her. After a few months on the Fresno streets, she got hauled in by a police officer who caught her sleeping in a park late one night. He shook her awake, arrested her without trying to mess with her, and tossed her in the back of the patrol car. On the ride to the station, he advised her, not unkindly, to get her shit together.

He seems like a good person, she thought. She studied the back of his freckled, balding head. He turned to the right just a bit, and she saw in a narrow alley the flash of movement that had caught his eye. He muttered into his little radio in secret police code, and she felt a flip in her stomach. She didn't want to be in the back of a police car. She wanted to be in the front. She wanted to talk the secret code into the little radio and drive through the dark streets with a swiveling head and eyes that took in every detail of the ghettoscape. She wanted to see the little movement and know what it meant and how to keep things safe for the good guys. She never knew the cop's name, but she never forgot him, either. When she put on her uniform for the first time after the academy, she felt the same flip in her stomach and knew that she was one of the good guys, finally.

Her dream circled back to that night at the trailer park, again and again, and her daddy's laugh was still sounding in her ears when a knock at the door startled her awake. She paused to grab her weapon before she heaved off the bed and loped to the door.

"Crap, it's dark out?"

Phan's face, distorted through the peephole, was a welcome sight.

***

Lola debated whether or not to go into Del's room and finally decided to duck her head in. The two detectives were hunched over the small table tucked into the corner of the room, and Tom Phan smiled at her to enter. He was handsome, tall and tanned and sporting an engaging smile. His warm brown eyes smiled at her and searched her at the same time—maybe it was a cop thing.

"Detective, it's nice to see you," she heard her own voice saying. "Thank you so much for helping me like this."

"Inspector Mason and I were just going over the physical evidence from your house, Ms. Bannon—what there is of it. Would you like to have a seat?"

Lola smiled and nodded. "Please, call me Lola." *Inspector?*

She perched on the edge of the bed. Del's bed, she thought, picturing Del asleep, her tanned skin golden against the white sheet. She looked away from the bed and gazed at the two detectives. Inspectors, she corrected herself.

"All right, Lola," he said easily. "But only if you promise to call me Tom."

She nodded.

"How are you, Lola? I understand you got hurt the other night."

"It's nothing. A few stitches, that's all."

Del finally looked at her and said, "There's not much here. I wish we could tell you he left fingerprints or a neighbor saw him or something, but no."

Lola nodded. "Okay."

So, she thought, all business. She forced her eyes away from the tempting sight of Del's long, muscular limbs, her solid torso, her angular face. She kept pushing her curls back in impatience as she talked with Tom. She must need a haircut. Lola wanted desperately to see Del after that haircut, with her long neck stretching above her broad shoulders and her long arms and her mysteriously undefined breasts.

What did she look like underneath the jeans and polo? Somehow, the way she kept her body under wraps made it even more enticing. Lola would like to be the one person who knew what Del looked like without the men's jeans and a big, square shirt. Her pulse was racing, and Lola forced herself to look at Tom and try to concentrate. He was watching her, and Lola hoped he didn't know what she'd been thinking.

"So, Lola, do you mind if I ask you some questions?"

She shook her head and tried to keep her mind off Del for the next two hours. He asked her about each incident, taking her slowly through every detail, following up on her every impression.

He asked her about Orrin and his brother, his partner, his girlfriend, and his money. He asked about friends and lovers, pressing when she insisted there'd been no one in her life for the past twenty years but Orrin and his family, and before them, only foster homes and social workers and teachers.

Somehow, he managed to pry into every facet of her life without seeming to intrude. Lola listened carefully to Phan and answered his questions with thoughtful care. Phan developed a rhythm, and Lola found herself responding to it. She imagined that cops did that all the time with witnesses and suspects. The rhythm lulled people, calmed them, helped them feel safe, allowed them to remember and reveal more. It was smart.

Finally, Phan closed his notebook and thanked Lola for her help. She smiled, visibly relaxing, and thanked him back.

"Well," Del said wearily. "I can't think of anything else, can you?"

He shook his head. "But we're still working in the dark."

Del frowned in agreement. "So, how do we fix that?"

Lola saw her tiredness and wanted to say or do something to

help. She'd been toying with an idea, one she knew Del would hate, and she decided to share it anyway.

"Um," she began, avoiding Del's gaze and focusing on Tom, "I was thinking. I mean, you guys are obviously the experts, of course, and I don't know what the best way is, and you do."

Tom just looked at her.

"So, anyway, what I was thinking was, you know, he wants to get to me, right?" No answer, but Lola saw Del sit back in her chair and narrow her eyes. Tom flicked a glance at Del but nodded at Lola.

She rushed, "Why not use that? Why not throw him off balance, draw him out?"

Del's head was shaking, but Lola continued, "Tom, the department will tolerate a certain amount of time, right? I mean, if we keep running around from one hotel to another, he won't be able to find me, maybe, but eventually, I'm going to have to go home. Del's going to have to go back to her job, her real job, and you'll get a more urgent case. If he doesn't kill me in the next week or so, the department will figure he's moved on. Your boss will say he's lost interest, and he'll cut the funding. Then Del will get in trouble, because she'll argue with her boss, and he'll just wait a little while and then kill me. Or he'll really move on, and then some other woman will be dead."

She paused. She'd never said so many words at once, and she was exhausted from the effort of not looking at Del, who'd risen abruptly from her chair and was standing at the window. "Use me, please."

CHAPTER TWENTY-ONE

"As what," Del spat out, "live bait?"

She whirled around, stopped, and forced herself to calm down. When she continued again, her voice was low.

"Phan," she began, "it's not an option." She was prepared to fight but saw that Phan agreed with her.

"No," he replied levelly, "of course not."

He turned to Lola. "Lola, I appreciate your courage. I understand that this—" he waved around the room, "isn't a fun lifestyle. That you're tired of being scared and being chased out of your own home. None of this is fair, and of course you want to get back to your normal life. I also suspect that you're concerned about Mason, about Del, getting hurt."

Del started to protest, and he shook his head. "You might

not like it, but she's obviously worried that you'll cowboy up and get yourself killed. Right?"

Lola shrugged a reluctant yes, and Phan continued, "Lola, I'm here to keep the situation as controlled as possible. Del can't go on a tear," he eyed Del, "and neither can you. This guy has already shown us that he's unpredictable and dangerous, and we have to get a step ahead of him. Not by staking you out in the forest like a little rabbit and waiting for him to show up with his stomach growling."

He waited for Lola to smile at his analogy. "Del and I will find him. That's our job. Your job is to stay here, watch TV, eat takeout and listen to us. Okay?"

Lola nodded. After a few minutes of small talk, Phan asked her for privacy. She nodded, repeated her thanks, and left the room.

"You handled that well," Del commented in a quiet voice.

Phan met her eyes. "She's too attached to you, Mason. And you're way too distracted by your personal feelings." He sat back.

"I know," Del agreed, biting back a reflexive argument.

He raised his eyebrows. "I thought you'd fight me on that one."

She shrugged and waited.

"Did you tell her about the cameras?"

"No reason to."

"You don't think she has a right to know?"

Del waggled her hand in a maybe gesture. "When things are settled down, when she's not scared anymore. What's the point of creeping her out? Besides, we're playing it like we didn't find them, and she can't lie for shit. So if we tell her, and he knows we know, because we told her—"

"How would he find out from her? How could it matter if he's gotten to her?"

Del made a face. "Listen, I'm not as objective as I should be, okay? But I do realize there's a possibility she's dirty and she knows or suspects who this is and isn't telling us. And this is all some kind of setup for who the hell knows what. I just figure there's no payoff to telling her until we know more."

"Pretty damn cynical," Phan said, shaking his head. Del was about to defend herself when he smiled. "Smart, too."

She smiled back at him. "Is that a compliment?" She faked a heart attack, and he laughed.

"You don't completely suck as a partner," he admitted with mock grudging, and she smiled again.

"See? Was that so hard?"

"My turn," he said and batted his eyelashes at her.

"I'm glad you're here."

"You're too kind," he intoned in a Southern belle's coo.

She ignored that. "You're smart," she said, "a good listener. You don't have a big ego. You keep your cool. You have a good mind for sifting through a mountain of information and knowing what's important. I noticed that on that domestic. And again tonight." She hesitated. "But I think maybe you wish you had someone else with you on this."

She saw him consider before answering. "I like working with you. I think we have similar styles. But you're an alpha, and so am I. And that might not work out too good. We both like to be in charge, and I need you to know that I'm in charge, here."

"Well," she answered slowly, trying not to get defensive. "You may be right. But I don't wanna have a pissing contest with you. I know where I stand. This is your investigation. I happen to be involved because the vic is my friend, but you're the big dog. You won't have any problems with me." She held his gaze and tried to project sincerity.

Whether it worked or not, he nodded and rose. "Okay, enough mutual admiration," he said, "call me if you need anything. I'll talk to you tomorrow."

"Thanks, Phan."

"Yeah," he said, opening the door and cocking his head to the side. "Mason?"

She met his eyes with a questioning look.

"No solo flights," he said with a grim smile, and she knew he didn't believe her. She couldn't be mad. In his shoes, she'd have the same concerns. She nodded as he let himself out without looking back.

"You hungry?" she called, and walked in to find Lola perched on the edge of her bed, grinning at her with a guilty face. She held up half of a chocolate bar. It was funny, seeing her perched there like that after having that dream. Lola couldn't be any more different from Momma if she tried.

"Nice dinner." Del smiled as Lola made a face.

"Want some?" She held out the chocolate, and Del reached down and snapped off a piece.

"S'good," Del mumbled around the candy, "but I need some real dinner. By the way," she forced her voice to sound casual, "you don't have to worry about me getting hurt."

Lola looked up with clouded eyes.

"I've been a cop for twenty years, Lola. I know how to take care of myself."

Lola reddened. "I didn't mean to suggest that you don't."

"I know."

Del sat down next to her. She didn't want Lola to think she was mad, but she wanted to make sure of her mindset. That was too hard to do while staring down at her big eyes and the hint of cleavage that peeked out of the top of her blouse. She needed to focus.

"You knew I wouldn't let you play bait."

"I knew you wouldn't like it," Lola admitted. "But it doesn't seem so crazy to me. What's wrong with taking control of the situation? Why not force his hand?"

Del took her time answering. She would feel the same way, in Lola's shoes.

"It's too dangerous," she said finally, "too many variables. And Phan agreed," she added. She watched Lola closely, wanting to be sure that Lola had dropped the idea.

Lola nodded. "He seems nice."

"Yeah."

"You like pizza?" She broke off another piece of chocolate and watched Lola nod and do the same. *So she can eat in front of me now. She's starting to trust me.*

"What kind?"

Lola shrugged, and Del watched her. "Cheese? Pepperoni? Veggie?"

"I don't care. It's up to you."

"No way." Del's voice was teasing. "I mean, I know you're Miss Polite and everything, but you have to know what kind of pizza you like. Pick!" she commanded, and Lola rolled her eyes.

"I don't know. What do you like?"

"Doesn't matter. Pick!"

Lola really didn't know, because she hadn't eaten pizza since she was maybe thirteen or fourteen. Orrin hated fast food and pizza in particular. She almost started to explain that, but she didn't want to bring Orrin up to Del again.

"Veggie?" She picked one at random.

"Veggie, it is." Del rose to order the pizza, and Lola realized that she had to rebalance herself on the bed. She'd been leaning closer to Del as they'd talked and hadn't even been aware of it. When Del looked directly at her, Lola felt unbalanced in her brain, as well as in her body. Her eyes were the strangest color—like the ocean, blue and green and gray, too. They darkened or lightened with Del's mood, and Lola sometimes tried to lighten them with teasing.

Knock it off, she told herself. Del feels responsible for you. She feels sorry for you. But she doesn't like you, not like that.

But she kissed me, her hopeful side protested.

Orrin t'sked her. "Lolly, she's bored. She's stuck in here with a stupid, boring cow, and she was just amusing herself."

She wanted to tell him to be quiet, but she wasn't at all sure that he was wrong.

She went to the window. The parking lot was nearly full, the restaurant across the street was crammed, and people were waiting outside for tables. Too bad they couldn't go there and just be two normal people having dinner in a restaurant and complaining about the wait or talking about movies or doing whatever it was that people did in restaurants. What was Del's favorite restaurant? Did she ever get dressed up and go out to a nice restaurant? Maybe she would wear a suit. She pictured Del dressed up in a nice suit with a haircut and a spring in her step and a gleam of pride in her eyes. She could see that but not herself at Del's side—she didn't fit into that picture. Someone better, someone beautiful and confident and smart, that was the kind of woman who belonged at Del's side. Someone good enough to walk into some lovely restaurant on Del's arm and smile up at her and make her heart beat faster. She swallowed hard. Was it wrong to wish she were good enough to be that woman?

Del's breath smelled like chocolate, as, she supposed, did hers. What if we kissed now? Would it taste like Del or like chocolate? She was startled when Del grabbed her arm and pushed her onto the bed. Her side burned, and she couldn't get out more than a strangled cry. She flashed her eyes at Del's face. It didn't look angry, and Lola was confused.

"Sorry." Del pulled the curtains shut. "I realized how visible you were from the outside, and I guess I overreacted."

Lola still had her hands up in front of her, shielding herself. Did she even realize she was doing that?

"Sorry," Del repeated through tight lips. Lola nodded and apologized *and* thanked her.

Lola eased into a sitting position, wincing.

"Oh, damn, your stitches. Let me see." She kneeled and eased up Lola's shirt. Lola flinched a little, and Del frowned. She peeled back the bandage.

No sign of infection, and the stitches were intact. It seemed to be healing. There was a scar not far from the edge of the bandage. Was that from a cigarette burn? It looked like it. There was another like it a few inches down. Another on her wrist. Del patted the bandage back into place and eased the shirt down with shaking hands.

"Looks okay. Does it hurt?" Her voice was hoarse.

Lola shook her head.

"I didn't mean to hurt you," Del choked out the words. "That night. Or again. Or, you know, ever."

Lola frowned. "I know. It's okay."

Del needed a distraction. She suggested they play cards until the pizza came, and she explained the game of poker to Lola. Not surprisingly, Lola was a terrible poker player. Her face was an open book. Del tried not to smile when Lola, examining her cards, tried to cover an exultant smile with a neutral expression. Within a short while, Del had let Lola win a huge pile of pennies from her.

Lola made a face. "You let me win, didn't you?"

Del raised her eyebrows. "Who, me?"

Lola rolled her eyes.

"You're a really terrible liar, Lola."

She made a face. "For all you know, I could be a very good liar!"

Del laughed at her indignant response. "It's not like that would be a good thing."

"I don't know." Lola looked thoughtful. "I wouldn't mind being able to feel things without advertising them."

Del shook her head. "People lie all the time, especially to police. Pretend to feel things they don't. Pretend not to feel things they do. It gets to where I figure everyone's lying all the time."

"That's terrible. How do you know who to believe, who to trust?"

Del snorted. "Yeah, well, good question." She wished they hadn't started the conversation. She needed to talk to Lola about what exactly she was hiding, and this conversation wasn't making that any easier.

"I'm sorry, Del." Lola's eyes were warm, sympathetic, kind. Del forced herself to focus on the questions she needed to ask.

"Listen. I wondered if maybe the guy might have been looking for something in your house. Like maybe the little pipe bomb was to scare you out. Maybe that's why he didn't actually hurt you with a more destructive explosive. And he did it while I was in the house. Maybe he figured I'd make sure you didn't get hurt, the house didn't catch fire, I don't know. If, uh, if he was looking to find something in the house, any idea what that could be?"

Lola frowned. "What do you mean? Like, money or jewelry or something?"

Del shrugged. The timing was wrong. She should have waited.

"Who knows?"

A knock on the door stopped her, and she waved Lola into the bathroom before she opened the door for the pizza guy.

"Okay, all clear," she called after he'd left.

Lola held out two cans.

"Root beer or diet?"

"Root beer, all the way."

"Good. I like diet."

Del laughed. "Nobody *likes* diet soda, not really. Y'all just drink it to stay skinny."

"Skinny? Ha!" Lola puffed out her cheeks. "I didn't know you were a comedian."

Del snorted. "Oh, God, you're not one of those, are you?"

"One of what?" Lola smiled, but she looked nervous.

"Women who don't eat."

"Ha, again!" Lola rolled her eyes. "Hand over the pizza, or you're in big trouble, lady."

Del laughed. "All right, tough guy, I give. Sure you have enough room after all that chocolate?"

Lola flushed, and Del realized that she'd taken it the wrong way.

"Kidding, kidding," she said, setting the pizza down on the table. "I had as much chocolate as you did, and I'm starving!"

Lola smiled, but it was reflexive. Del washed her hands and took a second to remind herself that Lola was still flinchy. It would take time before she stopped thinking she was about to get attacked any second. Those raised hands, those scars. She had to stop giving the girl a reason to be scared. She pushed her hair back with an impatient hand.

"Oh, Del, there aren't any plates. What should we do?"

Lola was standing by the table with a look of genuine distress on her face.

Del laughed. "Oh, my, whatever will we do? The governor and the queen are expected any minute, and where *is* our fine china?"

Lola smiled, her real smile, and, God, that smile was worth everything. Del dried her hands on her pants and headed over for dinner wearing a gomer grin a mile wide. *I'll question her tomorrow.*

***

Eating with Del was a strange experience, and Lola felt self-conscious when they sat across from each other at the small table. They ate over the pizza box, and Del teased her about trying to find a fork to eat with. She grabbed a slice and heaved it at her mouth, and Lola giggled and rolled her eyes. Del's face had worn a haunted look since they'd left the house, but now she seemed to relax a little. After the last goodnights had been said and the last silly jokes had been exchanged, Lola lay in her huge, empty bed and imagined that they lay in the same bed. She imagined that Del's hand held hers, Del's lips sought hers, and the cold sheets were warmed by the heat of their bodies.

Orrin started to make some snide comment, but Lola turned onto her unhurt side and away from where he perched on the edge of the bed.

"Leave me alone," she whispered. "You can't talk to me anymore. I'm not listening to you." She covered her ears, feeling silly, and tried to recapture her little daydream, but The Creep was there, too, and he and Orrin chased her into her dreams with their greedy, grasping, hurting hands.

CHAPTER TWENTY-TWO

Del shook her head. "It's like looking for a needle in a giant fucking mountain of needles!"

Phan frowned. "That's exactly what we're doing. We just need to find the one that's bent the right way."

He left for a while. To do what, Del couldn't have said. She was distracted, pinging without knowing why. What he'd said about how they had to find the one that was bent the right way kept nagging her. What was it about that thought that kept clicking for her? She couldn't put it together.

The next several days felt like an exercise in futility. Del went over everything, compared notes with Phan, and went over everything again. She checked in with the team going through Lola's hate mail, but nothing stood out.

Jones continued his work on Lola's computer, which he'd

nicknamed the Lolasaurus. He also set up an online trap, looking for "Joan."

"Get her to buy something from this millennium," he complained. "This thing runs on dinosaur shit."

"You should see her car," Del muttered.

He would continue to work on it, but he didn't seem hopeful.

Of the rest of the team, Johnny Dominguez was focused primarily on Lola's life. Everyone she'd ever met, talked to or lived near went under the microscope. He pulled Del aside and asked if he was supposed to look into Del herself, too. He looked away, shuffled his feet. Del thought all he needed was a cap to twist in his hands or a cowlick to tug on.

She nodded. "Of course." She smiled in what she hoped was a friendly way. He nodded, looking more unsettled than reassured. She saw that Phan and a couple others were watching, and she kept her cool on the outside but walked away fuming. *Sometimes being a cop's like living in a damned soap opera.*

The list she gave Dominguez was pretty long. A few dozen cons, of course, and suspects who'd gotten away with their crimes but who might consider her a burr under their saddles. There was also Janet, or maybe somebody mad at or about her. There was a drug dealer-cum-politician whose nose she'd broken a few years before, and her old landlord, who'd made the mistake of walking unannounced into her apartment while she was in the shower. She'd reached out to the back of the toilet tank, grabbed her weapon and pointed it at him, and he'd pissed his pants. He might have held a grudge. And, of course, there were a few guys on the job who wouldn't mind if she fell down a well, but she didn't include their names. They wouldn't do it this way, any of them, and it would be unfair to put Dominguez in the position of having to clear them.

It took her a while to type all the names, and she looked over the list with dismay. It was disheartening to see how many people might want her dead, and she was glad to be done with the task. She itched to ask Dominguez if she could see Lola's list, but he'd flag any serious candidates.

She could ask Lola, too, follow up on the question of who

exactly had been in her life all these years. It was hard to believe that she hadn't developed any relationships except with that fucker, Beckett.

She had to take her to get the stitches out of her side, anyway, and brought it up afterward.

"No coffee with a neighbor, Lola? No lunch with the ladies? Nothing?"

Lola shook her head, her mouth a tight line. Del knew she should follow up, but she didn't do it. There was something else to talk about: they would share a room with two beds. It was easier and cheaper that way. Del told Lola about this while parking the car in front of yet another beige building full of strangers. She kept her eyes on the windshield and her voice steady.

"You don't have to worry. Nothing inappropriate is going to happen again."

Lola looked at her with dark eyes. Not wanting to rehash what had happened, Del opened the car door, eased it carefully shut, and walked away.

***

Both of them craved some kind of physical activity, and late one restless night Lola started jumping on her bed. Del laughed and watched Lola as she hopped, pink cheeked, on her queen bed in the dingy hotel room of the day.

"You're nuts, you know that?"

Lola just smiled. "Join me!"

"Doesn't it hurt?" She pointed at Lola's side.

But Lola shook her head. "Nope." She in turn pointed at Del, her finger wavering up and down. "Chicken?"

Del jumped up, startling Lola into a laugh, and the game was on. They jumped, one on each bed, leapt across, trading beds, jumped, and leapt back again. Del was careful not to bump Lola, but she was laughing too hard to do much more than lunge away from her. They grew breathless with laughter, finally falling onto their separate beds.

"That was fun!" Lola smiled, and Del could only grin back at her.

Del didn't think she'd ever jumped on a bed in her life, and she realized how little she really knew Lola. At first she'd seemed like a compliant little mouse, but underneath it all she was playful and funny and just a little bit wicked. It was a damned sexy combination, as far as Del was concerned.

She couldn't help but wonder, later, as Lola's breathing slowed in the late-night darkness, what Lola would be like if she'd had a normal life—no lousy foster parents, no Dr. Orrin Beckett. Then a small murmur escaped Lola. She talked in her sleep sometimes, cried too. Once or twice she'd screamed, startling Del awake, and once she'd sat up in bed and started pleading with an invisible bad guy. Del had felt like an intruder, invading some private nightmare. She turned over, hoping for a peaceful night.

Not only was it heartbreaking, but also it made her want to hold Lola, comfort her. And that was not okay. She shook her head. No touching. No kissing. And definitely no holding Lola in her arms. A good person doesn't take advantage of someone who's scared and confused and traumatized. She closed her eyes.

***

It was nearly midnight when Lola sat on the edge of her bed and watched Del sleep. Her hand was outstretched like it had been at Lola's house that morning, fingers curled slightly over her palm. Lola wanted to hold her and kiss her and protect her. Without thinking about it, Lola rose and stood by Del's bed. She leaned over and softly kissed the tender palm of Del's lightly calloused hand.

"Good night," she whispered and slipped back into bed, her heart pounding.

***

Del felt a strand of Lola's hair sweep across her arm before she felt her soft, warm mouth. It took every ounce of her control to stay still, pretending to be asleep. She waited until Lola lay back down on her own bed and her even breathing indicated that she was totally out, and then she exhaled loudly. It had been so tempting to grab that silky hair and pull Lola's mouth to hers! She closed her eyes and groaned in frustration. This was killing her!

All she wanted to do was get it over with. She'd feel better if she slept with Lola. The mystery and the idealizing would be over. Sex with her would be like sex with any other woman, wouldn't it? Then she'd be able to stop thinking about her. It wouldn't be any good, she told herself. She's like a frightened child. She's afraid of her own body, and she's definitely afraid of mine. If I could just have her once, I'd be over it, and then I could focus! But as her mind wandered back over the memory of their kiss, she could almost feel Lola's body pressing against her own, Lola's hands in her hair, Lola's warmth and softness. Now, she relived this newest sensation, Lola's lips on her palm, and knew she was lying to herself.

Lola would be soft and lush and warm. She would be self-conscious and shy when Del explored her body. She would need to be petted and kissed and reassured with loving words and soft hands. But she would respond. She would open up and trust Del. Del could imagine Lola's skin growing warm from gentle caresses, her breath quickening in response to tender kisses.

She pictured Lola leaping from one bed to another, her hair wild, her skin flushed, her eyes sparkling with pleasure. She was sensual, underneath it all. She would be like a kitten, skittish at first and, once she'd grown more confident, would end up purring under Del's hand. She would—Del groaned again and buried her hot face under her pillow.

It was maybe an hour later when she was startled awake by a sudden screech. Lola! She rushed over and saw that Lola was actually awake—usually her bad dreams didn't wake her.

"You okay?"

Lola's face was white. She reached over and turned on the light. "I—in the ambulance, I remember!"

Del just looked at her.

"I saw him. In the ambulance. He was there, very close, and he was mad. He was really mad. But I forgot."

"It was a dream, Lola."

"No." Lola shook her head. How could she make her understand? She cleared her throat. "Listen, I forgot, but it wasn't a dream. It was real. Del, I need you to believe me."

Del nodded, but it was clear that she didn't, not really.

"It was The Creep. He wasn't the nice man, he was the other one, the man in the ambulance. He was there, Del. And he didn't have glasses, and he didn't have black hair. His hair was blond, and his eyes were blue, and he smelled the same, and his voice was the same. I swear! It was the same man. The one who killed Buttons and Queenie. And he wanted to talk to me, but I got scared and went away. He put his hand on my mouth, and he was holding me down, and I went away. I mean, I fainted."

Del pursed her lips. Her eyes measured Lola and told her that she'd failed. Del didn't believe her. Lola hugged herself. She was too frustrated to think.

Del's voice was soft. "That sounds pretty scary." She pursed her lips. "Listen, you've been through a lot lately. It's totally normal to have wild dreams when you're going through so much. I'm not saying you're wrong. I just think it's possible that your dream seemed really, really vivid, that's all. Does that make sense?"

Lola took a second to answer. "You're managing me, Del. Handling me. You know? I remembered something in a dream, but that doesn't make it less true."

"Tell you what. In the morning, if you're still sure it wasn't a dream, then fine. I'll get you back together with a sketch artist and follow up on this. But right now, it's the middle of the night, and there's nothing we can do about it. Okay?"

"But, Del, I'm telling the truth!"

Del looked down at her. Her expression communicated nothing. "I don't think you're lying, not at all. I believe that you think you saw him. But he's not here now, right? And it's too late at night to do anything about this. So, we'll get some sleep, and we'll talk about it in the morning. Does that seem reasonable? Okay. Good night." She turned off the light.

Lola watched Del climb back into bed and turn away to go to sleep. She didn't believe me at all, she thought miserably. She thinks I'm crazy and stupid and not reliable. And maybe she's right. Maybe it was all a dream. But it didn't feel like it. Part of her wanted to turn the light on and make Del listen and convince her that The Creep had been in the ambulance. But what if she got mad? What if she told Lola she was crazy? What if she just looked at her that measuring way again? Lola wasn't sure she could stand that.

Orrin whispered in that new, gentle voice of his. "Maybe she's right, Lolly. Maybe it was just a dream. Isn't that at least possible?"

It was. Lola had to admit that she'd had more than one dream that had bled over and seemed like it was real. So, maybe The Creep in the ambulance was just another one of those dreams. She shuddered. She didn't think that was true, but there was a part of her that really, really hoped it was.

***

Del got up extra early the next morning, punishing her body with a grueling run that left her breathless, dizzy, exhausted. They were in the suburb of Daly City, just south of the city, and the fog was so close to the ground that Del could barely see the parked cars as she headed for the room. It cooled her, though, and a jagged laugh escaped her. A long run, a foggy version of a cold shower, and none of it was helping. She was still burning for Lola. She turned around and did another few laps around the block. She got ready for work as quietly as she could, not wanting to wake Lola and have to pretend not to want her. It was almost a relief to head to work and look for the bad guy.

***

Lola was going crazy. She woke up to find that Del had already left for work. Something was nagging at her, and she couldn't get a fix on what it was. There was something she wanted to tell Del, wasn't there? That seemed right. That seemed like the answer. But she couldn't figure out what it was that she wanted to tell her.

After pacing the room for over an hour, she came to a decision. They had almost run out of clean underwear and Lola had been wearing the same top for two days. It smelled like sweat and pizza and felt like sandpaper. Her hair was a mess after days with no conditioner, and her lips were chapped from her nervous chewing on them.

"I've got to get out of here," she said to no one. "I'm losing my mind."

Orrin started to make some joke about that but she waved away his voice.

She called Del's cell phone and got no answer. She tried her precinct number, no answer. She called Tom, no answer. Where were they? Had something happened? What if Del was in danger, what if she needed help? Her eyes darted around the room, which seemed to be shrinking.

She scolded herself, "Keep it together!" She forced herself to breathe slowly, to sit down and stay calm. "The last thing anybody needs," she reminded herself, "the last thing Del needs, is you freaking out." She started to giggle. "You're a lesbian, start acting like it." She touched her lips with her fingertips, remembering the salty taste of Del's palm.

She wondered what it would be like to touch and kiss Del's body. Was she very different from her? What did her skin smell like, feel like, taste like?

Certainly she would be different from Orrin. He used his body as a weapon. He knew that Lola was afraid of being crushed because she'd told him before, when he was her friend, Dr. Beckett. When he became Orrin, he enjoyed pressing his weight down on her, watching her struggle to breathe and panic and try not to cry. Did he watch her go away? Did he try to make her go away? Lola hugged herself tightly, shaking her head.

Del wouldn't do that. She wouldn't want to hurt her. She would be strong and soft, all at once. Lola thought about the day they'd kissed. Had Del really been attracted to her, or would she have enjoyed making out with any available woman? It was hard to tell. Lola rolled her eyes. Okay, enough! She sat at the table again, with the laptop in front of her. But her mind kept wandering back to thoughts of Del's mouth, Del's hands, Del's skin.

***

Del had been stuck in meetings for what seemed like years, with everyone checking in to report a collective lack of progress, and Lola's messages alarmed her at first. She sounded fine, but she'd never called before. Del held her breath, waiting for Lola to pick up her cell, and exhaled loudly in her ear at the sound of her voice.

"Sorry," she said, "you okay?"

Lola was fine. Cabin fever, she said, and Del's heart resumed its regular rhythm.

"I know," she said, "I'm sorry. We should have caught this guy by now."

They chatted for a few minutes. Lola was, understandably, cracking under the pressure. Thank God she'd dropped the whole business about the dream. Del had seen the hurt in her eyes and felt guilty for it, but Lola was obviously susceptible to whims and would have just worked herself into a state over nothing.

Hanging up, Del turned to Phan. "Hey," she said. "I've been thinking about what Lola said the other day."

He looked at her, nonplussed.

"You know, the bait thing?"

His eyebrows shot up. "What?"

"No. I mean, not her. Me."

"Explain."

"Let's assume for a minute that he doesn't know we found the cameras. Okay? Obviously, he's seen me. He knows we're friends. Maybe he figures we're more than that. It's been well over a week. Maybe he's desperate enough to come after me."

Phan considered. "Maybe, maybe not. If he knows you're a cop, and he must, he might figure it's too high a risk."

"Maybe. But I was thinking. I don't know." Del waggled her head.

"What'd you have in mind?"

"I go to her house, like I'm checking on things. Clean out her fridge, get her mail. Water her plants. I go tonight. Go back every other night at the same time. Like I'm stopping by after work, on my way to go to her. He's bound to go for it, sooner or later, see if he can follow me to her. We could route him to a location we choose ahead of time."

Phan asked some questions and offered some suggestions for how she could do it, and she began to feel a little bit hopeful. She was surprised to hear excitement in Phan's voice and laughed. This might actually work! Or, she reminded herself, it could be a total bust, and they'd be stuck right back at nothing.

They spent the next couple of hours working out the details, getting approval from their captain to test it out on a trial basis. They spent a long time figuring out how to minimize the risks so that he would approve it without half the department having to be on scene.

Del called Lola. "I've got a hot lead," she said, "I can't leave until I run it down." She hated the disappointment in Lola's voice as she said that of course she understood, don't worry about her, she was fine. She could hear Lola's absolute trust. It would never occur to her that Del might be lying, would it? She rolled her eyes as she disconnected from the call.

"Shut up, Phan," she spat at him as he t'sked her with his finger. "I'm only lying to protect her."

"I know," he replied, "I'd do the same thing. But, Mason," he made a rueful face, "doesn't it ever bother you, how the job has made you such a good liar?"

CHAPTER TWENTY-THREE

As the afternoon turned to evening and Del didn't call or come back, Lola's nerves continued to fray. She felt sure that something was happening. Is she facing The Creep right now? Is she in danger? What is she keeping from me? Suddenly, a thought occurred to her. Closing the curtains as the sky darkened, she grabbed her cell phone and called her own house.

***

Del was just opening the front door when she heard the phone ringing and raced in to see the number. It took her a moment to realize that the alarm wasn't on. And the house was a mess—it had been tossed.

She wanted to ask Phan who was on the other end of the

phone, but she was mindful of the cameras and pressed her lips together. The button in her ear was tickling her, and she suppressed the urge to scratch.

"I'll try to get it, but I don't know. Play to the cameras." Phan's low voice was calm, reassuring. She pulled on gloves and booties and looked around the room warily. Her hand wandered near her weapon and then away.

She pulled out her cell phone and called her own house to feign leaving a message. "Hey, Phan, listen, I stopped by Lola Bannon's place—you remember, my neighbor with the pipe bomb? She asked me to get her mail and stuff, and it looks like somebody broke in and tossed it. Uh, I'm gonna just water the plants and get the food and garbage outta here, okay? I'm gloved and bootied. I doubt there's anything here, but maybe you could send a forensic team in the morning? Thanks. Bye."

Phan's voice crackled in her ear. "What was he looking for?"

She let her silence speak to her ignorance and turned her attention back to the mess before her. Okay. He had broken in. He'd turned the alarm off. He had taken his time, hours from the looks of it, tearing the house apart. Del was upset for Lola's sake, not only because she would be devastated by the destruction in her home, but also because it was such a violation. It angered and scared Del and started a whole new line of speculation in her head. She took dozens of still pictures of every room, and with every press of the button, she felt herself stepping closer and closer to the conclusion that she was missing something important.

She hummed "Jingle Bells" as she placed a second video camera, inches from the bad guy's, above the fireplace. She covered this by blocking her hand with her body. This might be unnecessary, but she wasn't taking any chances. She had requested surveillance on the house, but the captain hadn't approved the request. A patrol was supposed to drive by every couple of hours, but that hadn't helped, obviously. Del shook off her frustration. Now wasn't the time.

She picked up and watered the very dry Christmas tree, leaving the broken ornaments on the floor. She fought the urge to right the tables, chairs and lamps, to pick up the gutted couch cushions, to put the slashed pictures back on the walls. She turned lights on in every room she passed, using the back of her gloved hand.

The kitchen was a foul disaster. She cleaned out the fridge, which had obviously been standing open for a while. There was food everywhere—on the floor, on the counters, even spattered on the walls and ceiling. Nothing had been left untouched. Same with the cupboards. Every drawer and cupboard had been emptied. She ignored everything but the perishables and filled and emptied the trash. She stepped around the broken dishes and mugs and glasses. The can she left out on the sidewalk. Garbage day was tomorrow, but they'd get a guy to pull the bags before then. Poor Lola, a crew would be digging through her trash like she was a criminal.

She felt like an intruder as she headed up the stairs, flicking on the lights. Lola was very private. She would hate the thought of anyone wandering through her house, digging through her garbage, nosing around. It's my *job*, Del told herself. It's what I have to do to protect her. Still, she felt guilty. Had he felt guilty? Or had it been a thrill, roaming freely through the house, touching and breaking things?

Upstairs, the bed in the guest room was the worst. The mattress was destroyed, and the bedding was torn into rags. The empty drawers of the dresser had been left upside down on the wreckage of the bed. Two had been broken. Whatever he was looking for, he'd gotten pissed off when he couldn't find it. Or had he gotten excited, smelling Lola's perfume, seeing her things? Del felt herself getting angrier and angrier. Who did this asshole think he was? And a moment later came the despairing question: *Lola, what the hell are you hiding from me?*

People got their houses ransacked because they'd stolen something or because they knew secrets they shouldn't or because they had something to hide. He'd searched the house when he'd killed the cats. She'd seen that and never followed up on it. How many times had he searched the place that she didn't know about?

Del's stomach twisted. *Innocent people don't get ransacked. Not twice. She's hiding something from me.* Del had no right to be angry and knew it. But she was. *Deal with it later. Draw her out. Get her to open up. Then, when it's all over, when she's safe, I can worry about how I feel about her. About the fact that she's been lying to me.* Her stomach twisted again at that thought, and she fought a second, stronger wave of anger. *She's scared. Whatever she's done, whatever she'd hiding, it's because she's scared. I have to do a better job of making her feel safe, letting her know she can trust me.* She rubbed her face, forgetting for a moment that she was supposed to be playing to the cameras.

It was hard to be casual and vigilant at the same time, but she had to assume that he could be watching. Did he have a live feed? Or would he watch later? Hard to tell, without pulling his cameras out of place and letting him know they'd been found. She continued to place a department camera near each of his, doing so as covertly as possible.

"Doing good," Phan whispered. Del had almost forgotten he was there.

Lola's room was virtually untouched. So, obviously, he had time to search it completely when he did the cats. That took some time. *I wonder...* Sure enough, when she lifted the mattress, the underside was slashed open in a giant X. Should have seen that before, Del told herself. Forensic team should have too. She grimaced.

"Knock if off, Mason," she muttered inaudibly. "You're supposed to be her pal, not on the job."

Phan was right. Del refocused. She opened the windows that flanked the bed, as though the room smelled bad and needed airing out. Which, actually, it did. The stink from the opened fridge had filled the upstairs. He must have been here at least a day or two back—the food would take that long to smell so bad. She turned on the overhead light and both lamps. From the outside, she would be completely visible. And Phan now had a good view of every room in the house.

"Good. I got you. Time to bait the hook, Mason. I got your back."

She hesitated, then shrugged off her pullover and wore only a wifebeater, no bra. This was the hard part. She and Phan had argued about this, and she'd been forced to accept that he was right. She had to act the part, try to provoke him. But she still felt uncomfortable. You better not say anything, she silently warned Phan. I do have a weapon.

I trust him, she realized. I trust him enough to listen to his ideas and let him watch me. *He says he has my back, and I believe him.* It was a weird feeling. Good, but weird.

Stretching her spine before the oval mirror above the dresser, she fluffed her hair and gazed at her reflection. She felt like an actor in a play. For an audience of one. In character, she leaned forward and pursed her lips. Lola kept a small basket of makeup on the dresser, and Del casually snagged a lipstick and applied a thick layer of it to her mouth. She leaned forward again and kissed her reflection. Shit, she thought, I look like the world's worst drag queen.

Ohhh, big boy, she silently pleaded, come and get me. Please, come and get me. I'm a helpless female, all sexy and weak. Plus I'm a nasty old dyke. You straight guys love that, right? Look no bra! I'm ready for a big, strong man to come on in and get me. *Come on.* Come and get me. Get off your couch and come after me, so I can kick your cowardly, pathetic, bullying, animal-torturing ass.

She powdered her nose, which made her eyes water. Less, maybe? She broke character for a moment, trying to figure out how the whole powder thing was supposed to go. Why hadn't she anticipated that this might be harder than it looked? Her eyes itched like crazy, and she blinked hard to clear them.

"Shit, Mason, act like a girl." Phan's disembodied voice and the strange play-acting made her feel like she was in a dream. She tried the powder again, a lot less this time. "Good." It sounded like he was trying not to laugh.

She only ever bothered with brownish mascara, and that only because a girlfriend had once bribed her into it with kisses and sweet talk. Del had been surprised at how much more innocent and trustworthy she looked with it on and now incorporated it into her routine whenever she had to be in court. She wished she had some now. It probably would have gone with the rest of the stuff. She sprayed her neck with perfume, getting some in her mouth.

"Mason." Phan *was* laughing now, but she heard the tension in his voice. "You *are* a woman, right? Haven't you ever had a girlfriend? Do what they do."

She fluffed her hair again and ran her hands down her body. Come on, asshole, don't you like tits? Come and get 'em, asshole. Please, please, pretty please? She turned her back to the mirror and looked at herself over her shoulder. Shit, her weapon was nearly visible! She discreetly nudged her holster back down inside her waistband a bit and looked in the mirror again. Her arms were getting flabby. She would have to get back to hitting the weights again when the guy was locked up. She wondered what Lola's arms looked like—she was always wearing so many damn clothes!

One more thing on Phan's list, and she could give it up for the night. This whole thing was ridiculous, clearly artificial. She couldn't imagine anyone thinking she was actually being herself—she felt *queer*, doing all these girly things.

"Mason—Del, don't think. Just do it. And, remember, girly and pervy. Whatever flavor of fucked up he likes, you gotta look like it."

I know, Phan, she mentally responded, we talked about this. She hesitated before opening the top drawer in Lola's dresser. Again, though she wasn't doing this lightly but out of what felt like necessity, she felt like the world's biggest creep. She wasn't sure any of this was a good idea, all of a sudden. She knew her face was bright red. Her heart was banging around like it was trying to beat her ribs open.

Really, this was a risky operation and they should have been a lot more specific when they'd gotten approval, but she'd been impatient. She'd also worried that Wonderbread would say no. Not to mention how much it would've sucked to have half the department watch her girl it up. It was bad enough knowing Phan was watching. She stopped palavering and yanked the drawer open and eyed its contents. Sure enough, there was Lola's underwear. Del had assumed it would be all cotton briefs and sensible bras and was enchanted to find a rainbow of silk and ribbons and satin, inches from her fingers.

"Oh, Lola," she groaned, "you lovely little femme!"

"Perfect, Mason, now do it."

She recalled herself to the moment in a snap. Luckily, she'd been supposed to act all horny.

"Good. Just do it. Now."

Okay, Phan, she thought, as she did the last thing on his list. She lifted handfuls of Lola's silky panties and let them rain down between her fingers. *Oh, God. Thank you, asshole. I never would have done this if it hadn't been for you.* She tucked one pair into her pocket.

Phan's voice was quiet. "Good, Mason. He's gotta be all lathered by now. If he's close by, he's on his way."

But he wasn't. Del was sure of it. She'd been hyperaware, all through her little performance, every invisible antenna quivering in alertness, and there hadn't been a single ping. Hopefully he was recording. She blew herself a kiss in the mirror before she grabbed her pullover and closed the windows. She turned off all the lights and set the alarm before she left.

She and Phan assessed the effort as she drove them back to the station, and she was grateful that he didn't refer to her actions in Lola's room other than to hand her a paper towel to clean her face off and to tease her about her lack of finesse with makeup.

"Shit, Mason," he muttered, "Kaylee could have done better, and she's twelve!"

"You don't let her wear makeup, do you?"

"Hell, no! But you know how kids are."

Del nodded and smiled as he related a long story about clever ways Kaylee had found to get around the rules. She resisted the urge to touch Lola's silky panties. Just knowing they were right there in her pocket felt both creepy and incredibly erotic. She had to work hard to focus on what Phan was saying. He'd finished with the subject of Kaylee and moved on to something job-related. Something about a federal agent?

"Leave it to the Feebs," Phan muttered, "it's none of their business if some creep stalks and terrorizes an innocent woman, but if there's money to be found, they're all over it."

"No shit."

"Name's Christopher James. Sounded a little overeager, you ask me. I almost wonder if he's making a play for a promotion."

"Do we have to meet with him? I doubt he has anything for us."

"You sure you wanna take that chance?"

Del shrugged. "I guess not."

"Here's the thing," Phan said, "he wants to meet at a coffee shop near the Federal Building, not at his office. I figure he's trying to scoop his boss, get the credit, move up the ladder. Best way to do that is run his own investigation in the shadows."

"What an ass." Del was still distracted but tried to focus.

"That's what they force them into," he claimed, "that's the way they work—you have to always think about how you're gonna look from the top of the ladder."

It was, he said, yet another reason to distrust the Feebs. "They can't just do police work. They have to make it look good politically, too."

Del shrugged again. As long as he didn't waste too much of their time or interfere, she didn't care if he found Beckett's money or not. And maybe he could help them, whether he planned to or not. "He may know something that can help us. He might be able to help us without even knowing he's doing it."

It was Phan's turn to shrug. "It's worth a half hour of our time, at the most. After that, we can ditch or stay, depending on what we're getting."

"There are some questions I'd like to ask of someone who saw the interviews or read the reports before they were redacted." Del rubbed her forehead. "It feels like there's a lot missing."

"Okay, like what? Is Lola a suspect in Beckett's death?"

Del stared at him. "You can't be serious!"

"Do I think Lola offed the old guy? No. But if they do, it'd be good to know it."

"Yeah, I guess." She narrowed her eyes. "Have they found the partner? Was he connected to Lola? Could he be the attacker? Maybe he and Lola were supposed to take the cash together, and she didn't want to share."

It was Phan's turn to look shocked. "Del, do you honestly believe Lola's been playing you?"

"Do I want to? Hell, no. But it could still be true." Just saying it felt lousy.

"Does James think Beckett is still alive? Does he think Lola is still in contact with him?" Phan asked these questions without looking at her. "Or that she really has the money, but she's playing dumb?"

"What do you think, Phan?" She swallowed hard. "I want to know what you think."

He rubbed his chin. "Okay. She seems basically honest. A nice person. But I don't think she trusts us all the way. You more than me, but I think she might be scared of making you mad, of causing a conflict for you, of getting you in trouble or putting you in danger. I think she'd lie through her teeth to protect someone she loves."

Del didn't know how to respond to that. "What if she still loves Beckett—and he's still alive? Or even if he's not, but she's trying to cover for him, anyway? What if she's lying to protect him?"

"Well, that could be, I guess. But you know her better than I do. What do you think?"

"I think..." She paused, shaking her head. "I think my head is all muddy where she's concerned. I don't want to think she's been playing me all along. Shit, as you know, I have been down that road before."

Phan eyed her, his expression soft. "We've all been there."

Del didn't respond to that. "Yeah, well. I'd rather think that, at worst, she might be hiding something because she's scared and doesn't trust me. And that she could get killed because she didn't trust me."

"Maybe," Phan offered, "she knows something without knowing it."

Del frowned. "What do you mean?"

Phan hesitated before answering. "Listen, I don't want to put my nose in, okay? But you said it, your head's all muddy. You don't have the distance to be objective, here. She was married to this guy for a long time. Whether you like it or not, they had a history together. There are secrets between couples—jokes, old grudges, memories, things you don't even know are important because you've known them for twenty years. She may know about an old safe deposit box or a cabin or a family vacation home or an old college buddy's boat or something. She may not realize it's important, because she's a widow who's just lost her husband, and she's still getting over that. Whether he was the asshole you think he was or not, he was her husband. They ate dinner together, they slept together, they talked about shit."

Del grunted and gestured at him to continue.

"She knows more about him than she realizes, and the Feds pushed at her the wrong way. They tried to bully her, right? That's what I got from the reports. It was the wrong approach. You and I both know she's the kind that responds to the soft touch. If you worked this right, you could find out every single detail of the guy's life—how he liked his steak, what kind of shampoo he used, where he hid his porn. She knows all of it, but she hasn't been tapped right, not yet. Odds are, she could find that money if she really wanted to. And my guess is, very Special Agent Christopher James knows that. He'll want a crack at her. If you want to spare her that, you should try to ease her open first."

Del rubbed her forehead. He was right. She had been looking at this with blinders on. She didn't want to think about Lola lying side by side with that creepy old man night after night, whispering secrets, kissing good night, all of that shit. And if the Feds were looking at her hard, they might just decide that the stalker was related to the money and put her in protective custody. Lola would fall apart under the strain. They'd start out playing nice with her, but the pressure to produce would mean that they'd end up pushing her hard. They wouldn't care if it hurt her. Del stared out at the traffic that rushed passed. She had to push Lola or sit back while someone else did.

"I'll give it a shot."

He nodded. "Maybe you'll get something out of her, and we can take it to James tomorrow and get them out of the picture. Or at least give them somewhere to look besides her."

"Maybe." Del realized she'd been holding her breath and let it out in a long exhale that left her exhausted. Her shoulders were tight, and her stomach was flipping. She hated that Phan was right. And glad, again, to be working with him. She told him so as they said their goodnights, and he shrugged.

"What the hell kinda partners've you had, Mason?"

She frowned at him. "Whaddya mean?"

"Every time I manage not to piss my pants, you give me a gold star."

She laughed as he walked away.

***

As soon as Del was within twenty feet of the hotel room, Lola opened the door and stared at her. "Well?"

"Well, what?" Del tried to remember her lie. "Oh. Uh, it didn't pan out. Lots of leads turn to crap like that. Sorry. Gotta clean up."

She headed straight for the shower. She felt like Lola knew what she'd been doing. She felt guilty. She felt like an intruder and a pervert. *How would I feel if someone came into my house, my bedroom, rooted around in my underwear?* The warmish water splashed weakly over her face, and she closed her eyes, picturing her own cotton boxers rubbing against Lola's sexy silkies. Without warning, that image changed, and she saw Orrin Beckett grabbing at Lola's soft body, bruising her pale skin, scaring her. She grimaced and shook her head. She tried to erase that picture from her mind and couldn't.

What had their life together been like? Was it always bad, or did it start out good? Or was it good all the way through? She kept assuming that Beckett was abusive and that Lola was a victim, but she didn't have a lick of proof that this was true. For all she knew, Lola was a lying, manipulative criminal who'd conspired with Beckett and his partner to steal and launder millions. And now she was playing a game to find out how much Del knew. Lola had been in the laundry room just before the pipe bomb went off. She could have signaled a co-conspirator. Hell, she could have set the bomb herself. Rigged the window to blow in. It wouldn't be that hard to do.

She reviewed every time she'd seen Lola. Every conversation, every look that passed between them, every moment. Nothing pinged as a lie. Except her evasiveness about Beckett's temper, and that was standard behavior for a victim.

She cut short her shower and dressed quickly. Her dirty clothes were on the floor, and she snagged Lola's panties out of the pocket where she'd stowed them. Almost forgot those! She stuffed them in the pocket of her sweats and smoothed the outside of the pocket. She was shaky. Would this crazy day never end?

CHAPTER TWENTY-FOUR

Lola was ready to climb out of her skin. First Del had been gone for hours, then she'd come back and ignored her, and now she was still distracted, brushing her teeth. What was going on? Then Del's cell buzzed, and she dropped her toothbrush in the sink, grabbed the phone, and headed outside. Was it about The Creep? Or was it a personal thing? Was she involved with someone, and that someone was getting tired of sleeping alone?

Del was attractive. Rachel and, Lola would bet, plenty of other women, found her irresistible. Maybe one of them had caught Del's eye. Maybe she wished she'd never gotten herself roped into babysitting detail. Maybe she was out there, right now, laughing about poor, pathetic Lola pining away in a hotel room while Del was wishing she were with a hot, young blonde.

Fine! Whatever! I don't want to be here, either. I just want this all to be over with. I want my kitties back. I want to feel safe again. I want to go home! The truth of this, that her new house had finally begun to feel like a real home, made the reality of being chased from it even more painful. She knew she was being overly emotional, but she felt off balance and unsettled and uncertain of how to change those feelings.

Del finally came back in, her expression still distracted. She sat on the bed.

"Lola, I need to talk to you."

Her tone made Lola cautious. Suddenly, her worries about Del liking some other woman seemed selfish and silly. Maybe something bad had happened. Maybe Del was scared or upset. She sat next to Del, trying to hide her disappointment when Del moved to the other bed and sat facing Lola.

"So, I'm really sorry to tell you this, but somebody broke into your house." Del kept her voice neutral and watched Lola's reaction closely.

Her shock seemed genuine. She hugged herself and searched Del's face with wide, worried eyes. That was real fear and a real sense of violation. Del was sure of it. You were sure of Janet, too, she reminded herself. She pulled the wool over your eyes for months. Are you really so positive that Lola isn't doing the same thing? She couldn't keep vacillating about Lola's trustworthiness like this. It was making her stomach hurt.

"Why? Did he write on the wall again?"

Del shook her head. "No. He kinda tore the place apart. We're thinking he was looking for something."

She was on high alert, though she worked hard to hide it. She assessed Lola's breathing, her eye movements and pupil dilation, her mouth, her hands, everything. She felt like a human polygraph machine, trying to read the subject. Lola read as true, but could Del really trust her own perception? As Phan had pointed out, she wasn't objective.

"Like what?"

Del hesitated. She didn't want to do this. "Listen, I'm gonna be very direct with you, okay?"

She watched Lola nod, noting her lack of wariness.

"Okay."

"Most of the time, if somebody's in trouble, it's for a reason. You know? Like drugs or infidelity or money or something." She waited, but Lola just looked at her like she was waiting for more. Then Del saw comprehension darken her eyes.

"You think I must have done something wrong? That this is all my fault?" Her eyes grew huge, and she sucked in a deep breath. Did Del really think that? Was this her fault? Had she done something to cause The Creep to come after her? She rose and walked over to the window, though the curtains were closed. She wasn't sure how she felt, what she thought. When she heard herself speaking, she was surprised by her own words.

"This one time, I had some trouble at a foster home." She felt so cold! Her voice shook. "And then I went to another one, and I had some trouble there." She felt far, far away, as though her cold body and her quiet voice were separate from her real self. Del seemed a million miles away. Everything did. "The social worker was really mad. She said I caused too much trouble. She said there were too many kids like me. We always end up having trouble wherever we go. There's no helping us, because we always make the wrong choices and end up being in trouble. That we like being victims or maybe we're programmed that way. That we would always be victims. That we were a waste of time."

The defeat in Lola's voice, the faraway look in her eyes, the way she seemed to be floating around inside her head gave Del a sick feeling.

"That's not what I'm saying."

"Isn't it?" Lola seemed to zoom back into focus. She looked directly at Del.

"No."

"You're saying that most people only end up involved with bad people because they did something wrong. Because they're bad." Her sudden bark of bitter laughter startled Del, who stood up.

"That's not—I swear, that isn't what I'm saying, Lola."

"You wanna know what I've done wrong?" Hysteria edged Lola's voice up to an ugly screech. Then it broke to a barely audible whisper. "Everything. I've done absolutely everything wrong." She sank onto the bed, her face a blank.

"Tell me," Del whispered.

She could barely hear Lola's muffled voice. "I let myself trust Dr. Beckett and lean on him, and then I couldn't get away. And it's my own fault. That social worker was right—people like me always end up circling back around to the bad end of things."

"Tell me what the bad guy wants. Tell me what he's looking for. Once you tell me, you'll feel better. I promise."

Lola pulled away and looked at her. "You think I'm some kind of criminal? You think I'm a—a drug mule or a gambler or a thief or something like that? You think I stole that money?"

Del just looked at her.

"I don't know what to say. I've made a million mistakes in my life. I've been stupid and weak and a coward. But I'm not a criminal. I'm just not."

There was a long silence.

"I don't know what that man wants. I don't know what he's looking for. Maybe it's my fault he came after me, because I went online. Or there's just something wrong with me, and he saw it, and it made him mad. I don't know. But I'm not hiding anything from you. I wouldn't do that. I wouldn't put you in danger like that." Her voice broke again, and she cleared her throat. She stood and walked to the bathroom, easing the door shut behind her.

If she's hiding something, Del thought, she's a way better liar than I thought.

The surprise of Lola's sexy underwear slipped into Del's consciousness unbidden. What else was hiding underneath that innocent exterior?

Lola walked back into the room. "I don't keep a lot of cash in the house, just a few hundred dollars." She had her arms wrapped around her, but her eyes were clear, her voice steady. "I don't have any jewelry or expensive art or, you know, drugs or anything. And I don't have that money. What could he want from me?"

"That's what I'm wondering," Del said, letting her voice harden, and she saw Lola's eyes cloud over.

"Del," she wailed, "I don't know what you think I'm keeping from you. I haven't done anything criminal. I promise. I swear!"

Del tried to steel herself, but she couldn't. If she's lying, she's lying. I can't do this.

She put her arms around Lola, who buried her face in Del's chest.

"Why is this happening?" Lola started to sway. "You don't believe me, but I'm telling the truth. I swear, I swear I am."

Del eased her onto the bed, still holding her tightly. "It's okay. I believe you. It's not your fault." She repeated some version of this over and over for several long minutes. Her words ran together and formed a soothing lullaby, and she slowly felt Lola relax into her.

Her soft hair tickled Del's throat, chin, arms. Her body went limp against Del's. Her breathing slowed and deepened. Del leaned back against the smooth, cold headboard with Lola cradled against her and closed her eyes, still murmuring mindlessly. She was so tired. Her mind felt like it had been racing in circles for hours.

They fell asleep like that. In her last moments before giving in to slumber, Lola felt Del's breath on her forehead like a warm kiss. She tried to lean up into Del's lips and couldn't force her tired body to move.

Tomorrow, she thought. I'll kiss her tomorrow.

She dropped in and out of nightmares. In one, she and Del were riding a roller coaster. Up and down they whizzed, and voices behind them hooted and screamed and laughed. Lola knew that the track was worn and rickety, and she could hear the creaks and groans of the rotting wood. The whole structure swayed as the small cart rattled around and barely clung to the crackling beams. It was dangerous but no one else seemed to realize it.

A huge crowd watched from the ground, seemingly blind to the danger. They cheered and waved, and Lola couldn't figure out how to signal to them or the operator, who was hidden behind a cutout of a giant whale. Lola was rigid with rising terror. She tried to warn Del, who was laughing and cheering with her arms upraised, a jubilant smile lighting up her face.

Lola tried to scream, but she had no voice.

Del, watch out! Hold on! Del! Del!

She struggled against the heavy metal restraints that held her pressed against the hard plastic of the seat.

Del! Del, no, watch out!

But Del didn't hear her. She waved her arms and cheered. The restraint that held her, Lola saw, was only a thin, frayed rope. Lola plucked at her sleeve, but Del didn't seem to notice.

Nooooooo! She screamed as the rope gave way.

Del's body shot up out of the car just as the track dropped and they careened into a sharp downturn. Lola's fingers clawed the air, searching for Del's arms, legs, feet, but she was gone before Lola could get her. She tried to look up to see where Del had gone and was blinded by the bright sun.

No, no, come back! Del! No!

***

Del was awakened early by Lola's whimpers and gasps. She wasn't sure how to respond when Lola suddenly bucked violently upward and screamed.

Del tried to calm her but couldn't seem to wake her up. She shook Lola, called her name, but nothing worked for what felt like several minutes. Finally, clawing at Del's shirt, her face streaked with tears, Lola startled awake and stared into Del's eyes in shock. Her skin was white and cold, her eyes dark with fear and shock.

"Y'okay?" Del's voice was gruff.

"Oh, Del!"

Lola's arms were wrapped around Del's neck. She didn't think. She reached up and grabbed Del's face and kissed her. Del was stiff and unresponsive at first, but then her mouth softened, and she started kissing Lola back. Suddenly she pulled away, and Lola opened her eyes.

"Del, I—"

"Gotta go," Del muttered, pushing free and grabbing the black duffel and fleeing the room.

Oh, no. She must despise me, thought Lola, still slouched on the bed where Del had left her.

Damn, thought Del, racing down the stairs and to the car.

I should have questioned her about the money. I should have pushed her away.

She dumped her stuff in the car and stood at the open door for a moment. She trudged back up the stairs, opened the door, and stood outside.

Lola headed toward her, but Del held up her hands.

"Okay," she started, "we can't do stuff like that. I have to focus on finding this guy, and I can't do that if you, if we—"

"All right. I'm sorry, Del."

Del frowned. "We have to talk about something."

"Something else?" Anxiety made Lola's voice rise a little too high, and she blushed.

"Yeah." So, Del thought, she's uncomfortable too. Use it.

She eased inside, and Lola sat on the edge of the bed. Del pulled a chair over to sit in front of her, rubbing her hands together. Lola leaned forward, her eyes fixed on Del's. She looked so trusting! Del hesitated. Stop stalling!

"Phan got a call from a Feeb, uh, an FBI agent, Christopher James—do you recognize that name? Like, from when Beckett died, maybe?"

Lola considered for a moment and shook her head. "Sorry. I don't. But that doesn't mean he wasn't one of them. There were so many, and I was kind of in shock, I guess. My lawyer might know. I have his card in my wallet."

She handed Del the card, and Del pretended to study it.

"Because he was dead?"

"What?"

"You were in shock because Beckett was dead?" Del watched her closely. "You missed him? You loved him?" Was that really relevant? She told herself that it was.

There was a long pause. Lola hugged herself, looked down, crossed her legs. Uncrossed them, crossed them the other way.

"It's hard to—I was alone with just him for a long time. Then he died, and I was relieved, and I felt guilty for being relieved. Mostly, I couldn't believe he was gone. It was like God dying or something. I know it sounds stupid."

"Okay," Del continued as though Lola hadn't said anything.

"This guy, James, he says that they might have a lead. The Feds were investigating Beckett for a while. They started a couple years before he died. Did you know Henry Davis well?"

Lola shook her head. "No! Listen, the lawyers and whoever, they kept insisting that I must know Dr. Davis, that we conspired together, that we had an affair, that I was part of some big conspiracy to steal money or something." She took a deep breath and forced herself to speak slowly. "I never went to Orrin's office. I never met his partner. I didn't even know he had a partner. I never met the nurses or patients. We didn't go on vacations or out to dinner or to people's houses. I went to his brother's house once a year, and I went to the grocery store every Friday. Orrin would call me at ten o'clock and tell me to go. Then I had to call him by eleven o'clock and say I was back, or—that was it. I didn't go to lunch or to the movies or talk on the phone, except to Orrin and only when he said to. I cooked the dinner he told me to cook, and I wore the clothes he told me to wear. He picked my toothpaste and my deodorant and my underwear. He controlled everything I did."

Del didn't react. She filed the disclosures away for later, refusing to process them beyond storing them. She kept her muscles relaxed, her face blank.

Lola chewed her lip. "I don't think, I mean, maybe Orrin wasn't the nicest person in the world, but he wasn't a thief. I don't think he was a thief." She shook her head and lowered it. Her voice was a barely audible murmur. "I don't."

Del waited for Lola to lift her head. "Thank you. I have a better understanding of what things were like." There was more she wanted to say, more she wanted to ask. But now was not the time. And this was not the way. She took a deep breath, and she saw the way Lola braced herself for whatever Del might say next. *God, I hate that. I hate that kicked dog look.*

"Lola, the Feds seem pretty sure that Beckett was embezzling a lot of money. James told Phan that maybe somebody killed him—sabotaged his car, maybe—and maybe killed Davis too. That this somebody figured out what they were doing and has been trying to find the money. James says the guy might think you know where the money is. He might have been trying to get you out of the house. He thought you might have the money in your house."

Lola shook her head. "I swear, Del, I don't know anything about any secret money. If I knew anything about it, I would have told you way back when this whole thing started. I'm not keeping anything from you. I wouldn't do that."

"Listen, I gotta go. I'm meeting with Phan and the Fed in a little while." She rose and started to leave. One hand on the door, she paused. "Lola, what did you take with you?"

"What?"

"When Beckett kicked you out?"

She tilted her head. "Nothing. I mean, Orrin packed me a bag, some clothes. That's all. The key to my car. Cash, three thousand dollars. My purse. Oh!" She laughed and flushed bright red. "The next day, I snuck into the house. I took my computer." She shrugged.

Del eyed her. "Nothing else?"

Lola shook her head. "No. I was trying not to make him mad. I thought maybe it was a trick. I thought he was probably going to kill me anyway, but I didn't want to give him a reason. So, just the computer. And my music box. It isn't worth anything, it just has sentimental value."

Did Beckett give it to you? If it has sentimental value, then you loved him, once. Dammit. I'm focused on all the wrong things. She watched Lola watch her.

"Can I see it?" Del's voice was even.

Lola crossed over to her purse and fished out a little wooden box. She handed it to Del.

"Where did you get this?"

"Dr. Beckett gave it to me."

"When?" Dr. Beckett? Not Orrin?

"Um, when I was sixteen. At the time, I—" She shook her head. "Anyway, like I said, it isn't worth any money."

Del held the small box in her open palm and looked at it. It was maybe three inches square, two inches tall. Pressed wood, the varnished surface rubbed almost bare. Cheap, the kind of thing an indifferent relative gives a little girl for Christmas.

"Can I open it? Is that okay?"

At Lola's nod, she lifted the lid. "Daddy's Little Girl" tinkled out until she held down the trigger. *Gross.* She suppressed a grimace.

"At the time, you what?"

"Huh?" Lola's eyebrows rose, "Nothing." She flushed. Her arms were wrapped around her middle again.

Del waited her out. *Come on, sweetheart, just tell me. I already know the story, anyway. You were a kid, all alone. And he was nice to you, and you thought he cared about you. You trusted him, and then he turned out to be a monster. How else could it have gone?*

"It's embarrassing. Stupid. I guess I thought Dr. Beckett wanted to be, like, my dad, sort of. He was very kind, then. He was my friend back then. I thought so anyway. It was my birthday and he bought a cake, and he gave me this beautiful music box, and I was thrilled. There was a key inside for a car—you know, my car, the brown one? He was never creepy or mean, not then. And I thought, you know, it's like I have a dad now." She laughed. "Stupid. It was my own fault. I should have known better."

Del shook her head. Filed that story away for later along with all the rest of it. Pretty much what she'd figured, but still—the pain and shame in Lola's voice, in her eyes. It was worse, somehow, hearing the way Lola blamed herself. Even though the victims always did. She flicked her finger around the bits and pieces that filled the tiny space—there wasn't much. A button, a necklace, a ring, and a picture of Lola as a little girl—big eyes and a hesitant smile. She closed the lid before she could get caught staring at those big, sad eyes, that tiny child's fragility.

"Well," she said, "I don't see anything worth killing for."

Lola reached for the box. "Sorry," she said, "it would have been nice to find something in there that explained all this."

Del pulled it away and put it on the table. "I wanna have this checked over. Maybe there are fingerprints or something. Um, can I have your purse, too?"

Lola nodded.

"Del," she began, "you don't think that this is what The Creep's after, do you? Something in my purse? My music box?"

"'The Creep?'" Del sounded amused.

"That's what I call him. Remember? I told you, after I remembered him from the ambulance."

"Oh, right."

"You still don't believe me."

Del searched her face again. "I think you believe it. And I don't want to hurt your feelings, but it was the middle of the night. You've been wound up, losing sleep, scared. You've been through a lot, and you dreamed it. I know it felt really real to you, but I think it was a dream."

It was a dismissal. Lola chewed her lip.

Del was distracted. She got a towel and wrapped the box in it. "I gotta go, okay? I'll call you later." She held Lola's purse aloft, grimacing at the unfamiliar weight.

"I can tell you what he looks like," Lola said, her voice too loud. "I can talk to the sketch artist again, and this time I can do a better job. I promise!"

Del looked at her with shielded eyes. "Lola."

"Del, do you trust me or not?"

"It's not about trust. It's about being realistic."

"But I can tell you now. I couldn't before, because he had on a wig, I think, and glasses. But now I can tell you what he looks like."

"Lola." Del's jaw twitched. "You want to help, right?"

Lola nodded.

"So, isn't it possible that your mind tried to put this all together, tried to fill in the blanks?"

"It's possible, I guess, but that's not what happened." Lola started to cry. She hated that. Whenever she tried to explain something, or tried to fight for something, or got too upset about something, she would start to cry. And she saw that Del lost what little respect she had for her when the tears started. Still, she had to try. "That's not what happened," she repeated. "It wasn't a dream. It happened, I swear! Can't you just give me a chance?"

"Okay." Del shrugged. "I'll set up an appointment for you to meet with the sketch artist." But it was clear that Del was just placating her.

She was angry and frustrated and wanted to push the point,

but suddenly the feeling of dread that had overtaken Lola after her bad dream resurfaced. She was embarrassed and unable to explain her fear, but she drew nearer to Del.

"Please," she whispered, "don't go. Just stay with me, please?" She knew she must sound crazy, but she couldn't shake the feeling that if she let Del walk out that door, she'd never see her again.

Del just looked at her, frowning. "I can't do that, Lola."

"I just have a really bad feeling. I know it's stupid. I know you have things to do. But I need you to stay. Del, please, Tom can come here and get the box. We should go to a new hotel, anyway. We've been here too long. Please, Del?" She gripped Del's arm with rigid fingers.

But Del disengaged herself. "Don't be scared. I made sure no one followed me here, I always make sure."

Lola shook her head. "That's not what I'm saying."

"Lola, don't worry about me. I know how to take care of myself, remember? And we'll change hotels soon. It'll be fine. You're just getting a little cabin fever." She paused. "Beckett—he sorta kept you locked up, right?"

Lola looked at her with wary eyes.

"I know it feels like that again. I hate—but it's almost over. I can feel it." She leaned over suddenly and kissed Lola hard.

Lola's lips yielded under hers, and she felt a charge run between them.

Del hesitated. *This is* wrong. *Don't do this. She's scared and confused. Stop this. Leave now.*

But her body had taken over. All it wanted was more Lola. *Don't do this. Don't be an asshole, Mason.* Pulling away, she held Lola away from her and saw the disappointment in her eyes. She should say something. She should reassure her and explain herself and establish an appropriate boundary. She opened her mouth and closed it again. Lola stared at her.

She shook her head and slid out the door as quickly as she could, gripping Lola's purse and music box in her hands and trying not to look like she was running away.

CHAPTER TWENTY-FIVE

Lola was still catching her breath when Del swept out the door.

"Wait," she called, but it was too late.

She couldn't think clearly. She forced herself to eat, brush her teeth, shower and comb her hair. She straightened the room, packed their bags, and put them by the door. She looked around the room. Opened the curtains. Closed them again. Turned the television on and tried to stare at the nonsense on the screen. Turned it off. Checked all of the drawers and under the beds and in the bathroom. All the time, her anxiety kept building.

"Okay," she told herself, lying on her back on the neatly made bed, "just breathe. Empty your mind. Stop letting your emotions rule your thoughts. Let your mind speak." She leveled her breathing, relaxed her shoulders and unclenched her jaw. "Be an open jar. Just let the truth fill you."

The main character in her book did this, and it worked for her. Lola felt stupid and self-conscious and childish. She waited. For a long time, she couldn't do it. She scratched her arm and looked around the room.

She remembered the first time she looked at Orrin and realized he was an old man. His hands had become arthritic, and his hearing was getting a little weaker, but those things hadn't seemed to bother him. One morning, she saw him rubbing his knees and frowning. She pretended not to see, but he flew into a rage. He shot up from the bed where he'd been putting on his socks and shoes. When had he started sitting down to do that? She didn't remember. He growled and shoved her into the dresser. She hit her elbow and side and fell, and he screamed at her and hit her with his shoe while she cowered at his feet. Then he got tired. She felt it. The shoe hit her, but not as hard. He was out of breath.

It was afterward, waiting for him to leave for work, that she noticed his slight limp. Getting up so quickly had hurt. Now, lying on the hotel bed, months after Orrin's death, Lola felt as though she were back there on the floor in Orrin's bedroom, blood running down the side of her face, realizing that Orrin was almost seventy and an old man.

At some point he would be really elderly, and she would have to take care of him. She imagined her future self, saw a future Lola with thick streaks of gray in her hair, a nest of wrinkles around her eyes. Orrin would have to retire at some point. He wouldn't be able to drive anymore. Whether that was five years away or twenty, it would happen. He would depend on her for meals, for medicine, for washing up. She would have to turn him to prevent bedsores. She would have to put his pills in little boxes, one for each mealtime, one at bedtime. She would have to drive him to the doctor and ask questions and fill prescriptions and get him to take the pills. She would have to take care of the money and the bills and the insurance and the house, and he would question how she did everything, and she would always have done it wrong.

There would be temptations, moments when just a bit of extra morphine, a hapless foot on an IV line, some small bit of what could be error or neglect or carelessness would free her of him forever. Would she be strong enough not to give in to these temptations? She agonized over the possibility that she might kill him if she could get away with it. And maybe even if she couldn't. She could see herself planning it, figuring out how to make sure he was dead before calling for help. Could see herself accepting condolences and walking away from his cooling body without a backward glance. A shudder of horror ripped through her, and she recoiled from the images in her mind.

She was back in the present again, her back settled against the lumpy bedspread in a hotel just outside of San Francisco. Orrin was dead and had been for months, and she was no longer that woman who was contemplating whether or not she would murder her husband as soon as he had grown old and weak enough. She was not a murderer. She had not done the terrible things she had thought about. Orrin had died, but she hadn't killed him.

"Thank God," she whispered.

Why in the world was she thinking about Orrin? He had nothing to do with her life now. What she needed to do was focus and figure out if Del really needed help or not. And for some reason she was sure that if she just listened carefully enough, the answer to that question would come to her. She waited until silence filled her. She stopped fidgeting and worrying and remembering. She stopped fighting. Her body seemed far away, but she didn't let that scare her. Her breathing was slow and easy and regular. She waited. She waited. Suddenly, she knew. Del was in danger. Lola had to save her.

Bolting up, she used the bedside phone to call Del. And got no answer. She left messages everywhere she could think of. She started to call a taxi and then remembered that Del had taken her purse. What was she going to do, with no money, no credit cards?

***

Unaware of Lola's panic, Del met with Phan at the station. To her relief, he didn't make a big deal out of her failure to get Lola to talk about Beckett's routine. Like Del, he seemed to think it was probably a dead end. The hate mail seemed like a much more viable lead, and they thumbed through the most likely nutjobs.

"Nothing," Del muttered. "All smoke, no fire."

"I sent her purse and music box to the lab." Phan shrugged. "But you know how slow that is."

"The clock is winding down on this thing."

"You think?"

It was Del's turn to shrug. "Don't know why."

Phan eyed her. "You can hardly claim to be objective."

"I can't argue with that." She rubbed her forehead. "But I'm right."

They met with Dominguez to prepare for their meeting with the Fed. Dominguez had developed detailed profiles on everyone connected with Orrin Beckett. It was impressively comprehensive and completely useless.

"The problem," Dominguez complained, "is with Lola Beckett."

"Bannon."

"No family," he fumed, "no friends. No job. No trips. No bank account or debit card or checkbook. No credit cards. Nothing. Nobody. Listen, I can tell you the name of the doc's favorite boat wax, what brand of shoes he liked best, where he bought his scotch, and who he stiffed for a grand after last year's Super Bowl. But I can't find shit on her until a year ago. Either she's hiding a whole secret life, or she lived in a cave for twenty years."

"Cave," grunted Del, and the two men exchanged a look.

"Mason," started Phan, "I don't want to step on anything here, okay?"

Del eyed him, her face a mask of rigid control.

He signaled to Dominguez, who left. "I don't care if she's your friend, or your girlfriend, or whatever. Not my business, okay? But you know her. You're the only one who does. She trusts you, at least a little. If you tell me something, I swear I'll help you protect her. But don't shut me out. Don't make me find something on my own, or I'll have to make it all official and public. See what I'm saying? I don't have any interest in fucking over a nice lady who already got fucked over enough, you know? Just tell me—is she hiding *anything*?"

Del spread her arms, palms up, fingers spread. "Seriously, I'm not holding out on you. She's an innocent. From what I can tell, Beckett owned her from the time she was sixteen."

There was a short pause.

Phan made a face. "Kaylee's not much younger than that. She still plays with Barbies."

"Listen, Phan." Del tried not to sound defensive. "She's not hiding anything criminal. She doesn't know anything. I poked all around and didn't find anything but a nasty old man and a scared girl."

"Abuse?"

Del shrugged.

"He was a doctor," Phan commented.

"Probably patched her up himself." Del examined the laminate that peeled off the edge of the chair. She didn't want to talk about that. Think about that. It clouded her thinking too much.

"Hmmm." Phan grunted. He leveled his gaze at her, his expression remote. "One thing is off."

She looked at him with narrowed eyes.

"Okay." He ticked off on this fingers, "One, dirty old man finds a pretty little orphan. He grooms her, wins her trust, isolates her. Two, locks her up with a wedding ring. Says he's her lord and master, whatever. Three, uses threats and maybe violence to keep her under his thumb. Four, he owns her—no friends, no family, no job, no money, no way out. He'll kill her if she leaves, all that shit. Well, what's number five?"

"He kills her." The answer was automatic, and Del heard her voice saying the words before she knew she'd thought them.

"Right. But does he kick her out and hop in a car with his girlfriend? He's been embezzling for five, six years. He and his partner have been defrauding Medicare for twice that long. They have all this money stashed. Together? Or do they each take a cut and keep their shares separate? Where's the money? Play it out. Which is more important to Beckett, the money or the wife? He could have just buried her in the backyard, and no one would have missed her. So why let her go, all of a sudden?"

"Lola says Beckett didn't take the money. What if she's right? What if the partner is the thief, and he just sucked Beckett into it? Maybe he blackmailed the partner or something. Maybe—"

"Hold on," Phan interrupted. "Can you trust her assessment of him? She probably has Stockholm Syndrome. All those years under his thumb, you know how this shit works."

Del shrugged. "Maybe. She was freaked when he died. She might not want to think of him as a thief."

Dominguez strutted over, a huge bagel forgotten in his hand. "Davis, the guy's supposed to be on some kinda RV trip? Only he hasn't used his cell phone, his credit card, anything for over two months."

Phan turned and frowned. "We knew that."

"Yeah," Dominguez retorted, "but did you know he took ten grand outta his credit union this morning?"

"Where?" Phan and Del demanded, together.

"Oakland." Dominguez grinned. "I'll have him by dinnertime. Assholes always get stupid, sooner or later. Especially rich guys. Can't go ten minutes without a manicure or a hooker or some nice designer blow."

Phan looked at Del and smiled. "We'd love to join in the fun, but we have to meet with the Fed."

Del rolled her eyes but rose and tipped a wave at Dominguez as she and Phan stalked out to the car.

"My turn," she muttered, and Phan took the passenger seat. "Let's get this over with."

"Try not to lose your shit, Mason."

She made a face. "Me? I'm cool as ice."

"Not where Lola is concerned."

She grimaced. "I'll try."

His reply was a quiet grunt, and they joined the crawling line of cars headed toward Market Street. Del tapped her fingers against the steering wheel in impatience. Traffic was exactly why she loved her bike so much.

"Relax, we'll be there in two minutes."

***

Lola gripped the seat belt, trying not to look impatient. She didn't want to be rude, especially after Marco had been kind enough to come all the way to the hotel in Foster City and pick her up.

"Thank you so much," she said, smiling at him. "I hate to impose on you like this." She took in his paint-spattered clothes. "And to interrupt you while you're working."

"Don't worry about it," he murmured, merging onto the freeway. "I was just glad to hear your voice! I've been so worried. You both dropped off the face of the earth! I've been calling you every day. I don't like having to guess what's going on with you, Lola—things have been pretty scary."

"It's been a weird couple of weeks," she replied. "Sorry I haven't been staying in touch. Del said we had to lay low."

"I understand. Your house?"

"Please. Last time I couldn't get in touch with Del, that's where she was. And I want to see the damage—I told you about that, right?"

"I have to say, the neighborhood was pretty boring until you moved in."

She made a wry face. "Well, hopefully, it can get boring again really soon."

"Amen," Marco muttered, reaching over to squeeze her arm. Lola swallowed hard. Marco's kindness made her feel weak, and she needed to stay strong.

When he dropped her off, handing back the spare key she'd given him the month before, she thanked him again and waved off his offer of help. Then she gingerly pulled the crime scene tape off her front door.

She looked around and found that the house wasn't nearly as bad as she'd thought it would be. Things had been knocked over and pushed aside, but her books were okay. Unfortunately, most of the furniture would have to be replaced, and all of the artwork. She inspected the kitchen. Several dishes had been broken, and a cupboard door hung askew. She opened the fridge. The food was all gone, too. There wasn't even any coffee in the house. Orrin chuckled, and Lola waved him away.

Del obviously wasn't around. Lola called and left her a message apologizing for deviating from the plan and explaining that she was at the house.

"Oh," she added, "don't worry, I'm setting the alarm." She punched in the numbers, but the light didn't blink. Well, she thought, maybe Del had it disconnected altogether because of the other cops coming and going.

She looked around. Okay, what now? She had to figure out where Del was and what the source of the danger was. She was sure that the truth was somewhere in her own mind, that she was inches away from grasping it, and her frustration mounted.

"This couldn't possibly be more aggravating."

***

When Del and Phan returned from meeting with James, they were both frustrated. He'd had little to tell them and had seemed more interested in picking their brains. They'd felt like he was stonewalling them and had responded by doing the same.

"Typical Feeb," Phan griped, and Del nodded.

James wanted to take custody of Lola, shake her down. He was clearly convinced that she had the money or knew where it was.

Del kept her cool throughout most of the fruitless meeting but ended by bursting out, "Listen, asshole, we don't care about the money. That's your problem. We're trying to keep this woman alive. Got it? I mean, okay, you don't give a shit if some innocent civilian dies, fine. But we do."

She'd stormed out, leaving Phan to smooth things over and say their goodbyes. She regretted losing her cool, but it was done. James was useless, a bland blond bureaucrat in a blue suit.

"Sorry," she muttered to Phan as they entered the precinct.

"Guy's an ass," he responded companionably. "Funny, he looks a hell of a lot like Beckett's old partner."

"You think?" She frowned. "Davis?" She sat at her computer

and pulled up Davis's picture. "Yeah, I guess. A little younger, though. And less... I don't know what."

"Gin soaked." Phan raised an eyebrow, and Del shrugged. "Yeah."

"You know, Lola—never mind. It was just a dream."

"What?

Del was embarrassed. "She woke up night before last with a bad dream, hollering. Said her attacker was in the ambulance with her after the pipe bomb. She wants to meet with the sketch artist."

Phan frowned. "You never said anything. You don't believe her?"

"I think it was a dream. She has a lot of crazy dreams, Phan. I think she just wanted to be able to help, you know?"

"Still," he started.

Their cell phones buzzed at the same time, and they both listened to Lola's messages. The desk sergeant handed them each a message from her, rolling her eyes.

"She's at the house?" They looked at each other.

Del called the house and got a busy signal. Was the phone off the hook, or had it been messed with? There wasn't enough time to check.

They raced to the car, and Phan shoved Del toward the passenger side with a grunt. As they tore out of the parking lot, Del dialed the security company and was told that the alarm system had been turned off the night before.

"No. I turned it on myself. And the resident just turned it on."

The manager patiently said, no, the unit was not activated.

"Do it remotely."

That wasn't possible.

She hung up and tried the house again. Busy signal again. Phan, who had the roof light flashing as he wove through the heavy traffic, pushed the laptop at her. He was on the phone. Of course, the cameras! Del pulled up the program and switched from camera to camera, searching for Lola.

"She's in the kitchen." Del heard her voice shaking and steadied it. "Looks fine. She's cleaning up. She's alone."

"Check."

"No one in any other rooms."

They were only minutes away, and Del wanted to push the car faster. Maybe she should have told Lola about the cameras. She would have stayed away from the house if she'd known the guy could see her in there.

"Come on," she muttered as a delivery truck veered in front of them and forced Phan to brake. She called the house phone again. Busy signal.

"Okay." Phan's voice was calm. "Civilian alone. Gotta figure he can see her. No landlines. Cell?"

"It was in her purse when I took it." Stupid, she told herself. *Really* stupid.

"That's okay. Mason? Del! I need you to focus. Should have had more eyes on the place. Can't see the garage, the laundry room or the side yard. There's a part of each hallway, up and down, that's outside camera range. And the front of the house is blind." He shook his head. "Listen, she's fine. She's alone, right?"

Del shook her head. "For now. As far as we know."

CHAPTER TWENTY-SIX

Lola heard a faint noise, footsteps on hardwood floor. Del! She was relieved but a little nervous. Del might be angry with her. As she started to call out a hello, she saw a tall figure heading toward her. Not Del. A man—a bad man, moving fast.

She shook her head, too frightened to think.

Move! She turned around and started to run toward the laundry room, the back door. But time seemed to slow down. She felt like she was wading in molasses, and before she'd gone two steps he was on her.

He grabbed her around the waist, lifted and swung her. She saw the wall coming straight at her and tried to twist away, but there was no time. She hit the wall with her head, her shoulder, and the side of her face.

He let go as she hit, and she bounced off the wall and hit the floor. She grunted and watched tears and blood drop from her face onto the linoleum. She tried to scrabble away from him, but he was too fast and too strong. He grabbed her arms, squeezing them and pulling her up backward. She bit back a cry of pain, pressing her lips together.

"Time to be a good girl, Lola."

His voice sounded familiar. She hadn't seen his face well enough to be sure, but he smelled like The Creep. This recognition broke her limited control, and she whimpered. She couldn't remember how to move her head, her body.

He was talking, but she couldn't make out what he was saying. This had always been the case. When things were too scary, she couldn't hear what the bad people were saying. This usually made them even madder. She heard one word, "whore."

She finally remembered how and twisted her head to try and see his face, but this just made him grip her even tighter. She felt like she couldn't breathe and panic set in. She didn't want to panic. If she did, she would go away. But it was too late. The old helpless feeling washed over her, and she stopped struggling. Into the hole she slid, and everything went away.

***

As Phan brought the car to an abrupt stop in front of a house several doors down from Lola's, Del was still flipping from one camera view to another, unable for a moment to locate Lola. Then she spotted an intruder and switched gears. Her mind recorded: white male, over six feet, medium build. Dark blue hooded sweatshirt, hood up and almost covering a dark baseball cap, pulled low. Dark blue pants. Slacks? Dress shoes, too. Weird. He was carrying an unconscious victim, female, toward the stairs.

She turned the computer toward Phan and gestured at the screen without a word. They watched as the assailant disappeared out of range. She scrolled through the images until she saw him in the master bedroom. He came in and raised his arms higher, then dropped the victim on the bed. She almost rolled off, and he stopped her with his knee. Del's breath came in short puffs as the man stood over the unconscious victim—Lola—for a long couple of minutes. Del strained to see. She heard Phan shooting short bursts of words into his phone.

"He's trying to wake her up," Phan guessed.

"Then she's alive."

"Or he thinks she is."

Del's gaze flicked to Phan's face and back to the screen.

"Is she breathing?" Del heard Phan's question but didn't answer. The doer seemed worried, too, because he checked her pulse. Apparently satisfied that she was alive, he touched her hair, her lips. He wiped something off her face—was that blood?

He obviously hadn't anticipated her being unconscious. Had he hit her too hard, or had she fainted? Maybe she'd gone a gomer. It was hard to tell. Now he'd have to adjust his plan, whatever it had been. That made things worse. When bad guys had to improvise, it made them impulsive, reckless.

This was too personal. She'd known that from the beginning, but now it was too late to change things. Her mind raced, going over and rejecting several possible approaches. What was the best way to handle this? She knew procedure—wait for backup, establish a perimeter, wait for a negotiator, wait for a SWAT team. Wait, wait and wait. While that fucker had Lola to himself. Acid boiled up her esophagus.

"There's no way in hell I'm sitting on my ass while this shithead hurts her."

"Wait," he said. "She's out. He doesn't know we're here. He's not planning to kill her, or he'd have already done it. He cleaned off her face. You saw that, right? He wants to talk to her. We have time."

Del was about to argue, though he was probably right, when she saw that the holding pattern had broken. The assailant had taken off his sweatshirt and tossed it out of camera range.

White dress shirt, no tie. The baseball cap stayed on, but when he leaned down she saw his hair. It was dirty blond, short. She wished she could see his face, but the camera was behind him. He reached down and lifted Lola, moving her further toward the middle of the bed. Del grunted. *Fuck.* He set her down and pulled his arms out slowly, sitting on the edge of the bed. Del still couldn't see his face. He reached over and stroked her hair. He pulled a strand up and leaned over to sniff it.

Like I did, thought Del. Her stomach was boiling with liquid fire. *That woman is not Lola. She's just a female victim. Not Lola. Or she pays for your distraction.*

He caressed the victim's face, ran the tips of his fingers back and forth along her lower lip. He shifted closer on the bed. There was a glint of metal as he pulled a knife from his pocket and stroked the handle. Del heard a small animal sound.

"Mason!" Phan's voice came from far away.

"Mason? Fuck. Del!" He grabbed at the computer, and she grabbed him by the throat. It was a second before she realized what she was doing and released him. He ignored what she'd done and looked at her. "Stay or go?"

"Go," she said, but her body wouldn't move, and neither would her mind. She wanted to see the computer.

"Exigent circumstances compel us to alter procedure to ensure—I saw a knife. Do you agree?"

"Uh." Her brain was on vacation.

"You wanna just sit there, or should we go play cops and shitheads?"

Del felt that penetrate her mental fog. "Yeah. The garage. I have a key to the side door."

They sidled down the street, close to the residences. She eased the side gate open, glad that it didn't squeal in protest. Phan followed as she crept along the outer wall. The windows were closed. No noise from inside the house. She checked her weapon.

Adrenaline had burned through the last of her mental haze, and she felt sharp and energized, almost high. The victim mattered, but it was the bad guy she was focused on. Her daddy's voice coached her: watch the predator, not the prey.

He looked taller than herself and Phan, but not by much. Phan might have a few pounds on him. He was wearing business clothes, so he might be softer than he looked. Something about his clothes bothered her. The pants, the shirt—there was something about the way his clothes fit that pinged for her, but she couldn't figure out why. She shook it off. Later. Think about it later.

She slid her key into the garage's side door and eased it open. Thank God Lola was a neat freak. The garage was empty of clutter that might have impeded their nearly silent progress toward and then up the stairs into the house. The same key opened that door, and Del was just inserting it when she felt Phan's hand on her arm. He held something in front of his face, and she peered back. It was a Smartphone, and he was checking the cameras.

The bad guy was still in the master bedroom, but it was hard to see what he was doing on the small screen. As long as he didn't have an accomplice in the house, they would be fine. The entry hall was empty, so were the stairs. They cleared the downstairs in seconds.

Two and a half minutes since she and Phan had left the car. They heard voices, the victim's and the bad guy's. The victim was conscious and on the move, heading toward the upstairs hallway. Phan gestured at Del to follow him into the laundry room.

***

"Please, I don't know what you want." Lola hated the way she sounded, weak and craven. But The Creep had a huge black gun pointed at her, and she was lightheaded.

The hole was there. It wanted her, and she wanted it, too. But she couldn't give in to that, could she? Wouldn't that be wrong? It would, she was sure of it, though she wasn't sure why. She stared up at The Creep, whose face was partly hidden by dark sunglasses and a baseball cap. He was holding her arm and hustling her toward the stairs and then down them. At the bottom, they passed within several feet of the front door, and she considered running for it.

She must have signaled her intention in some way because he tightened his grip on her arm and rushed her even faster toward the kitchen. The moment passed and her momentary hope of escape was dashed. What would he do to her?

She'd woken to find him leaning over her, and she'd felt his hot breath on her face, smelled his toothpaste and soap and that other smell. She remembered the first time he'd stood over her, cursing at her and trying to drag her into the house. And the encounter in the ambulance. It had been real, she was sure of that—he looked just the way she remembered. Her legs buckled under her—now he had her. He yanked her back up with a jerk, and she bit her lip to keep from crying out.

"You're in trouble now, girlie," said Orrin, and his voice was indifferent, neither exultant nor concerned. She looked around but didn't see him.

"Orrin?" But no, she remembered. "You died."

The Creep laughed and shook her. "You are one crazy little bitch, aren't you?"

She arched her back and twisted her legs, catching him by surprise and wrenching free of his grasp. He grabbed her hair and slammed her head into the wall with an almost casual movement.

There was a blank moment. Then she was floating and breathless with shock. She forgot how to breathe, how to speak, how to think. She couldn't even register the pain for several seconds. Her vision went white, and everything was eclipsed by the need to flee the sudden tsunami bouncing off the inside of her skull. It was like a loud sound inside of her head, only with no noise, and it was nauseating and dizzying. She was falling but didn't know how to react to this. What are you supposed to do, when you're falling? This seemed a theoretical question, and she tried to focus on it but couldn't seem to care about the answer. And then there was nothing.

Some unknowable quantity of time went by. She was sitting in a chair. She tried to remember where she was. She tried to stand up and was stopped short. Her wrists hurt. Her head was swimming. Her arms hurt. Her head hurt. Her eyes hurt. She sucked in air. It hurt, but it cleared her head a tiny bit.

Oh, good, she thought. I can breathe. Her vision was coming back in watery, broken pieces. She couldn't remember where she was or why she was afraid, and she wasn't sure *when* she was. She tried to focus, to ground herself. She started by wiggling her toes. That was always good. If she could wiggle her toes, then she could maybe think. She wiggled her fingers. Blinked. Breathed slowly and deeply.

Focus, Lola. Find the up and the down. Figure out where you are.
Figure out when you are. And who's here.

She knew that her hands were bound behind her back and
that there was something stuffed in her mouth. She felt the chair
being pulled sideways. Something swam in front of her, and she
tried to focus on it. It was a face, she thought, though there was
something wrong with it. There were no eyes! She panicked and
reared backward, trying to flee the scary face with no eyes, but
the chair, and she with it, slammed back down. She cried out in
pain and fear. The sound was strange—why? Oh, the thing in her
mouth. No Eyes Man had put a hurting thing in her mouth.

He was talking. His voice was quiet and pleasant sounding,
but there was menace behind it. She was glad that she couldn't
hear his words. No Eyes Man was a bad man. He wasn't Orrin,
but he was bad like Orrin. Like Orrin was before he died. He
would hurt her. She was sure of this. And that she would be
unable to stop him. She started sliding toward the hole.

Something stopped her, and the going away feeling left with a
snap. She was irritated. In the hole, she would have been safe. No
Eyes Man couldn't hurt her there, not really. But the irritation
warred with gratitude. There was something she wanted to
remember, wasn't there? Someone.

Del! Del was coming. She would get Lola's message and
come here, and the bad man with no eyes would kill Del. It was
like in her dream: she couldn't move, couldn't speak, and Del
would come and she would die, and Lola couldn't stop it.

She was here to stay but helpless to save Del. Tears burned
her cheeks, and she began to cry big, ugly sobs. This made her
choke on the rag in her mouth. She twisted her wrists in the iron
bands of the handcuffs—that's what they were. It was useless.
She was useless. She tried to rise out of the chair, and the man
slapped her and sat her back down hard again. He was talking,
asking her something, but she still couldn't understand him. He
had eyes now. They were wide and wild, but she barely registered
this. It was the gun she saw, big and black and round. It seemed
impossibly large, like a gun in a cartoon. Every time he stopped
talking, he gestured at her with the gun, and her eyes were fixed
on it.

Then she realized that he wanted her to talk to him. She nodded and locked eyes on him. He stared into her face for a moment and pulled the rag from her mouth with a sneer of disgust at her gagging.

"You finally done playing around?"

Lola nodded again. Whatever he wanted, she needed to convince him to leave here, so that Del wouldn't come and find them and get killed. He was looking for something.

"Orrin's money," she said aloud, and the man jabbed at her shoulder with the gun.

"Get on with it. Where's the money, bitch? Where the fuck is it?" His voice was rising in volume and pitch, and it was almost comically high by the end of his question. Lola's mind raced. What would he believe? She hadn't decided what to say when she heard herself speaking.

"He put it in a storage unit in Daly City."

"Bullshit. Don't play games with me, whore. I'll start getting creative."

Creative? What did he mean by that? He put the gun somewhere, and then he had a knife. He used it to lightly draw an invisible line from her collarbone to her pelvis, and she gasped in horror. The kitties! Bile rose in her throat, and she gagged. He laughed, but she could see that he was disgusted. She watched as he put the knife back on his belt. Then the gun was in her face again.

"Lola, you have one chance here." His voice was calm now, almost friendly. It was scarier, for some reason.

"No, mister, I swear. Orrin made me get a storage unit in Daly City. I used a fake name and paid for two years in advance. I'd never even been to Daly City before. Orrin drove me there from Folsom, and he made me get a storage unit and use a fake name. He didn't tell me what it was for. But I figured it out. I figured it out when those FBI agents—oh!"

Her mouth dropped open. She stared at the man who held a gun in front of her face. He was the man with the newscaster hair and the piggy eyes and the shark's smile. Who was he? She wasn't sure. She should have paid more attention to who all those people were, but she had let the peacock, her lawyer, talk to them as much as possible. I was such a weak, stupid, cowardly ninny!

"What's the address?" If he noticed her realization, he gave no sign of it. Maybe he had decided to kill her a long time ago, whether she knew who he was or not.

"I don't know. Orrin drove there. He waited in the car while I rented the unit. But I know where it is."

She searched her memory. Hadn't there been a storage place near that mall? It seemed like a million years ago, that day when she'd forgotten her cell phone and Del had been mad at her, and she'd been such a baby.

There had been a lot of cemeteries, she remembered. But there had been a storage place too. Right by the freeway. She'd gotten lost and had turned around in the driveway, and there had been a metal gate. "That street, the one with the man's name, the Spanish name. There's a freeway with the same name—it's Spanish. Uh, there are two words, like a first name and a last name, something, Herrera Serra?"

He knew what she meant. She could see it in his face. She watched him consider her with a kind of cool detachment. He wanted to believe her.

She fought impatience and rested against the back of the chair. Don't let him see that you want to leave. She saw him decide and let out her breath. They would go. They would get in his car and drive to Daly City, and he would be somewhere that Del wasn't. She almost smiled but instead chewed on her lip.

"You have the key?"

She hadn't thought of that. Storage units have keys? She had assumed there was one key for all of them and you showed a receipt to the man and he opened it for you. She tried to think of a key she could present as the right one. Did they have special keys, or did they look like regular keys? She couldn't think. She licked her lips.

"Orrin kept the original one and made a copy for me in case of an emergency. He said I could only open the unit if he told me to. I kept the key in my music box. In my purse." She was babbling, but she couldn't stop herself. "He didn't kick me out for real. It was all part of his plan to trick his partner. I went to the motel, and he was supposed to fake his death. When I saw the story about the accident on the news, I thought it was staged, and that he'd show up any minute and tell me we were going to get the money."

Del listened to this from the laundry room and bit her lip. Lola was the worst liar in history. Her voice gave her away. And Del would bet that her face was giving it away too. *How could I have suspected she was a criminal?* She shrugged away the question. She could castigate herself later, when Lola was safe. Lola was still babbling away.

"But he never showed up. And I thought maybe he decided to get the money by himself and leave me behind. That's why I came down to the Bay Area. I figured I'd check on the place, and it would be empty. But I was afraid to check it. I didn't know for sure if Orrin was still alive, if he was going to show up someday and kill me if I'd taken the money. So I've been waiting. I didn't know what to do."

Del chewed on the inside of her cheek. *He was the Feeb, and he'd been across the table from her, two feet away, not two hours before. How could I not have seen that he was the guy? What did I miss? Again, that was a question for later.* Del signaled to Phan and snuck forward.

"Well, Lola, that's not half bad." James's voice sounded amused. "Really. I admire a bitch with a good imagination. I bet you like to use that imagination in bed, don't you? I bet you do, you clever little whore."

Lola gasped, and James laughed. Del tightened her mouth. *The woman's not shocked by a gun in her face, but a reference to sex knocks her on her ass?* She shook away the thought. *That wasn't Lola in there. It was a victim. Anonymous. Not Lola.*

She could see James's back now. He had a Luger trained on the victim's chest. But his stance was off. He was distracted, wasn't paying attention. If she and Phan could get close enough, if the victim didn't look at them and give it away, they might have a chance at ending this without firing a shot. She glanced at

Phan, and he eased to the right. He would cover her. She crept forward and saw that James was off purpose again.

Del forced herself to relax, to slow her breathing, to steady her weapon hand. All we have to do is keep her alive. That's all. If she gets hurt, it's okay. I'll take care of her. She just has to be alive. He wants her alive too. Not Lola, she reminded herself yet again. A nameless victim.

He was breathing hard, standing too close to Lola. Not like a Feeb. Not like a cop. Not even like a regular bad guy. He could have grabbed her months ago, if he'd wanted to. But he'd been playing. She imagined a cat batting around a helpless little mouse. He wanted the money, but there was something else. Something about Lola had turned him on, twisted him off purpose. Otherwise he would have just taken her that first time. He'd been watching her, enjoying her. He'd gotten distracted. Turned on.

Darkness swirled around her vision, and she swallowed hard. That wasn't Lola. She was a victim, someone with no face and no name and no soft lips and no big, pleading eyes. She shook her head to clear it. It worked, she noted with some detachment. It was a bad guy and a victim, and she'd only lost a second to her distraction. She flexed her hand. She'd been gripping her weapon with tight fingers, like a rookie. She softened her knees, blinked until her focus on James was sharper than a razor.

He was standing right in front of the victim now, grinding his pelvis against her head. His breathing was hectic, and his weapon hand was playing with her hair, barely holding the Luger. He was murmuring, pushing against her. Del ignored the victim's crying.

The kitchen was too small, too enclosed. Del's breathing accelerated, and she slowed it down. She was only three feet from James, but he was practically on top of the victim who was trying without success to pull away from him. Del felt black flames of rage flare inside her head but squelched them. Hate him later.

"Think you're clever, huh? You think you're a clever little bitch, don't you? Oh, my Lola, you're a good little whore. A clever little whore." He was whispering now, a lover sharing sweet nothings. His voice was husky. He wanted to put the gun down. His weapon hand kept twitching down toward the knife in its belt sheath. He wanted to play with his new toy. He'd been watching her for weeks, imagining what he would do with his pretty toy and his ugly knife.

Del was two feet away now. She felt Phan's position rather than seeing it. He was three feet to her right and back maybe eight or nine inches.

"I figured you must have stashed the cash someplace clever. A clever little whore like you loves to play games, don't you? I knew you'd make it tough. Someplace most people wouldn't think of. You wanted to make me work for it, didn't you? That's exactly what you whores do, isn't that right? Nothin' for free? Huh? Yeah, that's right."

Del realized that the victim had seen Phan. Her one visible feature was a puffy, blood-smeared, teary eye. It widened, but she gave no other sign. Good girl. Not that James was looking at her face. He was too busy humping it.

James slipped his gun into the holster at his waist and pulled the knife up. He ran it lightly over the victim's hair in what could have been a gentle caress. His breath was a shudder. The victim's eye followed the path of the knife, and she moaned. This seemed to get James all worked up, and he started pushing harder against her, bouncing her head back further and further.

Del worked to suck in air, but it felt like wet concrete. Her body was loose, her weapon hand steady. It was time. She took the last step before the go as lightly as possible, easing the ball of her foot down.

"You were a bad girl, weren't you, Lola? A bad little whore. You tried to trick me, didn't you?" He laughed, a breathless gasping wheeze. He was speeding up, jamming his groin into the victim's face, bending her neck at an impossible angle, his balance off as he braced against her body. Del tried to pick her moment, while he was off balance, but the knife was too close to the victim. If Del went at him, he'd slice the victim's neck open without even meaning to.

Lola's neck hurt, her face hurt. Her shoulders were jammed against the back of the chair, and it felt like her spine would snap. The chair tipped back an inch or two, landed, tipped and landed, over and over. A jarring pain ran through her whole body every time the chair's front legs hit the ground again. She couldn't see through her tears, but she knew that Tom was right there, which meant that Del was right there too. He would kill Del and Tom, just like he killed the kitties.

She shuddered as he pressed her open, crying mouth harder against him. She couldn't breathe. She was going to choke to death on his pants while he ground himself against her. A high keening rose in her body as she struggled to free herself and get air. He reached down behind her, and suddenly her hands were freed from the handcuffs. He pulled one of her hands up and pushed it toward his groin. She didn't try to resist. Then he was grabbing for her hair again. At least with her hand there, she could breathe.

Del forced herself to wait another second, to let his knife hand wrap around the victim's head to hold it close. She didn't like seeing the knife right there by the victim, but James was too focused on getting off to think clearly, and that gave her the advantage she needed. She finally saw the right moment. She lunged forward in silence and pressed the barrel of her service revolver against James's spine. Phan was there, reaching to snag James's gun. His weapon was trained on James.

"Drop the knife." Del's hand and voice were steady.

She was okay until she saw Lola's face, and she wasn't the victim but Lola, and she drew in a quick breath that hurt. She was refocused in only a second, and it should have been okay.

But James seized the chance she gave him, and he was fast. He grabbed the victim, spun around, and stood her in front of him before Del could react. How had that happened? How had she let that happen? Lola's eyes were dark and wide, her skin chalky except where it was stained with blood. Bruises were already sprouting on her neck, her face, her arms. Her pupils were huge. She would, if she survived, look like one of those kids who've been tortured past what a human being can withstand without going insane. Black, black eyes with no color and nothing in them but pain and fear and emptiness. Del's heart stopped.

***

Lola couldn't understand what anyone was saying. Del and Tom were talking to the bad man. They seemed quiet and calm, but Del's eyes snapped. The bad man was holding her tight against his chest. His arm was crushing her. Something bad was by her neck. He would kill her. Or he would use her as a hostage to get to a car and leave. That wasn't great. But he used to have a gun, and the gun could have hurt all of them. Now that was gone, and the knife could only hurt her, not Del. So that was better. And while being held too tight by the bad man was scary and painful, it was better than choking on his crotch. His pants had tasted really, really bad.

Lola got the giggles. She tried to stop, tried to summon Orrin's angry voice to say, this is inappropriate, how could you, but she couldn't seem to muster it. The giggles got worse, and she was gasping for air, really losing breath, and she began to panic. She felt herself collapsing. The bad man was trying to hold her up and hold his knife, and he was having a hard time.

"Because I'm too fat."

Was that out loud?

"My lips hurt."

They really hurt a lot. From, she realized, being rubbed against his crotch! Lola laughed almost hard enough to pee her pants. Which the embarrassing possibility made her laugh again. She remembered Orrin's face when she peed on the carpet. He was so angry! And now he was dead. She couldn't remember the last time she'd heard his voice. What made him go away?

"It was you," she explained to Del, who was pointing a gun at the bad man and ignored her. "You made Orrin go away."

***

James frowned, and Del saw that he was reassessing the situation. He looked from Lola to Del and back again.

"What's she talking about?"

Del shrugged, trying to play for time. "Listen, James, we can work something out, the three of us." She gestured with a casual wave at Lola. "She'll do what I say. Phan and I want this to end well for everyone."

James was trying to decide, and Phan jumped in. "You figure it was a coincidence, Beckett's wife moves in down the street from a cop? We had to keep an eye on her."

James shook his head. "Bullshit. You think I'm stupid?"

Del rolled her eyes, eased back on her heels, tried to look relaxed and friendly. Well, as relaxed and friendly as a person can look while pointing a weapon at a bad guy. "Remember the partner, Davis? We found him two months ago, put him on ice. We just needed to wait a while for the heat to die down. We're not as impatient as you are. Fuckin' Feebs can never play things out, always rush in. Premature, if you know what I mean." She made a face, and Phan laughed.

"Bullshit. This is bullshit." James's gaze shot from her to Phan and back again.

"Think about it, James. You pulled the case because you saw a chance to make a little money, right? Think you're the only one who wants to make a little money? Davis was a suspect in a fraud case. One of the patients has a daughter who lives here. She came in, made a big stink. Phan was working fraud at the time. He kept an eye on Davis, saw some hinky shit, and then the old man was dead. He pulled me into it, knew he needed somebody to work the bitch." She gestured at the victim, who gaped at her.

He was thinking about it. Del held her breath, waited one beat, two. "Nobody has to die, here, James. But we can't let you take our money. I don't have a problem with sharing. There's enough to go around."

He shook his head. "You must think I'm a fucking retard."

***

Lola realized that Del and Tom were trying to trick the bad man, and for a moment she thought it might be working. But the man was crushing her to him even harder, and it was hard to breathe. She started to struggle in earnest, and her body started to jerk and flail in its fight for air. Panic filled her and emptied her mind. She started to slide into the hole. But she heard a voice, was that Orrin? James was crushing her chest, just like Orrin, just like that bad man when she was a little girl. *Why do some men think they can hurt people and get away with it?*

"Because we can," Orrin breathed hotly into her ear. "We always get away with it too. You know we do. You're either a sheep or a wolf, and you, my sweet little Lolly, are a sheep."

Lola shook her head. "No!" She thought she'd yelled, but it came out as barely a whisper.

Orrin's laugh filled her head, and it was what she'd always thought of as his ugly laugh, the annoying chuckle of the superior know-it-all.

Lola was angry. Not angry, she thought. "Pissed off."

James's grip loosened slightly as he shifted.

His gaze flicked over her dismissively and went back to Del.

He doesn't consider me a threat, Lola realized. They all see me as a sheep. As someone who can be bossed around and shot and knifed and crushed and worked and pushed around like furniture. She was starting to hyperventilate and forced her breathing to slow.

"I'm not a sheep." She glared at Del.

James shook her. "The grownups are talking, sweetheart," he said, and then he laughed. It was Orrin's laugh, that ugly, derisive sound that she hated.

Orrin—no, not Orrin, James, Christopher James. Who was The Creep. Who had attacked her and killed her poor, innocent kitties. Who thought he could do whatever he wanted because he was a wolf and she was a sheep. He was talking with Del. They were talking about her, talking about her like she was, as he'd implied, a helpless child whose fate would be decided by others. Del clearly agreed. And Tom did, too. They all ignored her and acted like she was just a helpless, useless child.

"I'm not a child," she whispered, and they all ignored her.

James's knife was inches away from her throat, and that was scary, but her rage made the knife seem less like a danger and more like an insult. Lola didn't think about what she was doing. She jutted out her chin and bit James on the fleshy thumb pad of his palm. There was a moment when she almost let go. He tasted very, very bad, and she realized that she was tasting his flesh and his blood. She fought a wave of nausea, but it faded when she thought about how he'd held her mouth against his pants. It was better to taste the bad man's blood than his pants. Plus, it was satisfying, the way he screamed and dropped the knife and tried uselessly to pull away.

Who's the sheep now? She held on with dogged determination, and she was not a victim but an animal with strong, sharp teeth that were clamped on his helpless flesh and not letting go. *Who's the bitch now, bad man?* He screamed again, and she smiled, feeling his blood drip from her lips as she continued to clamp down.

***

Del felt like she was moving in slow motion, like they all were. James wasn't the only one who was startled when the victim suddenly bit his hand. Del couldn't quite process that, but she did see the knife drop, and that was the important part. James screamed like he was on fire, and Del lunged forward.

Del reached for the victim as James's knees buckled and he pulled her down with him. At the same time, Phan lunged forward in a back alley tackle: his forearm hit James in the throat, and his knee hit him in the groin. James, already off balance, fell backward with the victim. Del grabbed her and pulled hard to get her to let go with her teeth.

"Let go. Come on, it's okay."

But she held on. Blood streamed from between her lips, and her eyes were glazed. Del shook her, yelled at her face, tried to pull at her jaw. But she wouldn't let go. Del changed tactics.

"Good job, little darlin'," she said in her daddy's drawl, "you did real good, honey. Now you can let go, okay? All right. Honey, can you do that for me, please?"

***

Lola was stunned. She was thrown sideways. She felt her throat burning as she scraped air into her lungs in quick, desperate gulps. She was sore and nauseous and laughing and crying. Her knee hurt. Her throat hurt. Her head hurt. Her lips really hurt a lot. Her teeth had clamped of their own accord on the bad guy and wouldn't let go. If she let go, then James was right. If she let go, then she was a child and helpless and a victim. And Orrin would have been right all along. She didn't think she could let go if she wanted to. Her mouth tasted like blood, and she was aware of how gross that was but still couldn't let go.

But then Del was there, and she was nice and was trying to gentle her like she was a wild animal. Or, Lola thought, an out-of-control child.

"I'm not a child," she said, glaring at Del. James's hand went away, and Lola watched as Tom handcuffed him.

Del put her hands up in a gesture of surrender. "I know that." She sounded surprised.

"Do you understand what I'm saying?"

"Yes," Del said, but Lola wasn't so sure.

"I don't think you get it at all. I really don't." Her words were mushy.

"Hey," Del said, "you're the one who got the bad guy."

Del smiled, and she saw the victim consider whether or not to believe her. Then she nodded and made a face and was Lola again.

Del rubbed her thumbs gently on Lola's reddened wrists. They'd bruise and would hurt in a day or two, but for now they were probably numb. Lola pulled her hands away.

She was still feeling riled up, touchy. Her mouth was still covered with blood, and she absently swiped at it with the back of her hand, smearing blood on her hand and across her face.

Del wanted to clean off the blood—was James carrying anything Lola could catch? HIV? Hepatitis? She'd have to get the doctors to test for everything.

"Are you dizzy? Can you see okay?"

"Del?" Was she real? Lola was feeling strange. Her mouth tasted very, very bad, and she gagged.

"Let's get you to the hospital."

Del sounded strange.

"Are you okay? Did the bad man hurt you?" She pressed her face against Del's, feeling her breathing and listening for her heartbeat. Del was shaking, but she was breathing. She was alive. The bad man hadn't killed her.

She tried to explain things to Del. He had two first names, and he was from the FBI. He wanted money from Orrin, but she didn't have it. Could she please have some water? She had a dream, and there was a roller coaster, and Del flew away. That's why it was important to come here. She was babbling, she could tell. But she didn't know how to stop.

As Del held Lola there on the floor of the kitchen, listening to Phan read a cuffed James his rights while Lola mumbled incoherently, she felt tears on her face. Were they hers or Lola's? She should be calling it in. She should do any of the ten things that needed to be done now. But instead she sat and watched Phan and felt Lola shake and cry and breathe and be alive.

CHAPTER TWENTY-SEVEN

Del walked into the station and found Phan sitting in her chair. He held a cup of coffee out to her and smiled at her surprise.

"I see you finally found something you're good at."

He rolled his eyes and tossed a file at her. "Kiss my ass."

So things were okay between them, even though she was a dipshit and had lost her focus. Mostly because everything turned out okay. The victim was alive, the bad guy was in a box, and nobody had gotten killed, seriously hurt, written up or suspended.

Thank God. Every time she'd closed her eyes to sleep, all she had been able to see was Lola's face, drawn and white, her eyes wide and dark with fear, and James holding that ugly knife. At the time Del had mostly blocked out Lola's face and replaced it with a cardboard cutout of a victim's face. But her mind had recorded it for later, obviously.

Thanks a lot. I really needed to remember that forever. It had been luck, not skill, that had saved them. And that wasn't good enough. If she'd listened to Lola and gotten her in to work with a sketch artist again she'd have recognized James, and he'd never have gotten close to Lola again. If she'd put it together faster. If she'd done a dozen things smarter, better. Phan had been a rock. She'd thanked him a dozen times, and he'd finally told her to shut up and stop acting like a goddamn girl.

Dominguez had managed to track down Davis, but the Feebs were making noises about taking the collar. They seemed pretty smug, according to Dominguez. They weren't sharing, but he thought maybe they had a line on the money. Del didn't care. What did it matter? The money was beside the point. Didn't anybody understand that?

Del looked over at Phan and saw that he had a picture of his little girl on the desk. When had he put that there? Did it mean he wanted to be her partner, long term? She stopped, hands immobile, staring at the photo of pretty little Kaylee Phan in a plum-colored dress and a silk flower over one ear and a wide smile that showed a mouthful of braces. She saw Phan watching her and went back to work. Don't make a big deal out of it, she told herself. Don't act like a "goddamn girl" and say something about it. But she smiled a little when he wasn't looking.

She hadn't had a permanent partner in over three years, ever since Buchanan got hooked on prescription drugs after his second knee surgery. She'd called him on it, privately, threatened to turn him in when she realized that he was lit up on the job. But she didn't do it. She couldn't work with him knowing he was wrecked half the time, but she couldn't rat on him, either. A county mountie had popped him for a DUI and she was off the hook. No one ever asked her about him. He went to rehab on the city's dime, took a job upstate, and she was a pariah.

Were they pissed because she didn't turn him in, or because they thought she did? She couldn't be sure. Nobody ever said anything to attack her. She just wasn't invited to the bars and the barbecues and the softball games and the lunches. She was just not one of them anymore, and it had taken two long, lonely years for that to change. Then, just when everything had started to get normal again, when she wasn't invisible anymore, she'd met Janet and became nobody again. So maybe now she wasn't nobody anymore. Maybe. At least to Phan and Jones and a couple of the other guys.

It was several hours before the mountain of paperwork associated with the case was almost finished, and by then it was a federal case and out of their hands. Captain Wonderbread got them a ringside seat for the last half of James's intake interview.

He looked like a prince on a throne, Del thought, watching him through the interview room mirror. Legs wide apart, hands on his knees—one hand was bandaged, and she chuckled at that. Phan flicked a glance at her and smiled. He had his hands in front of him, almost touching the glass that shielded them from James's view. She had her arms folded over her chest. James twitched his bandaged hand, and Phan snorted.

"Remind me not to mess with Lola," he said, and somebody shushed him.

"Women don't steal money unless there's a man driving them," James was preaching to the agents in front of him in the tiny interrogation room. He explained how he'd found her online, searched her house, planted the cameras.

"She's definitely a crazy little bitch," he said. "Talks to herself. Talks to Beckett." He shook his head. "Cute, though." He shifted, smiled. "Smells nice."

He looked at the mirror. Del knew that he couldn't see her, but it looked like he was staring right at her. "Sexy, too. Soft in all the right places, right, Mason?"

Del shook her head. He was still playing games.

A Feeb was asking him something, but Del was watching James's smile. He licked his lips, grinned like a dog in a henhouse.

"The cat thing? Oh, shit, yeah." He laughed. "No, hell no, that wasn't something I planned. It just came to me." His eyes were gleaming. He was flushed now, excited. Now he was aroused. He'd been playing at being turned on by Lola, then. He was turned on by violence, blood, fear. Del made a face as James went on to describe the experience of luring and torturing the animals in detail for several minutes, but Del only half listened.

What was it about killing the animals that had twisted him and taken him off purpose? The feeling of cutting through flesh? The sound of it? The smell? Was the compulsion something he was programmed, genetically or however, to respond to? Was it, somehow, his fate? There was another unasked question—how many people thought they were normal until they stumbled over the one act of violence that would turn them on? Are we all potential sociopaths, just waiting to hit the right trigger? She walked out, ignoring James's continuing monologue espousing the joys of animal torture. She didn't need to hear any more. She realized Phan had followed her and exchanged grimaces with him.

"Ridiculous," Phan said. "Assholes cut him a deal to testify against Davis. So he gets away with everything. Not to mention he'll probably end up living in the suburbs in some nice neighborhood full of unsuspecting families. And our tax dollars will pay for that!"

Del shrugged. That part was out of her hands.

"Come on, Mason—tell me it doesn't piss you off."

She tried to find a way to explain. "I think he's seriously fucked up in the head. I think he's gonna maybe turn out to be a really dangerous guy. But he's off Lola, at least for now, and I can't do anything about what he does in the future. The thing I was worried about was if she caught something when she bit him. But she didn't. So, the rest I can't worry about."

He looked at her a moment longer, debating, and then she saw him decide to believe her. He shrugged and headed for the door.

"Hey, Phan," she called. "Nice work."

"Yeah," he said, not turning around. "I know."

She watched him, wishing she'd asked about his kid, found a way to cement the partnership, something.

"See you Monday," he called over his shoulder, and she nodded like it was nothing.

"Not if I see you first."

His laugh followed him out the door.

She left soon after that, fighting exactly the frustration Phan had expressed. To clear it away, all she had to do was picture James's face when Lola clamped down on his hand and shook it like she was a ferocious little poodle. She laughed and started up her bike.

***

Del had insisted that Lola stay with her, and Lola was grateful and glad. She wasn't ready to face her own house, and she didn't want to stay in another hotel, either. Del was working hard to make Lola feel welcome and normal and safe. She was being carefully kind and sweet and understanding. She spoke to her softly, moved slowly around her, and gave her plenty of space.

It was making Lola crazy. She understood that Del was still thinking of her as a victim. That it would take time before she saw Lola as someone other than a hostage or a victim or a duty. That she was berating herself for letting that man get to her, for not believing her. She had to be mad at Lola for going to the house when she'd told her not to. She was probably repulsed by Lola's marriage to Orrin and wasn't sure if she even wanted to be friends, much less anything more.

She only looked down the street at her own house once. Would she ever feel comfortable living there again? She couldn't stay in Del's guest room forever. She would have to face her fears sometime. Still, she turned away from the window and couldn't make herself face a decision about the future. How had she looked to Del? Scared and weak and helpless. That was not the person she wanted Del to see when she looked at her. That was not the person she herself wanted to be.

A careful, quiet, slow-moving and solicitous hostess was not the Del that Lola wanted to see and feel and know. It was the sleeping Del she wanted to know, the relaxed Del, laughing or eating pizza or jumping on a bed or just sitting quietly. The Del who had kissed her. She touched her fingers to her lips. But how well did she really know that Del? The house was the only clue in front of her, and she was almost afraid to see what it revealed.

The house was smaller than Lola's but had a similar layout.

Del had mentioned once that she'd rebuilt practically the whole thing, and Lola wondered what her choices said about her. The wood floors were very dark. No throw rugs, no carpet anywhere. The minimal furniture was dark and utilitarian. Everything about the house was dark and cold and square. It looked like a monastery. No personal photos. No paintings. No plants. No throw pillows. No knickknacks.

The whole house felt empty, as though no one lived there. Things were clean and organized, but there was somehow an air of neglect. The house felt cold, and this bothered Lola. Del was warm and passionate and funny and full of life, but none of that came across in her home. Del's house seemed so lonely!

Del brought home takeout, something spicy that Lola could only pick at. Del got a call and jumped up, almost knocking over a greasy container of noodles.

"Uh, gotta go. Homicide. Don't wait up," Del said, and Lola could hear excitement in her voice. Now that Lola's case had been solved, would Del lose interest in her? Had danger been the only thing between them?

She said goodnight to Del and waited a moment, standing close to her, looking up at her, but Del just said goodnight and walked away. She was avoiding looking at Lola's face. Lola tried to believe that it was because she didn't want to see the bruises, but she knew it was more likely that Del wished Lola would go away and never come back.

She wished she were brave enough to ask if Del liked her. But what if she said no? What if she said, Lola, you're a nice person, but you were married to a man, and you're old and fat and mousy and boring and stupid and a chicken who doesn't know how to do anything right.

Lola didn't think that there was any real chance that Del would want to be with her, but she couldn't help wanting to take a chance anyway. She felt like a third grader. "Check this box if you like me, this one if you don't." What if Del checked the "don't" box? How could she not?

When Del came back the next morning, she was carrying a paper bag. "I stopped at your place. Figured you might want some of your own things."

Lola gulped out a thank you. She wanted to talk, but Del said she had to get back to work. As soon as she was gone, Lola rushed to dress and walk to the store—there was nothing to eat in Del's cupboards or refrigerator but a wide variety of leftover spicy things, most of which appeared to be weeks old. Lola made a face. They'd been in the hotels for almost two weeks, so everything in the fridge was older than that. She grabbed the trash bin and started cleaning up.

***

Del was wiped out. She came home wishing she'd thought to order a pizza. But she smelled food cooking—had she ever walked in and smelled cooking in this house before? She doubted it. She started to head for the kitchen, sniffing like a puppy, and then there was a sound, a cough.

Del looked up and grinned at the sight of Lola in a pretty white dress at the top of the stairs. She looked like a fairy, a princess, a bride. Her hair was down around her shoulders, glowing in the light. She was pretty, if you didn't let your gaze linger long enough to see the bruises that showed even through the makeup she'd used to try to hide them. She wasn't smiling. She stared down at Del as though the two of them were strangers. The shadows settled in the bruised hollows under her eyes, at her temples. God, they were everywhere. Her cheeks, her mouth, her throat. Her arms too. Distinct, overlapping finger marks showed on her upper arms, her wrists. Even her hands were bruised.

Del's grin faded. I let that happen.

Lola didn't speak, didn't move.

She's worried, Del realized. She let her smile show her pleasure and saw Lola's response build by tiny degrees. Del suddenly felt shy herself. She wanted to race up the stairs and take Lola in her arms right there and then. She just watched Lola come down the stairs with care—she was still in pain, obviously, and still trying to hide it.

"Uh, I, uh." Lola laughed. "Hi."

"Hi." Del wished she could think of something to say, but

she was tongue-tied. God, when was the last time that happened? Maybe never.

"Do you like my dress?" Lola's voice shook.

Del shook her head. "No."

Lola's eyes widened.

"I like you. The dress is just a dress."

Lola smiled again, her real smile, the one that took Del's breath away. Lola flushed bright red, and her eyes searched Del's and dropped away, and she went pale again. That made the bruises look darker, and Del frowned.

What was wrong? Why was she so—Del shook her head. Lola was unsure of Del's feelings for her. But how could that be? How could she not know? Del inhaled deeply, tried to figure out what to do. But her mind was a blank, and she could only stand there and shake her head.

"Del, I don't know how to say this. I mean, I don't know what to say." Lola faltered. Her mouth tightened, and her gaze dropped.

Del didn't think. She didn't plan. She took Lola's hands in hers and kissed them, careful not to hurt her.

Lola didn't respond. She was still looking down.

Del carefully tilted her face up, crooking a gentle finger under her chin, and smiled into her wide, searching eyes. She ignored the bruises as much as she could and looked past them at Lola. Del kissed her forehead, the tip of her nose, and finally, finally her lips.

She forced herself to stay slow, to not scare her. She felt Lola's lips soften against hers and part, and her heart beat faster. Desire made her feel drunk, shaky. She kissed her for long minutes, not allowing herself to do more than this. She knew that Lola was attracted to her, but she also knew that Lola was afraid. She would have to be careful. It was like petting a wild doe that'd bolt at the first sign of danger. Del remembered the hunting trip with her father and sound of deer hooves dancing through the underbrush like little bugs lighting on flowers and zipping away.

She felt the same thing now that she had that day so many years past, that same connection with Lola she'd once had with her daddy. There were a million invisible threads holding them together and making them a part of each other, and she felt an ache inside her body ease, as though some part of her that had been holding its breath for a thousand years could at long last let go.

She felt dampness on her cheek and thought Lola was crying—she cried a lot, it seemed like—but then she realized that it wasn't Lola who was crying but she herself. *When was the last time I cried?* She couldn't remember. *Did I cry when Janet—no, I didn't. I'm sure I didn't. I think the last time I cried was at Mrs. Wendell's. What was that, thirty years ago?* She pulled away and allowed herself a small smile at Lola's uncensored look of disappointment.

"You are the most beautiful thing I've ever seen."

"No," Lola said, her voice hoarse. "You're the most beautiful thing I've ever seen." She smiled, a flirty little grin that made Del's heart jump.

Del kissed her again, a whisper of a touch that tickled and teased, and she felt Lola's intake of breath and felt her body ease toward Del's. It was uncalculated, that shifting forward, and Del deepened the kiss until she felt Lola start to tense up. She pulled back again.

Lola's smile was tremulous, and Del reminded herself again to take it slow.

"I smell food." If they stayed here one more minute, she wouldn't be able to control herself.

Lola's eyes widened. "The bread!"

She hurried to the kitchen, and Del followed more slowly.

Lola bustled around, occasionally stopping, a shadow of pain crossing her face. She talked a blue streak, explaining what she'd made, why she'd chosen this recipe, why she thought Del would like it. She was nervous as a cat, filling the silence with chatter, and Del just made the appropriate noises. This wasn't a conversation. It was a defense mechanism. How many was that? How many more were there? In a lot of ways, they were unsuited for each other. All the reasons why flitted through her mind like cards in a Rolodex. But they went by too quickly for her to read them. Or, she thought, maybe she just didn't want to.

She wanted Lola. But it was more than just desire, and that was the scary part. She felt like something not quite in her control was in motion, like she was being carried by a wave to some inevitable destination. *Everything* changes now, she thought. That thought left her breathless.

***

As they ate, Lola chatted about her day, about the food, about Marco and Phil's upcoming trip to Florida. She knew she was acting like an airhead, but Del's stony face and distracted air were unnerving her. What was she thinking? What was she feeling? If only she would say how she felt, she could stop this breathless, meaningless tide of stupid words about nothing.

But Del didn't. She ate, clearly without tasting a thing. She nodded and frowned and pretended to listen, but she was miles away. Was she thinking about Janet? Was she bored? Lola's stomach hurt. Every part of her body hurt, as a matter of fact, and she was becoming more aware of this by the second. This uncertainty was unbearable.

I'll go back home, she thought. I don't want to. I'm scared to, even though there's no reason to be, but I can't take this. Another hour of this and I'm going to just take off my head like a cartoon character and run off to the hills and let it scream and scream for an hour and then come back and she'll still be sitting there like a statue.

***

Del looked across the table. Lola was just sitting there, looking at her. How long had it been since she'd stopped talking? She wanted Lola with a kind of desperation, like there was something in Lola that she needed or she would die. It seemed melodramatic, even childish, but it was true.

Then Lola laughed at something—who knew what? It was yet another defense mechanism, probably, and Del forgot her questions and her fears. *I want to hear that laugh a million times. I want to taste and touch and smell and love every single bit of this woman.* She wanted to let the wave take her where it would, as long as it took her with Lola, whose laughing eyes did something to Del's insides. Don't be afraid, she told herself. Love her. Love? And she was afraid all over again.

Lola acted like she didn't notice Del's preoccupation. Once or twice, though, Del thought she saw Lola watching her, assessing her.

After dinner, she stood in front of Del and looked her square in the eye. If it had been anyone else, it would have seemed confrontational.

"Del, I haven't thanked you."

Del shook her head, surprised by a burst of frustration and regret and anger. "Jesus, Lola, thank me? For—for what? Letting James beat on you? For not believing you when you said you saw him? For not telling you about the cameras? How about for not getting there faster? I let you down. You might want to pretend you forgot that, but I haven't. I never will."

Lola gaped at her. "Are you kidding? What—you saved my life! That man was crazy. He was going to kill me, and you and Tom saved my life."

Del shrugged and crossed her arms. "If you want to see it that way, fine. But—"

"But, nothing." Lola rested her hands on Del's forearms. "Listen to me: no one could have done a better job than you. Period."

Del made a face. "We can agree to disagree." She knew she was being sour, and she knew this wasn't fair, but she couldn't change that. She was pissed and she couldn't have said whether it even had anything to do with James.

Lola grimaced. "Adele Savannah Mason, I mean, come on! You are human, you know."

"What does that mean?"

"You don't have to be perfect. You aren't perfect. You get to be imperfect and human and feel things, just like the rest of us. To make mistakes and be scared and all of it. Don't you?"

Del nodded. Somehow, the wind had gone out of her sails, and she was tired of fighting all of the craziness inside of her. "I was scared, Lola. I thought he was going to kill you." Her throat was trying to close, but she forced her voice through it. "I saw how scared you were, and it was my fault."

"No," Lola protested, "I was scared for you."

Del frowned, nonplussed.

She told Del about her nightmare. "I thought it was a kind of premonition or something. That's why I went to the house, to keep you from getting hurt. And that only made things worse. Oh, Del, I'm so sorry!"

Del kissed her to quiet her.

"We're okay, Lola, we're both okay, and the bad guy is locked up and he can't hurt you ever again."

"The what?" Lola got up on her toes to peer into Del's eyes.

"The, uh, bad guy."

Lola's laugh made Del smile. "Is that the official police term?"

Del smirked. "You bet it is."

"Silly." She was flushed pink and grinning and looked lighter and happier than Del had ever seen her.

"I want you."

Lola's breath caught. She was terrified and excited and impatient all at once. What if this was a mistake? What if Del kept getting angry all the time? What if she decided not to like her after a while? What if she still loved Janet, after all? What if—but Del was watching her, and her eyes were that amazing, hypnotic blend of greens and blues and desire and intensity, and Lola heard herself say the words, "I want you too."

They kissed again, easing together with agonizing slowness and care. *What happens now? I'm scared. God, I'm so scared! What if she hurts me? What if I hurt her? What if I'm not good enough? What if—I want this. I need this. I need her.* And their bodies took over, impatient with the nonsense that their brains put in the way.

It was Lola who broke the kiss. She pulled away. "I'm scared."

"I know." Del ran a finger slowly down Lola's cheek, easing back a strand of hair and steering around a large bruise. "Me too."

Lola frowned at her. "I want this, though. I want to be with you and get close to you and find out everything about you. I want you."

"I'm yours." Del shrugged, spreading her arms out and grinning. "Take me." She dropped her arms to take Lola's hands. They were shaking. Were her own?

"I promise to be honest with you."

Del smiled. "I promise to be honest, too." She swallowed hard. "I promise to not walk all over you."

Lola's eyes widened. "You—okay. I promise to be brave. And strong. And not to depend on you too much."

Del squeezed her hand. "I promise to listen to you."

"I promise to listen to you. And talk to you."

"Even if it's uncomfortable."

"Yes."

"Me, too."

Lola made a goofy face. "Can we just promise to try? Is that enough for now?"

Del let out the air she'd been holding in. "Yes, for sure, absolutely. And we'll probably screw everything up for a while. You know? But we'll keep trying."

"Sorry. I'm a sap." She rubbed her teary eyes.

"Hey," Del whispered, pulling her hands away. She used her thumb to lightly blot the skin under Lola's eyes. It was so delicate, that skin, soft and fragile and already bruised. Tears had washed away the makeup and exposed the purple and black, and Del's hand shook. She felt like her thumb would tear right through that skin if she weren't careful.

But she was careful, and she didn't hurt Lola, and Lola smiled at her with her guileless eyes unclouded by fear. She was so trusting! It was overwhelming, knowing that such soft stuff was in her hands.

"Be careful with that face," Del said, her voice breaking. "That's a face I happen to like."

Lola smiled. She couldn't speak. Instead, she reached up and kissed Del's soft, soft, lips. She tried to let go of all of her fear and feel only her courage and desire and hope, and then she forgot about all of that and could only feel Del's lips and Del's hands and Del's loud, hammering, fragile heart.

She pulled back to look into Del's eyes again. "One other thing."

"What?" Del breathed through the thrill of fear that ran through her.

"I want a ride."

"O—kay."

"No." Lola gave a wicked smile and raised an eyebrow. "I want you to take me out on the bike and show me how fast we can go."

Del grinned, and the grin turned into laughter. "Oh, darlin'," she drawled, "you're gonna get the ride of your life."

**Publications from
Bella Books, Inc.
Women. Books. Even Better Together.
P.O. Box 10543
Tallahassee, FL 32302
Phone: 800-729-4992**
www.bellabooks.com

CALM BEFORE THE STORM by Peggy J. Herring. Colonel Marcel Robicheaux doesn't tell and so far no one official has asked, but the amorous pursuit by Jordan McGowen has her worried for both her career and her honor.
978-0-9677753-1-9

THE WILD ONE by Lyn Denison. Rachel Weston is busy keeping home and head together after the death of her husband. Her kids need her and what she doesn't need is the confusion that Quinn Farrelly creates in her body and heart.
978-0-9677753-4-0

LESSONS IN MURDER by Claire McNab. There's a corpse in the school with a neat hole in the head and a Black & Decker drill alongside. Which teacher should Inspector Carol Ashton suspect? Unfortunately, the alluring Sybil Quade is at the top of the list. First in this highly lauded series.
978-1-931513-65-4

WHEN AN ECHO RETURNS by Linda Kay Silva. The bayou where Echo Branson found her sanity has been swept clean by a hurricane—or at least they thought. Then an evil washed up by the storm comes looking for them all, one-by-one. Second in series.
978-1-59493-225-0